SECOND WIND

Dick Francis

THE
WINDSOR
SELECTION

CHIVERS PRESS
BATH

First published 1999
by
Michael Joseph Ltd

This Large Print edition published by
Chivers Press
by arrangement with
Michael Joseph Ltd
2000

ISBN 0 7540 1363 4

British Library Cataloguing in Publication Data available

ALSO BY DICK FRANCIS

My sincere thanks to

JOHN KETTLEY
Meteorologist

FELIX FRANCIS
Physicist

MERRICK FRANCIS
Horseman

and

NORMA JEAN BENNET
ETHEL SMITH
FRANK ROULSTONE
CAROLINE GREEN
ALAN GRIFFIN
ANDY HIBBERT
PILAR BUSH GORDON
STEVE PICKERING

and

THE CAYMAN ISLANDS
NATIONAL ARCHIVE

SECOND WIND

PROLOGUE

DELIRIUM BRINGS COMFORT to the dying.
I had lived in an ordered world. Salary had mattered, and timetables. My grandmother belonged there with her fears.

"But isn't there a risk?" she asked.

You bet your life there's a risk.

"No," I said. "No risk."

"Surely flying into a hurricane must be risky?"

"I'll come back safe," I said.

But now, near dead as dammit, I tumbled like a rag-doll piece of flotsam in towering gale-driven seas that sucked unimaginable tons of water from the deeps and hurled them along in liquid mountains faster than a Derby gallop. Sometimes the colossal waves swept me inexorably with them.

Sometimes they buried me until my agonized lungs begged the ultimate relief of inhaling anything, even water, when only air would keep the engine turning.

I'd swallowed gagging amounts of Caribbean salt.

It had been night for hours, with no gleam anywhere. I was losing all perception of which way was up. Which way was *air.* My arms and legs had bit by bit stopped working. An increasingly out-of-order brain had begun seeing visions that shimmered and played in colors inside my head.

I could see my dry-land grandmother clearly. Her wheelchair. Her silver shoes. Her round anxious eyes and her miserable foreboding.

"Don't go, Perry. It gives me the heebie-jeebies."

Whoever listens to grandmothers.

When she spoke in my head, her mouth was out of sync with her voice.

I'm drowning, I thought. The waves are bigger. The storm is worse. I'll go to sleep soon.

Delirium brings comfort at the end.

1

AT THE BEGINNING it was a bit of fun.

Kris Ironside and I, both single, both thirty-one, both meteorologists employed to interpret the invisible swings and buffets of global air for television and radio audience consumption, both of us found without excitement that some of the vacation weeks allotted to us overlapped.

We both worked in the Weather Centre of the British Broadcasting Corporation, taking it in turns with several other forecasters to deliver the good or bad weather news to the nation. From breakfast to midnight our voices sounded familiar and our faces smiled or frowned into millions of homes until we could go nowhere at all without recognition.

Kris rather enjoyed it, and so had I once, but I had long gone beyond any depth of gratification and sometimes found the instant identification a positive drawback.

"Aren't you . . . ?"

"Yes, I guess so."

I used to go for vacations to lands that didn't know me. A week in Greece. Elephants in the Serengeti. By dugout canoe up the Orinoco. Small adventures. No grand or gasp-worthy dangers. I lived an ordered life.

Kris stabbed with his thumb the roster pinned to the department notice board. Disgust shook his hand.

"October and November!" he grumbled. "And I asked for August."

It was January at the time: August tended to be given to those with school-age children. Kris's chances of August had always realistically been zero, but with Kris hope often outweighed common sense.

It was his streak of wild unpredictability—the manic side of his character—that made him a good evening pub companion, but a week in his company once in the foothills of the Himalayas had left me glad to return to home soil.

My own name, Perry Stuart, appeared alphabetically near the bottom of the list, ahead only of Williams and Yates. In late October, I saw, I could take the ten working days still owing to me by then and return to the screen on the eve of Fireworks Night, November 5th. I shrugged and sighed. Year after year I got especially chosen and, I supposed, honored to deal with the rain-or-no-rain million-dollar gamble on fine weather for the night the skies blazed with the multicolored firework starbursts sent up in memory of Guy Fawkes and his blow-up-Parliament gunpowder plot. Year after year if I got downpours right I winced over sackloads of letters from reproachful children who reckoned their disappointment to be my fault.

Kris followed my gaze down the list and tapped my name with his finger.

"October and November," he pronounced without surprise. "Don't tell me! You'll waste half of that leave on your grandmother again."

"I expect so."

He protested, "But you see her every week."

"Mm."

Where Kris had parents, brothers and a coven of cousins, I had a grandmother. She had literally plucked me as an infant out of the ruins of a gas-exploded house, and had dried her grief for my dead parents in order to bring me up.

Where batches of my meteorological colleagues had wives, husbands, live-ins and one-nighters, I had—sometimes—my grandmother's nurses. I wasn't unmarried by design: more by lack of urgency or the advent of Cinderella.

As AUTUMN APPROACHED the Ironside manic-depressive gloom intensified downwards. Kris's latest girlfriend left him, and the Norwegian pessimism he'd inherited from his mother, along with his pale skin, lengthy jaw and ectomorph physique, was leading him to predict cyclones more often than usual at the drop of a single millibar.

Small groups of the great wide public with special needs tended to gravitate to particular forecasters. One associate, Beryl Yates, had cornered weddings, for instance, and Sonny Rae spent his spare time advising builders and house painters, and pompous old George told local councils when they might dryly dig up their water mains.

Landowners, great and small, felt comfortable with Kris, and would cut their hay to the half hour on his say-so.

As Kris's main compulsive personal hobby was flying his own light aircraft, he spent many of his free days lunching with far-flung but welcoming farmers. They cleared their sheep out of fields to give him landing room and had been known to pollard a row of willows to provide a safe low-trajectory takeoff.

I had flown with him three times on these farming jaunts, though my own bunch of followers, apart from children with garden birthday parties, had proved to be involved with horses. I seemed particularly to be consulted by racehorse trainers seeking perfect underfoot conditions for their speedy hopefuls, even though we did run forecasts dedicated to particular events.

By voice transfer on a message machine a trainer might say, "I've a fancied runner at Windsor on Wednesday evening, what are the chances of firm ground?" or "I'm not declaring my three-mile 'chaser to run tomorrow unless you swear it'll rain overnight." They might be pony club camp organizers or horse show promoters, or even polo entrepreneurs, begging for the promise of sunshine. They might be shippers of brood mares to Ireland anxious for a calm sea crossing, and they might above all be racecourse managers wanting advice on whether or not to water their turf for good going in the days ahead. The prospect of good going encouraged trainers to send their horses. The prospect of many runners encouraged spectators to arrive in crowds. "Good going" was gold dust to the racing industry; and woe betide the forecaster who misread the clouds.

But no weatherman, however profound his knowledge or intuition, could guess the skies right all the time, and, as over the British Isles especially the fickle winds could change direction without giving notice, to be accurate eighty-five percent of the time was miraculous.

Kris's early autumnal depression intensified day by day and it was from some vague impulse to cheer him up that I agreed to his suggestion of a Sunday lunch flight to Newmarket. Our host, Kris assured me, would be catering for at least twenty guests, so my presence would hardly overload the arrangements. "And besides," Kris added with mild routine sarcasm, "your face is your fortune, you can't get away from it. Caspar will slobber all over you."

"Caspar?"

"Caspar Harvey, it's his lunch."

"Oh."

Caspar Harvey might be one of Kris's wealthiest farming cronies, but he also owned three or four racehorses whose trainer twittered in nervous sound bites in my ears from Monday to Sunday. Oliver Quigley, the trainer, temperamentally unsuited to any stressful way of life, let alone the nerve-breaking day-to-day of the thoroughbred circuit, was, on his messages system, audibly in awe of Caspar Harvey, which was hardly the best basis for an owner-trainer relationship.

I had met neither man face to face and didn't much want to, but as the day of the lunch approached I kept coming across references to "that gift to racing, Caspar Harvey" or "Caspar Harvey in final dash to honors on the winning owners' list" or "Caspar Harvey pays millions at the Yearling Sales for Derby hopes": and as my knowledge and curiosity grew, so did my understanding of the Quigley jitters.

The week before the Caspar Harvey lunch was one of those times when I gave the top two forecasts, at six-thirty and nine-thirty each evening, daily working out the probable path of air masses and going in front of the cameras at peak times to put my assessments on the line. Many people used to think that all Kris and I and other forecasters did was to read out from someone else's script: there was often surprise when we explained that we were in actual fact forecasters, that it was we who predicted the weather ourselves, using the information gathered from distant weather stations and having discussed it with colleagues. We then went "live" and unscripted— and usually alone—into a very small studio where we ourselves placed the computerized weather symbols on the background screen map of Britain.

There were well over two hundred weather stations covering the British Isles, each reporting local wind speeds and direction and barometric pressure into a large central computer housed in the main Meteorological Office in Bracknell, near Ascot, west of London. Into that computer too came data from all over the world: and one could draw from it everything the world's weather was likely to do in the next forty-eight hours. But nothing was ever certain, and a lurch of high atmosphere pressure could let in a polar gust that would refrigerate our cheerful expectations into unconvincing explanations.

The late September Sunday of Caspar Harvey's lunch, though, dawned fine and clear with a chilly wind from the east, conditions that would remain that way all day while the farmers of East Anglia harvested their late-ripening barley. "Perfect for flying," Kris said.

Kris's airplane, a low-winged single-engined Piper Cherokee, was approximately thirty years old. He, he frankly acknowledged, was its fourth owner, the third being a flying club that had sometimes put six hours a day on the propeller log (Kris's only gripe) and rubbed old-age patches into the cracked leather seats.

My first reaction to the antique rig a couple of years earlier had been "No thanks, I'll stay on the ground," but Kris had introduced me in his home airfield's echoing hangar to a machinist who understood the relationship between loose screws and sudden death. I'd put my life in Kris's hands on the machinist's assurance that old though the Piper might be, it was airworthy to the last rivet.

Kris, in fact, had turned out to be a surprisingly competent pilot. I'd expected him to be as volatile in the air as in his general behavior but instead he was soberly responsible at the controls and only as high as a radiosonde balloon afterwards.

Many of our colleagues found Kris a difficult companion and asked me in mild exasperation how I dealt with his obvious leaning towards my company. I usually answered truthfully that I enjoyed his slightly weird views on life, and I didn't mention that in his depressive periods he talked familiarly about suicide as if discussing an unimportant life choice like what tie to wear for early breakfast broadcasts.

It was regard for his parents, and for his father in particular, that deterred him from the final jump into the path of a train (his preferred method of exit), and I reckoned that he had less self-hatred and more courageous staying power than many who'd given in to a death wish.

At the time of Caspar Harvey's lunch party, Kris Ironside at thirty-one had outlasted the macabre instincts of a succession of young women who had temporarily found the idea of suicide fascinating, and was beginning to face the possibility that he might yet make it to middle age.

In appearance, apart from the overall tall and willowy build, he was noticeably good-looking, with pale blue intelligent eyes, wiry blond stick-out hair that refused help from barbers, a strong blond mustache, and, on screen particularly, a sort of half-grin that dared you not to believe his every word.

He kept his flying pride and joy on White Waltham airfield and to its upkeep devoted the bulk of his income, gleefully informing anyone who would listen that it left aerobic exercises out of sight as a keep-fit heart-stresser. He greeted me at White Waltham with what I knew from experience to be supercharged happiness. His Cherokee, parked by the petrol pumps, was taking aboard fuel that was no more stable than himself, each wing tank being filled to overflowing to expel any water formed there by hot saturated air condensing as the aircraft cooled after last time out.

Kris, never one of the old goggles-and-white-silk-scarf variety of pilots, was wearing a plaid heavy wool shirt with a Norwegian-knit sweater on top. He eyed my dark pants, white shirt and navy jacket and nodded approval: in some way he considered my all-too-conventional appearance to be a license for his own eccentricity to flourish.

He finished the refueling, checked that the two wing tank caps were screwed on tight and then,

having with my help pushed the little white airplane a short distance from the pumps (a small
courtesy to other refuelers), he methodically
walked round the whole machine, intoning his
checklist to himself as he touched each vital part.
As usual, he finished by unclipping and opening
backwards each half of the engine cowling,
checking that the mechanic hadn't left a rag in
the works (as if he would!) and also wiping the
dipstick clean before re-inserting it down into
the sump, to make sure there was a satisfactorily
deep lake of oil there to lubricate the engine. Kris
had never been one to take foolish chances when
it came to flying.

Once aboard and sitting in the left-hand (captain's) seat he equally seriously completed his pre-
starting checks—all switches in good order, and
things like that—and finally started the engine,
gazing concentratedly at its gauges.

Used to his meticulous ways, I sat placidly waiting for satisfaction to relax the tension in his
backbone and hands, until at last he grunted,
switched on his radio, and informed the Sunday
controller up in his glass tower that Ironside in
his Cherokee required takeoff clearance for a simple flight to Newmarket, return expected at about

seventeen hundred hours local time. Kris and the controller knew each other well; the exchange of information was a courtesy, more than an obligation. Cleared to taxi, allowed the tower. "Thanks, kiddo," the pilot said.

Kris was right, it was a lovely day for flying. The Cherokee lifted off lightheartedly with its easy load and swung round towards the north as it climbed away from base. The noise of the engine in a cross between a growl and clatter made casual conversation difficult, but talking anyway was ever superfluous up there higher than eagles. Pleasure as always sat like a balloon in my mind, and I checked our progress against the map on my knees with unalloyed contentment. Maybe one of these days . . . why didn't I . . . learn to fly?

Kris had drawn two straight lines on the wipe-clean surface of the air map, a dogleg route to lunch. It was he who steered by the direction indicator, allowing for magnetic variation and a crosswind, and I with small triumphs who checked our passage over the roads and rivers two thousand feet below and pointed them out to him, earning grins and nods.

From White Waltham we flew north to avoid crossing straight over London, turning northeast where the north-heading multi-lane M1 high-way reached the outskirts of the sprawling town of Luton, with its busy airport to the east.

Kris yearned for some of the expensive avionic packages that would give him access to all the latest equipment that made air navigation easier. It cost him every spare cent, however, just to keep flying, so he navigated by dead reckoning and sharp-eyed passengers, and only once, he said, had he been disastrously lost.

Dead reckoning delivered us safely alive into the Newmarket area, where he sought out a large house some way south of the town and, descending to a thousand feet or so, circled round it twice, causing figures below to appear waving in the garden.

"Caspar Harvey's house," Kris shouted unnecessarily.

I nodded O.K.; and as he was circling clockwise, with the wing on my side low to give me a good view, I brought out the handy little camera I carried with me always and took enough shots, I reckoned, to thank and please our host.

Kris, breaking off from the circling, ascended again a few hundred more feet and gave me a Cherokee-eye view of the purpose-built town

that the racing world called "Headquarters."
I'd talked a hundred or more times on the telephone or voice mail to the trainers who worked
there. I'd corresponded with e-mail by the electronic ton. I knew voices and I knew characters,
and it wasn't only Oliver Quigley whose sharp
anxieties begged assurances from me that I
couldn't give.

Neither Kris nor I, as I'd checked with him before the flight, knew which of the many stableyards in Newmarket were identifiable from the
air, and once over the place and thundering along
at a hundred and twenty knots, I found I was
sure only of one or two of the biggest.

Oliver Quigley had told me often that his string
could trot straight from his yard onto Warren
Hill, but with the speed and the sunshine and
my ground-to-air ignorance of the town's geog-
raphy, I wasn't at all sure in which quadrangle
stableyard stood Caspar Harvey's equine invest-
ments, not to mention a filly due to run on Friday. To be on the safe side of pleasing the trainer,
therefore, I snapped as many stableyards as I
could.

There wasn't a horse to be seen, neither on the
well-marked gallops nor in the stableyards nor

on the horse walks (special paths for horses) which laced the town. There were upwards of twelve hundred aristocratic thoroughbreds down there somewhere, but at lunchtime on a Sunday they weren't doing much but dreaming.

Kris looked at his watch and headed south of the town, where he put the wheels down sweetly on the official grass strip that ran beside the part of the racecourse used in high summer—the July course. The Jockey Club not only allowed this but, to Kris's indignation, charged a fee.

He taxied back fast to where a Land Rover waited with a young woman in an ultra short skirt leaning against it.

"Shit," Kris said forcefully.

"Why shit?"

"He's sent his daughter. He promised she wouldn't be here."

"She looks O.K. to me."

Kris said "Huh" with pity for my ignorance and slowed the Cherokee, and, swinging it round neatly into a tidy configuration for parking, cut the engine.

"Her name's Belladonna," Kris said. "Poison."

I unclipped my seat belt, unlatched the door, climbed out and jumped down from the wing.

Kris, having checked his switches, scrambled after. I wasn't sure he meant it about her name but he casually introduced us. "Bell, this is Perry. Perry . . . Belladonna. Call her Bell."

I shook her hand. She said, eyebrows lifting, "Aren't you . . . ?"

"I expect so," I said.

She looked sugar-sweet, not deadly. Fair hair, more wispy than regulated. Blue eyes with innocuously blinking lids. Pink-outlined lips with a smile that never quite left them. Even without Kris's comment, I'd have been aware of witchcraft.

"Climb in," she invited, gesturing to the Land Rover. "Dad heard you circling overhead and sent me along. He's mulling wine. He'd never leave with cinnamon floating."

Kris, apparently deaf to the instruction, was walking round his aircraft and patting it with approval, listening to the small cracking noises of the metal cooling. Its white painted fuselage gleamed in the sun along with the dark blue personalized insignia of a lightning flash and the registration letters that identified Kris worldwide: and in fact he had flown in enough countries to be known (not without respect) as the "the fussy

English." After his final landing on wet days he sponged and dried the undersides of the wings, not just the tops, to get rid of any mud thrown up by the wheels.

"Get in, do," Bell told him, opening the Land Rover's front passenger door for him. "This party's today, not tomorrow."

The antagonism between them was faint but positive. I sat in the rear seat for the five-mile drive to Caspar Harvey's house listening to the semi-polite exchanges and wondering how far their mutual dislike would go, such as, would they save each other if it risked themselves.

Caspar Harvey's home proved to be more than halfway to grand but just definitely on the under side of ostentatious. The front, with small-scale Palladian pillars, seemed imposing, but the inside was only one room deep, and no one had tried to pretend otherwise. Entrance hall and sitting room, combined by a wall of arches, made a single space ample enough for the gathering of upwards of thirty people who stood around drinking hot red wine, eating handfuls of peanuts and talking about Newmarket's main profitable crop—racehorses.

Caspar Harvey, noticing Kris's arrival, eeled his

way, drink held high, until he could greet his guest within shouting distance in the throng.

"I heard your overhead pass." He nodded to Kris. "And welcome to you, too," he added in my direction. "My trainer swears by your nose for rain. He's here somewhere. Do I run my filly on Friday? My wife puts her faith in the stars. Have some wine."

I accepted the wine, which tasted melodiously of cinnamon and sugar, and followed his identifying finger to his trainer across the crowd, Oliver Quigley, a-quiver and visibly ill at ease.

"Tell him it will be dry until Friday," Harvey said. "Tell him to run my horse."

He was enjoying, I thought, his role of lavish host. Reprehensible of me to think also that the role itself meant more to him than his guests. His expansive gestures were like his setting: a conscious indication of wealth and achievement, but one that carefully fell short of a flourish of trumpets.

I told him I'd taken aerial photos of his house and would send them to him, and, pleased, he invited me to take as many shots of his guests as they would allow.

In body he was as substantial as in means, a

heavy-shouldered presence with a thick neck and a trim gray grizzled beard. Shorter by only three inches than Kris's willowy extent—as I was myself—Caspar Harvey would nevertheless have been noticeable at any height, or lack of it: he had, strongly developed, the indefinable aura that comes with success. I took his picture. He posed again, and nodded benignly at the flash.

Kris drank Coca-Cola as a good little pilot should and kept his manic extravagance within bounds. It was definitely an "up" day in his psyche; good for wit and laughter and with no question of despairing walks along railway tracks.

The non-poisonous Belladonna, appearing at my side and pouring from a steaming jug of replenishment, asked me baldly why a sensible-looking person like myself should bother with Ironside's mental switchback.

"He's clever," I said neutrally.

"Is that enough?"

"Why don't you like him?" I asked.

"Like him? I loved the bastard once." She gave me a twitch of a deeper smile and a shrug of shoulders and poured reinforcements for others and I, as one does at such events, in time fetched up in a chatting bunch that contained the ever-worried trainer, Oliver Quigley. What about this wind, he wanted to know. "It's cold," he said.

My harmless actual tangible presence—especially with camera—seemed to upset him. I was used to aggression and disbelief from the sort of horse-oriented people who seemed to think (like children) that bad weather was somehow my fault. I was accustomed to being the unpopular messenger who brought the bad news of battles lost, and I'd been often enough cursed for *smiling* while I forecast blizzards; but on the whole I'd not caused what looked unexpectedly like *fear.*

I must be misreading him, I thought. But then, I knew him only as an agitated weather-obsessed horse trainer, and he could have—who knew—all sorts of other problems.

"It depends on the Urals," I said soothingly.

He was mystified. "What does?"

"The wind from the east. It's early in the year for a polar continental blast like this, but there may be a clear dry day for Caspar Harvey's filly, if it goes on blowing until Friday."

"And will it?" The question was put slightly pugnaciously by a gray-haired fiftyish imposing American-sounding woman who'd joined the group with three rows of pearls and an apologetic husband.

"Evelyn dear . . ." he murmured patiently.

She persevered with questions. "And what do you mean by Urals?"

Her husband, a small round man in heavy dark eyeglass frames, answered her smoothly. "Evelyn, dear, the Urals are mountains in Russia. On a straight line from the Urals to London, there is no high ground to get in the way. Nothing to divert or deflect an east wind from Siberia." He assessed me with shrewd but amiable brown eyes behind the heavy-duty lenses. He said, "Aren't you the young man who flew here with the meteorologist?"

Before I could agree that yes, I was, Oliver Quigley told him with rapid emphasis and energetic hands that I too forecast the weather and was probably even better known to the television public than Kris himself. "Robin and Evelyn," he assured me, anxious to be understood, "are American of course, and, as they live mostly in Florida, they don't see much British TV."

"Darcy," said the small man, completing the introduction by shifting his wine glass carefully to his left hand and offering me the right, "Robin

Darcy." He made lunch-party small talk in a subdued Boston-type accent. "And will you be along with Kris Ironside on his vacation?"

Not that I knew of. "I don't think so," I replied. Robin, I thought, had just inquired very delicately about my sexual preference. And what, I wondered, was his own? Evelyn, matronly in black and seemingly older than her husband, was nobody's idea of a trophy bimbo.

"Be sure to look us up," she said automatically, but insincerely.

"Love to." I sounded falsely eager, as one does.

Her husband rocked a little on heels and toes, his wrists folded over each other low on his stomach. His interest in me, slight in the first place, was fading rapidly, and presently he drifted off, Evelyn in tow, in search of more responsive brains.

Belladonna reappeared with her jug, her gaze ahead on the Darcys. "If you like cleverness, he's your man."

"He's clever at what?"

Bell's pale eyelids fluttered. "It's like beauty. Born in him. He just *is.*"

Darcy wandered around, however, looking insignificant and unimpressive. Evelyn's socializing voice was the one that prevailed.

"Don't be fooled," Bell said.

"No."

"Kris said you saved his life a couple of times."

After a pause, I said, "He liked to play with trains."

"No longer?"

"Less and less."

"I wouldn't fly with him," she said. "So we quarreled." After a silence she added, "It finished us. Doesn't he scare you?"

There had been a time only a year ago when the trains had all but won; when I'd sat with him all night while he curled like a fetus and moaned with pain: when the only word he'd said, in a sort of anguish, had been "Poison."

A couple of paces away Kris was at the top of his upswing, telling a flying joke and raising eye-crinkling laughter. "So the air hostess said, 'Yes, Miss Steinem, of course you can go up to the cockpit during this flight and talk to our lady captain and our lady first officer, but there's just one thing, with our all-female flight crew we don't call it a *cockpit* any more . . .'"

"God," Bell groaned. "I told him that bit of feminism yonks ago."

"Good jokes never die."

"Did you know that sometimes he writes verses?"

"Mm." I paused. "Scientific, mostly."

"I've seen him tear them up," Bell said.

So had I. A form of suicide, I'd thought: but better to kill a poem than himself.

Bell turned her back on Kris and said there was food in the dining room. There were also white-clothed tables and caterers' gold chairs and an autumnal buffet suitable for millionaires and hungry weathermen. I collected a disgracefully full plate and was welcomed by an insistent Evelyn Darcy into a space on a round table where her husband and four other guests were munching roast grouse with concentration.

The four unknowns and I went through the usual recognition routine and a promise that it wouldn't rain before bedtime; and I smiled and answered them placidly because in fact I liked my job very much, and good public relations never hurt.

Two of the unknowns slowly identified themselves as George Loricroft, distinguished, forty-five, top-dog racehorse trainer, and his blonde and over-shapely young wife, Glenda. Every time Glenda spoke, her dominating husband either contradicted or interrupted her. Glenda's nervous titter hid some razor-sharp resentment, I'd have said.

Evelyn Darcy, who besides the three rows of pearls, the black dress and the gray-silver over-lacquered hair was decidedly nosy, had no inhibitions about question time. She wanted to know—and used her loud voice to get attention—whether Kris and I earned a fortune for our many onscreen appearances. How else could Kris afford the upkeep of an airplane?

Everyone heard her. Kris across the room gave me a comical look, half choked with laughter and yelled her an answer.

"We're both civil servants. We get civil service pay. *You* all pay us . . . and it's not enough to fund a month of condoms."

Reactions to this intimate and inaccurate revelation varied from laughter among the guests to distaste and embarrassment. I peacefully ate my grouse. Being a friend of Kris's meant being willing to accept the whole package. He could have said far worse. He had done, in the past.

Evelyn Darcy enjoyed the ripples. Robin looked long-suffering at her side. George Loricroft, the constant wife repressor, checked with me that we did indeed get civil service pay and I unexcitedly agreed that yes we did, and why not, we gave a public service.

Oliver Quigley at that point inserted a chair where there was hardly enough space for it between Evelyn and myself and behaved in general as if the military police were hot on his trail for unspeakable offenses. Did the man *never* relax?

"I wanted to say to you," he more or less stuttered into my lunch, "that I had a sort of pamphlet in the post yesterday from a new sort of organization that offers . . . er, well, I mean, it's worth a try, you know . . ."

"Offers what?" I asked without pressing interest as he rambled to a halt.

"Well . . . er . . . a personalized reading of the weather."

"A private firm?" I asked. "Is that it?"

"Well . . . yes. You give the . . . er, by e-mail of course . . . the time and place where you want to know what weather to expect and you get the answer back at once."

"Fascinating," I said dryly.

"Haven't you heard of it? Bit of competition for you, isn't it?"

If he'd had more courage, what he'd said would have neared sarcasm. As it was, I finished the excellent grouse and fried breadcrumbs and smiled without annoyance.

"You go ahead and sign on with them, Mr. Quigley," I said. "Fine."

"I didn't expect you to say that!" he exclaimed. "I mean . . . don't you mind?"

"Not in the least."

Robin Darcy leaned forward and asked me from across his wife and the shaky trainer, "How much do you charge Mr. Quigley for saying to run Caspar's filly on Friday?"

Oliver Quigley might be nervous, but not stupid. He listened, and understood. He opened and closed his mouth and would, I knew, continue to tap me for accurate info that he didn't have to pay for.

Robin Darcy, with seemingly genuine interest, then asked me politely when I'd first become interested in the weather, and I told him, as I'd explained a hundred times before, that I'd watched the clouds since I was six, and had never wanted a different life.

His amiability, I thought, was built on his certainty of his own mental superiority. I had long ago learned to leave that sort of belief unchallenged, and had received a couple of advancements in consequence. Only to myself could I admit my reprehensible cynicism. And to myself, often enough, I could also, with humility, admit that I'd more than met my match. I smiled weakly at Robin Darcy and couldn't decide where his cleverness ended—or began.

Evelyn asked, "Where did you go to learn meteorology? Is there a special school for it?"

I said, "It's called standing out in the rain."

Kris, on the move back to the buffet, overheard both question and answer and replied to her over his shoulder, "Don't listen to him. He's a physicist. Dr. Perry Stuart, no less."

Robin yawned and closed his myopic eyes, but somewhere in that sharp brain there had been a quickening. I had seen it and could feel it, and didn't know why he wanted to hide it.

Oliver Quigley hastened to assure me with many a quiver that he hadn't meant to insult me by considering an outside firm better, when we both knew he had come darned near to it. The difference was that although he appeared vastly disturbed by it, I didn't care at all. If Oliver Quigley would only take his shivery nerves and dump them on someone else's doorstep, I would be delighted.

Caspar Harvey played the genial host faultlessly to give his guests good memories, collecting me from table, taking me in tow and introducing me to everyone in turn, persuading them to let me take their photo. Those who disliked the idea were overridden: Caspar offered refilled glasses, and got his way.

I snapped Quigley and Loricroft together, the pair of racehorse trainers topping up on crisp roast potatoes and pausing briefly in passing to discuss their trade. I heard snatches of Quigley— "He never pays on time"—and then Loricroft— "My runner at Baden-Baden got bumped at the start."

Loricroft's bosomy wife confided proudly to others at the table, "George goes to Germany often and wins races there, don't you, George?" But Loricroft, coldly undermining her enthusiasm, cut the "often" to "only once" during the past season. "I win far more races in France, but I can't expect my dear wife to get things right."

He looked around to gather sympathetic responses and smiled with superiority down his nose. I thought Glenda a pain but her dear George an agony.

The splendid lunch narrowed down to coffee

and worthwhile port and eventually, with regret, the guests began to leave. Kris and I needed transport back to the Cherokee, though, and Bell was nowhere to be seen.

Caspar Harvey himself put an end to my hovering on one foot by halting in front of me and saying decisively, "While you're here in Newmarket you may as well take a peek at my filly. Take her photo too. Then you'll know what's at stake when you're looking at Friday."

He put a tugging hand on my arm and made it downright rude for me to pull away: but I had no reason not to see the filly, if that was what he wanted, and felt it a small enough courtesy after such a lunch, if Kris were not pressed for time for flying home before dark.

It wasn't time that upset Kris, but the realization that he was expected to travel in the Land Rover again with Bell. There seemed no logical reason for four of us to travel in two cars to see the filly, but that was clearly what Caspar Harvey wanted; and when he'd cordially waved a temporary adieu to Oliver Quigley, his last departing guest, that was what Caspar Harvey got.

He drove out through the front gates, following Quigley's pale blue Volvo, and leaving Kris behind for his daughter to bring in the Land Rover.

With only a six or so miles' journey to go, Caspar Harvey lost no time in saying what he'd maneuvered me into hearing.

"How unstable is your friend Kris?"

I said vaguely, "Um . . ."

Harvey announced, "I don't want him as a son-in-law."

"At the moment," I said, "it doesn't look probable."

"Rubbish! The girl's besotted. A year ago they fought like cats, and I'll tell you, I was glad of it. Not that he's not a brilliant forecaster; he is. So I went on acting on his weather advice and he's saved me thousands, literally thousands."

He paused, finding the question difficult, I guessed, but asking it just the same.

"Can you tell him to leave my daughter alone?"

The short answer was of course no, I couldn't. It didn't seem to me, though, to be the right question.

When I didn't answer at once Harvey said, "A year ago she was spitting mad. She went off and got a job in Spain. Then six weeks ago she came back wanting me to arrange today's lunch and not to tell Kris she'd be here, and I did it for her,

God knows why, thinking she'd thoroughly got over him, and I was wrong. She hasn't."

He paused gloomily, his big car purring, eating up the miles. "He asked if he could bring a friend to navigate today and when I saw you . . . and you're obviously sensible—not like him—I thought of getting you to tell him not to upset Bell all over again . . . but I suppose you'll think it was a bad idea. . . ."

I said a shade helplessly, "They'll work it out for themselves."

It wasn't what he wanted to hear, and we finished the six miles in mutually unsatisfied silence.

Oliver Quigley's stableyard, it transpired, was on the far side of the town, where shops and hotels gave way to the essential business of the place, to stalls for polished horses, and to the Heath galloping grounds, where they could practice winning and turn their gloss into procreation.

Quigley the trainer drove his pale blue Volvo into his own domain, and even there he looked ill at ease. The big quadrangle stableyard was alive with grooms fetching hay and water to each horse, and putting the straw floor covering clean and comfortable for the night. The groom in authority—clearly the foreman, the head groom—

was doling out scoops of food for each horse. Some of the stalls had open doors, some had interior lights on, some were altogether closed and dark. There was an air of wanting to finish the Sunday afternoon program and get off as soon as possible for more enjoyable pursuits.

Caspar Harvey had stopped his car beside Quigley's and made no more reference to his daughter's feelings for Kris.

There was a notable smartening of body language among the grooms at the sight of the two most powerful men in their lives, Oliver Quigley the trainer (and never mind his self-conscious fluttering, it was he who paid the wages) and Caspar Harvey, owner of four superstars that gave kudos not only to Quigley's stable, but to the whole sport of racing.

The filly who might run on Friday was to be found, it seemed, behind one of the closed doors, not yet put right for the night.

Caspar Harvey with pleased anticipation strode over to a row of six stalls separated from the others on one side by the path leading out from the yard and down towards the Warren Hill gallops, and on the other side by a path giving on to the large house where it seemed Quigley lived.

"This is the filly's stall," he said, beckoning to me to come as he unlatched the bolts of the top half of the split stable door. "She's in here."

And so she was. But she wouldn't race on Friday.

I watched Harvey's face change from pride to horror. I saw his throat constrict as he groped for air. His treasure, the Friday filly, the two-year-old preparing to take the females' crown, the possible over-winter favorite for the following year's 1,000 Guineas and Oaks, the future dam of champions, the golden chestnut with a single small white star on her forehead; this fast and famous athlete was down on her knees and groaning, sweat darkening her flanks.

While Harvey, Quigley and I watched in long stunned seconds she toppled over onto her side, labored breath wheezing, her pain obvious.

She looked on the point of death, but she didn't die.

2

DEEPLY UPSET ON many levels, Caspar Harvey took charge, and it was he who sent for the veterinarian, brushing Quigley out of the way and offering the veterinarian, whom he knew well, twice his normal fee if he abandoned his Sunday afternoon rest and appeared in Quigley's yard immediately.

There was nothing he could physically do for his filly because he didn't know what was wrong with her: he understood the power of money, though, and he would spend it lavishly if it would get useful results.

"Colic?" he speculated. "Oliver, shouldn't you be walking her round? Surely walking is what you do for colic?"

Oliver Quigley squatted down beside his horse's head and stroked her nose. He said he thought walking might do more harm than good, even if he could get the filly to stand up again, and that he would wait for the veterinarian. And it was noticeable, I thought, that, faced with a real and disastrous-looking crisis with his horses, his constant anxiety shivers abated and almost died away.

Caspar Harvey stifled his emotions and thought of the future.

"You . . ." he said to me. "I mean you, Stuart, do you still have that camera?"

I produced it from my pants pocket.

He nodded. "Take the filly, for the insurance. Pictures. Stronger than words."

I did his bidding, the flash bright inside the darkening stall.

"Send them to me," he said, and I assured him I would.

Belladonna, driving Kris into the yard in the Land Rover, reacted to the filly's plight with loving distress and absolute priority, and Kris infuriated her by saying his and my departure time was more important than waiting around for the veterinarian, because we couldn't navigate or land safely at White Waltham in fading light. Filly or no filly we needed to be off the ground by half past four, he said. Bell argued sharply that half past five would do. Kris said if she wouldn't take us to the plane when he wanted to go, he would call for a taxi. It seemed to me, listening to the vinegary exchange, that Caspar Harvey had no immediate worry about a son-in-law.

The veterinarian earned his double fee with screeching tires and, while listening through his stethoscope, metaphorically scratched his head over the filly.

"I don't think she has colic," he said. "What has she been eating?"

The head groom and all the others were immediately insulted at the slur on their care.

The filly had eaten nothing that day, they swore, except oats and bran and hay.

Kris argued insistently with Bell, who finally in a rage told her father she would be away for a while delivering the infuriating Kris to his transport. Her father nodded absentmindedly, his attention all now on his suffering animal, and he looked vague also when, on the point of leaving, I thanked him for the lunch and repeated that I would send the snaps.

Bell, braking with a jerk beside the Cherokee after a bad-tempered ride through the town, listened with a frown while Kris tried to explain yet again that as we were both on duty that evening it was essential to return in time. It was true that we were on duty, but it wasn't strictly necessary for us to leave Newmarket by half past four. A long-established loyalty, however, tied my tongue.

She watched Kris walk round the Cherokee doing the ever-necessary checks.

"He makes me lose my temper," she said.

I nodded. "I'll look after him. You go back to your father."

She stared at me concentratedly with the blue eyes.

She said, "I don't *mean* to be a bitch."

I thought that as she was dealing with two strong-willed men and was hardly pliant herself, she was not, even with the winsomely blinking eyelids, going to activate any sort of three-way equilibrium without a maybe volcanic show of strength first.

Kris finished his checks, and Bell and I both stood up out of the Land Rover. Bell and Kris stood looking at each other in a silence that crackled as if electric.

Bell said finally, "I've got a job as assistant trainer to George Loricroft. I'll be staying in Newmarket from now on."

Loricroft had been at the lunch table where I sat with Evelyn (pearls) and Robin (glasses) Darcy.

Kris considered it, scowling.

"I've a month's leave coming up," he said. "I'm going to Florida for part of it."

"Nice for you."

"You could come."

"No."

Kris turned his back abruptly and climbed into his flying machine, anything but, I thought wryly, a magnificent man as in the song.

I said goodbye awkwardly to Bell and said I hoped for the best with the filly.

"Give me your phone number, and I'll tell you."

I had a pen but no paper. She took the pen and wrote the number on her left-hand palm.

"Get in, get in, Perry," Kris shouted, "or I'll go without you."

"He's a shit," Bell said.

"He loves you," I commented.

"Like a tornado tears you apart."

Kris started the engine and, not wanting to risk

being actually abandoned, I climbed into the Cherokee, closed the door, fastened its hatch and buckled on my seat belt. Bell gave a vestige of a wave in return for my more vigorous farewell through the window, but Kris stared unforgivingly ahead until it was too late even for courtesy. When we were airborne, though, and while Bell still stood by the Land Rover watching us depart, Kris made a ceremonial pass in front of her and waggled his wings as we flew away.

Newmarket to White Waltham wasn't really very far. We had plenty of time and plenty of light when we landed, and the good spirits of the morning had returned to the pilot.

THE COLD WIND BLEW until Friday, its Sunday sunshine fading to a depressing iron gray. Caspar Harvey's filly clung onto life, her symptoms and progress delivered to me at first hand by Bell, who had at the last minute, she said, remembered to write my telephone number onto something more lasting than skin only when she'd already squeezed liquid soap onto her hands.

"Apparently the poor animal had been pressing her head against the wall, just pressing. . . . Well, I've never seen a horse do that and nor has her groom, but the veterinarian says that head-pressing is a symptom of *poison,* and now everyone's in a tizzy. Panic."

"What poison?" I asked, faintly teasing. "Not belladonna?"

"No. Thanks very much. Very funny. I've had to put up all my life with being named after deadly nightshade. The veterinarian kindly says belladonna would very likely have killed her."

Two days later Bell was back on the line with an update. It was Wednesday by then.

"Dad and Oliver Quigley are trying to keep this out of the papers, heaven knows why, there isn't a chance. News goes round Newmarket like the black death. The filly is up at the equine hospital and they're taking blood samples and her temperature, and poking around in manure, you name it, they've thought of it. I saw Kris doing the forecast at lunchtime. He looks so level-headed you'd never guess what he's like. Don't tell him I watch him."

Bell was right in that nothing was secret or sacred at Headquarters: on back pages from tabloids to broadsheets, the filly kicked football into second place for two whole days.

I'd taken my film of Sunday's happenings to be

developed the day after the lunch party, and I'd sent off a set of prints as a gift to Caspar Harvey. Bell reported her father as being horrified by the filly pics but on the whole grateful, and Oliver Quigley was moaning that the filly's state wasn't his fault. "But Dad's so angry we're heading for court, I shouldn't wonder," Bell said. "They spend hours arguing against each other."

My own days as usual were spent at the weather section of the BBC Wood Lane Television Centre. There each afternoon at two o'clock I and all other Meteorological Office forecasters working the same shift were connected together in a telephone conference to learn what was happening in the weather world, and what interpretation we should put on sometimes wildly divergent facts.

The skill that had unexpectedly transformed my life at about twenty-two had been an awakening gift for presentation. I'd been dumped "cold" in front of the cameras one evening at nine-thirty to give the longest solo appearance of the day, standing in at the ultimate last minute for a colleague with running diarrhea. Because it was unexpected I hadn't had time for nerves, and most luckily I'd read the weather signs right, so that it rained the next day where I'd said it would.

The resulting trickle of letters of approval had been enough to give me another chance. I'd enjoyed it. More letters followed. By the end of six months I was a regular on the screen and after seven years reached second place in the hierarchy. The top guy, the oldest of us all, held guru status and was treated by everyone with the deference due his postcard collection of Edwardian porn.

Both he and I could have shunted ourselves out of active forecasting and wafted our careers upstairs into organization. Neither of us wanted to go. The actor in both of us enjoyed the live performance.

My grandmother loved it.

My grandmother was in a way my Cherokee at White Waltham, or, in other words, the bottomless pit into which I chose to pour the shekels I should have been laying up in bonds.

My grandmother and I had no other relations left besides ourselves and both she and I knew that probably fairly soon I'd be alone. The energetic woman who'd picked an infant from the wreckage that had just killed her daughter, the able journalist who had persuaded a court to grant her custody of her grandson, the understanding adult who'd seen a boy safely through childhood, adolescence and university, she now, at eighty, used wheels for legs and needed a nursing attendant all the time for simple living.

I called to see her on the Thursday afternoon, kissing her lightly on the forehead and checking on her general state of health.

"How're you doing, Gran?"

"Absolutely fine."

A lie, as we both knew.

She still lived in the apartment where I'd spent my youth, on the second floor of a house overlooking the River Thames near the top of the tidal flow. At low tide there were acres of mud with screeching gulls scavenging; and at high tide steamerfuls of tourists charging past—with or without thumping music—for a quick trip up through the half-tide lock at Richmond into deeper waters above.

The ever-increasing rent stretched our joint resources painfully, but the living parade outside was worth it.

When I'd graduated from college and left the nest, as one does, she'd still been an agile employee of a travel company for whom she'd worked all my life. The travel company, enlightened beyond the normal, had relied on her changing age to give advice in their brochures to her peers. At fifty she'd written, "Those gorgeous boys teaching you tennis are playing for money, not keeps," and at sixty she'd said of Australia, "Climb Ayer's Rock if you're either a five-year-old kid or next best thing to a mountain goat," and at seventy gave her view that "It's now or never for Great Walls and pilgrimage. Do it now, or settle for never."

Fate had settled it for never. At seventy-four, disregarding warning periods of little feeling in her legs, she went out to assess the strength needed for white-water rafting in southern stretches of the Colorado River. She hadn't actually bucketed down the fiercest stretches; she'd asked the guides. She wasn't *mad,* my grandmother. She was paid to write about possible adventures for her age group, and if necessary to say, "Don't go." At seventy-four she'd been unenthusiastic about white-water down her spine, and, wanting to get home, had ignored subsequent fever and chills as just a nuisance. Then, delayed at the airport, she'd had to wait half a day for a replacement aircraft to be found for the return to England. She'd written me a postcard from the airport, which of course I didn't receive until three weeks later.

Dearest Perry, I have the screaming heebie-jeebies about this flight, but there isn't another for five days. Look after yourself. I've caught a cold. Eternally, Gran.

On the long overnight heebie-jeebie flight from Phoenix, Arizona, to London she had progressively lost muscular strength in her legs, and by the time the substitute aircraft landed safely at Heathrow the next morning the whole of her lower body felt numb. She had walked very slowly to immigration, and hardly ever again.

After hours of anxious investigations we were told that the trouble lay in a meningioma, a non-cancerous but hard tumor that had invaded and grown slowly inside the spinal column and was now compressing the spinal nerves. Friendly and clearly concerned doctors tried truckloads of steroids, but they did no good. Surgery, though discussed lengthily and carefully carried out, interfered with the vascular supply of blood to the spinal cord and made things worse.

My grandmother's heebie-jeebies were never to be lightly ignored.

She had had the heebie-jeebies the day she'd traveled eighteen hours to try by her presence to persuade my reluctant parents to leave their much-loved house, only to see it blow up with them inside as she approached. She'd had much milder heebie-jeebies the day I'd broken my ankle being run over by a golf cart, but because of some deeply foreboding heebie-jeebies, we had not gone skiing in a valley that could have killed us in an avalanche had we been there.

When the medical dust had settled on the un-helpful meninges, my no longer active grand-mother was making jokes about relative inability, and was afraid she would be forcibly retired by her employers. Instead, they had asked for columns on day-treats and holidays for the dis-abled; and I had shaken hands on a deal with an agency that supplied nurses; they agreed that a succession of angels would each live for a week in the flat, caring for my gran. They would nurse, shop and cook and dress their patient and drive her to column-worthy destinations. They would sleep in the small rear-facing room where my physics books still took up shelf space. They would wear uniforms if they wanted to. And, my grandmother insisted, they would watch the weather forecasts.

Only one of the nurses the agency sent had

been a failure: she'd been heavily unattractive and of gloomy mind, and she'd brought her dog. My grandmother preferred her angels to be of grand-daughter age, unencumbered and pretty, and to their surprise, the agency found their nurses *asking* to spend repeat live-in weeks with an old woman.

On the Thursday after Caspar Harvey's lunch I mentioned the sick filly to my grandmother and found her one step ahead of the facts; no real surprise, she read newspapers at vacuum-pump speed and from her own long experience at writing them, understood all the inferences they left out.

"Caspar Harvey will dump Oliver Quigley, don't you think, Perry?" she observed. "He'll send his horses to Loricroft, to be where his daughter's going."

As her hands and arms could deal fairly well with newsprint she habitually spread the papers open on her knees. I watched her wrestle, knowing she wouldn't thank me for assistance. Only when she laid the papers down on her lap unmoving with a cross little sigh could one expect to be allowed to help.

As always, though it took her and the current

nurse an hour or more to achieve it, she looked fresh, neat and striking, this time in a dark blue lace-edged gown with a silver and white artificial gardenia pinned to her left shoulder, and silver leather shoes on her non-functioning feet.

I asked, mystified, "What makes you think Harvey will move his horses?"

"He's in the game for glory. And you've always told me, haven't you, that Oliver Quigley has the permanent heebie-jeebies all the time?"

"I suppose so, yes."

I sat in a large armchair near the window, next to her, with her wheels locked in her favorite place, so that we could both watch the raucous seagulls chase one another over the mud, their display of basic aggressive instinct obvious and so informative that inter-human wars, my grand-mother observed, were natural and inevitable.

On that Thursday afternoon it seemed to me that the life force was as low as the ebb tide in my grandmother, however hard she might try to dis-guise it, and it alarmed me very much because I didn't want to imagine life without her.

She had been always not only stand-in parent with bandages for scraped knees, but also an in-tellectual teacher, partner and prompter of thought. The occasional rebellions of my teens were distant memories. I'd come to visit her by habit for years since then, listening to her down-to-earth wisdom and adopting most of it for myself. It was too soon for her to ebb. I wasn't ready to lose her. I supposed that perhaps it would always be too soon.

"If Quigley loses the Harvey horses . . ." I began vaguely.

My grandmother had her own questions. "Who poisoned the filly? Who's trying to find out? What is that mad friend of yours doing about it?"

I smiled. "He's off to Florida on leave. He has a love-hate thing going with Caspar Harvey's daughter. You might say he's running away."

She tired abruptly of the Harvey saga at that point and, closing her eyes, let the newspaper slide to the floor.

There was a new nurse on duty that week, one I hadn't met before, and as if called she came quietly into the sitting room and gathered the papers into a tidy pile. She had been introduced to me by my grandmother as, "This dear young woman is Jett van Els. She'll write it down for you. Her father was Belgian."

Jett van Els of the Belgian father easily filled my grandmother's requirements of youth and looks and was moreover tall and trim in a blue-and-white uniform with an upside-down watch pinned where I would get into harassment trouble looking at the time.

My grandmother's sleepinesses never lasted more than a few minutes, but that day it took her longer to wake up. Still, she suddenly opened her round blue eyes and as always came back to full awareness immediately.

"Stay away from Newmarket, Perry, that place is full of villains." She spoke as if without prior thought and looked almost surprised at what she'd said.

"Newmarket's quite a big town," I commented mildly. "Stay away from whom, exactly?"

"Stay away from that filly."

I said, "O.K.," casually and didn't mean what I said.

As far as I could remember she had only once herself been to Newmarket, and that years ago on a visit prompted by her writing a magazine article series on how to squander one's time and spending money on cheerful days out. After that, Newmarket had been consigned to her mental file of "been there, done that" and life was too short, she often said, for taking the same road twice.

"What's wrong with seeing the filly, anyway?" I asked.

"That's *exactly* the point. Whatever's wrong with the filly, stay away from it."

She frowned, however, and I reckoned she didn't clearly know what she meant. Worse than physical weakness, I always feared, would be the atrophy of her sharp mind: so what she'd said about the filly was either acutely perceptive or nonsense, and I didn't want to guess which.

To Jett van Els the exchange meant nothing as horses weren't her interest. She arranged cushions comfortably at her patient's back and showed in every fluid movement the expertise of a good nurse. Regardless of her un-English name, she spoke and looked like a homegrown rose, very much the type for whom I'd once ditched a tycoon's daughter, only to be dumped in my turn when the novelty of being escorted by a well-known face had worn off. Real life began when the screen went dark.

Jett van Els with composure said that Mrs. Mevagissey would be having fish pie with parsley sauce for supper: did I want to stay?

Mrs. Mevagissey was my grandmother.

"No, he won't stay," she placidly said. "But on past form you may find him asking you to share a pub sandwich in a week or two."

"Gran," I protested.

"I'm glad of it," she said truthfully. "So off you go, and I'll watch you tomorrow on the box."

I always left at her bidding so as not to exhaust her, and this time I collected on the way out a friendly and amused reaction from the brown van Els eyes, a visible message that if I asked I might get my sandwich.

Mrs. Mevagissey knew me a shade too well, I thought.

I SPENT FRIDAY in the Weather Center watching reports come in from all over the world. The steady continental wind from the east was breaking up, but the Newmarket turf would still have been dry and fast for Harvey's filly that afternoon if she'd been capable of benefiting.

Messages from Bell sounded as if frustration largely prevailed. The industry's busy news-diggers had broken off their filly chase for the weekend in order to report the races themselves, and by Monday the sick horse would be of backburner stature, if she got a mention at all. The transfer of all Harvey's other horses along the road from Quigley to Loricroft earned one strong paragraph: the engagement of Bell as Loricroft's assistant trainer merited a picture—of Bell, not of Loricroft, not of Harvey, and not of the horses. It was Bell who was pretty.

Poor Oliver Quigley no longer troubled my telephone twice at least every day: I received one pathetic call from him, a matter of a choking throat and barely swallowed emotion, the quivers back at full force.

Racing, though, even including the top two-year-old colts' races, the Dewhurst and the Middle Park Stakes, and the fillies' championship, the Cheveley Park Stakes, was not near my highest priority.

Winds around the globe were increasingly in turmoil as usual in that autumnal time of year, with a full-blown hurricane in the Pacific threatening the southwest California coast, and a destructively raging typhoon coming ashore and drowning people in the Philippines. Japan was suffering appalling waves, called tsunamis, caused by offshore ocean-bed earthquakes.

In the Atlantic the count of hurricanes and

lesser tropical depressions had reached thirteen for the year, with possibly the most active cyclonic weeks of autumn still ahead; and although roaring and massive disturbances of hurricane strength seldom reached the British Isles except as decaying systems of heavy rain, to us as to meteorologists round the world they were of ultimate interest.

Two weeks after Caspar Harvey's lunch the year's fourteenth cyclonic swirl of clouds formed off the west coast of Africa and crossed the Atlantic slightly north of the equator. The three essentials for its transformation into a full hurricane were all in place, being, first, a seawater temperature above 80 degrees Fahrenheit; second, hot air from the tropics converging with equatorial air full of moisture taken up from the sea; and third, winds caused by the warm moist air rising and letting cold air flood in underneath. The rotation of the earth kept the inflowing winds spinning, and the heat of the ocean went on intensifying the whole circling air mass.

Its identifying name, chosen years before to be given to the fourteenth storm of that season, was Nicky.

Kris watched its development moodily.

"It's heading westwards, straight to Florida," he complained, "and it's traveling quite fast at twenty miles an hour."

"I thought you'd be interested," I said.

"Of *course* I'd be interested, but it will get there ahead of me, won't it? I don't go for another eight days."

"It's getting more organized," I commented, nodding. "The surface winds are circling at about eighty miles an hour already."

Kris said, "I've always wanted to fly through a hurricane." He paused. "I mean . . . as a pilot . . . fly through one."

I listened to the fanatical relish in his voice: he wasn't making idle chat.

"People do, you know," he said seriously.

"It's crazy," I said, but I wanted to as well, badly.

"Just think of it!" His pale eyes glazed with growing excitement. "And don't tell me the idea of it doesn't get your own blood racing, because who was it who competed in the North Cornwall high-surfing contests? Who can stand upright on a surfboard? Riding the tunnel, isn't it called?"

"The tube. That was different. It was totally safe."

"Oh really?"

"Well, almost."

"I'll fly you safely through Hurricane Nicky."

To his enormous disappointment, however, he didn't get the chance. Hurricane Nicky, although intensifying to a Category 3 storm on the Saffir-Simpson scale, with circulating wind speeds between 111 and 130 miles an hour, not only didn't wait around for Kris to arrive in the States, but turned northwards before it reached the American eastern seaboard at all, and blew itself out harmlessly over the cold waters of the North Atlantic.

Kris nevertheless set off to Florida, with the rocketry at Cape Canaveral as his priority, followed by contacts with the National Hurricane Tracking Center in Miami; but no storms at all, to his great disappointment, were shaping up in their chief spawning ground, west of Africa.

During an otherwise uneventful week there he sent me a fax to say he was now staying for a few days with the people we met at Caspar Harvey's lunch, as arranged.

I couldn't remember at first whom he meant. The lunch itself had receded in my mind, semi-eclipsed by the poisoning of the filly, but a backwards-looking search came up tentatively with the Darcys; Robin the brains and Evelyn the pearls.

Confirmation quickly followed. Kris dispatched, "This is a casual place. Robin and Evelyn are adamant they want you to join us on Monday, to stay for a few days, so send a yes-thank-you pronto. Just to remind you, the minor disturbance now forming in the Caribbean will be called Odin if it develops. I intend to fly through it. Won't you come?"

The minor disturbance in the Caribbean, I judged from a swift trawl of the chaotic conditions there, would probably collapse into a fizzle, saving the name Odin for another day.

Next morning, though, the winds south of Jamaica gained speed, and the barometric pressure dropped to well below a thousand millibars, an ominously low reading considering that the average was nearer 1013. A wind sheer aloft that had been preventing an organized circling movement had disintegrated and stopped tearing the upper atmosphere apart, and the minor disturbance, as if taking stock of the possibilities, had begun a slow invitation to a dance.

Kris transmitted, "Odin is now designated a tropical storm. Pity it's not yet a hurricane, but come on Monday anyway." He included directions to reach the Darcys, and welcoming messages from both.

The Monday ahead was the beginning of my official leave.

I pondered over the meager savings I'd intended to devote to walking in Sicily, and then telephoned Belladonna Harvey. I learned about the state of the filly (feeble but on her feet, test results still not available); the state of Oliver Quigley (lachrymose); the state of her relations with her new employer Loricroft (he was chasing her); and the state of her father (fuming). And how was Kris doing, she finally wanted to know, as he'd been missing from the screen for a week.

"He went to Florida."

"So he did."

"He wanted you to go."

"Mm."

"He's staying with Robin and Evelyn Darcy. They've asked me to join them. Is that odd?"

There was a pause before she said, "What do you want to know?"

With a smile that I knew reached my voice, I asked, "For a start, what does he *do?*"

"Evelyn tells everyone he sells mushrooms. He never denies it."

"He *can't* sell mushrooms," I protested.

"Why not? Evelyn says he sells all the sorts of

mushrooms the food world's gone mad about. Portobello, cèpes, chanterelles, shiitake, things like that. He has them freeze-dried and sealed in vacuum packs and they're making him a fortune." She paused. "Also he sells grass."

"He *what?*"

"He sells grass. I don't mean *that* sort of grass. You may laugh, but in Florida they don't grow garden grass from seed. The climate's wrong, or something. They plant sods instead. They lay lawns like laying carpets. Robin Darcy has a sod farm. Don't laugh. That's what it's called, and it's a million-dollar business."

I said slowly, "You also said he was born clever."

"Yes. He was. And I told you not to be fooled. He goes around in those thick black eyeglass frames looking like a rather inadequate and cuddly little ninny, but everything he touches turns to gold."

"And do you like him?" I asked.

"Not really." She answered without hesitation. "He's Dad's buddy, not mine. He's too calculating. Everything he does has a purpose, but you only realize that later."

"And Evelyn?" I asked.

"She's his front man, like I told you. Well,

woman. I've known them for ages, on and off. Robin and Dad have always talked farming, though you wouldn't think mushrooms and sod have much in common with birdseed, which is Dad's major industry."

I said vaguely, "I thought your father grew barley."

"Yes, he does. It makes great whisky. He doesn't grow the birdseed. He buys every variety of seed by the hundred tons and has a factory which mixes them and sells them in small packets to people who keep budgerigars and things. You might say that both Robin Darcy and my father make millions four ounces at a time."

"So . . . er . . . Evelyn?" I murmured again.

"She and my mother get on fine. They both adore jewelry. If you talk diamonds to Evelyn you'll be her friend for life."

Bell hadn't persuaded me pro or con, but the thought of Florida, so far unvisited, easily won, and it was at that point that I thoughtlessly told my grandmother that Kris wanted to fly with me through a hurricane.

"Don't go, Perry. It gives me the heebie-jeebies . . . ."

But I'd kissed her and given her anxiety no

weight. It was years, by then, since the slow paralysis of the Phoenix-to-London flight, and no heebies or indeed jeebies had since that dreadful journey raised a threatening head.

"I'll come back safely," I assured her, and flew to Florida on the cheapest ticket I could find.

ROBIN AND EVELYN'S South Florida home, though apparently nothing extravagant for the area, was to eyes disciplined to a one-room third-floor attic bedsit (tiny bathroom and alcove-kitchen) a dazzling revelation.

To start with, there was the brilliance of color. I was used to the blue-gray northern light already afflicting the afternoons of London W.12, latitude between 51 and 52 degrees north.

In Sand Dollar Beach, at latitude 25 degrees, just north of the Tropic of Cancer but well north of the equator, pink was vibrant, turquoise blazed to the horizon on the sea and green palm trees swayed over white crumbling lacy waves.

I very seldom regretted the constraints I accepted in order to pay for my grandmother's comfort, but I felt, on that beautiful sparkling evening, that the English screaming seagulls fighting on the ebb tide came expensive.

I had thanked the Darcys for their invitation and they'd warmly greeted my arrival but, even allowing for the legendary generosity that Americans displayed by habit, I still wasn't sure why I was there in Sand Dollar Beach watching the golden sunset, drinking an exotic intoxicater and eating canapés the size of Frisbees.

Evelyn talked about diamonds, as Bell had foretold. Evelyn, silver hair immaculate, wore shimmering ice-blue silk pants with a loose blouse of the same silk, embroidered all over with pearls and little silver tubes that my worldly grandmother had educated me to recognize as bugles.

Robin, full glass of icy concoction in hand, lazed back in a vast thickly cushioned garden chaise longue that horizontally supported his bare ankles and feet. Robin had called me "Dr. Stuart" while meeting my flight in Miami airport and "dear boy" when pressing a piña colada into my hand, murmuring also "Pineapple juice, coconut milk and rum. Suit you, I hope?"

He wasn't sure of me, I thought, nor I of him. One could often perceive goodwill instantly. In Robin I saw a chess game.

We sat on a south-facing large terrace that overlooked the calm Atlantic Ocean on one side and was dramatically lit on the other by streaky gold clouds in a late afternoon sky.

Kris, who seldom drank alcohol even when not flying, restlessly wandered from terrace to lower-level deck pool and back again, searching the golden heavens as if in annoyed disappointment.

Robin Darcy said to him tolerantly, "Kris, go inside and watch the Weather Channel. If the great god Odin is stalking about in the Caribbean, you won't see him up here for days."

I asked Robin if he and Evelyn had ever sat tight through a hurricane and was smiled at with sad pity for my naiveté.

"You *can't* sit tight," Evelyn assured me. "You get thrown about. I thought you were a meteorologist. I thought you knew things like that."

"He knows in theory," Kris told them, pardoning me. "He knows how hurricanes form but no one knows why. He knows why they're called hurricanes, but not where they're going. He's a doctor of philosophy, which is rare for a weatherman, and he ought to be doing research like 'into the why, that no one knows,' and not sitting drinking in the sun, but I'll tell you he's here now because I said I'd fly him through a hurricane's eye, and not because he's researching coconut milk with pineapple juice and rum."

Robin swiveled his eyes my way, also the hand holding his drink. "Is that a fact?" he said.

"I wouldn't have missed this evening for anything," I replied. I raised my own drink towards the sun, but it was opaque like many questions and let no light through.

3

ROBIN, GENEROUS WITH his telephone as with his rum, listened with barely confined enthusiasm to my report on the weather brewing in the circle of sea named after the frightening Caribs, North American Indians, who invaded the islands and coastal lands, and ruled by torture there before Columbus and other European colonists drove them out in their turn.

There were still pirates, modern-dress variety, Robin said, infesting the warm blue waters as murderous predators, stealing yachts and killing the owners, though maybe they weren't quite as bloodsucking as in the past. He smiled, mentioning that the word Carib had the same linguistic root as cannibal.

I talked to the Hurricane Center in Miami, where a longtime telephone pal gave me an as-of-five-minutes-ago state of the upper winds:

"Odin is coming along nicely," he said. "There were signs of organization during the night. I wouldn't now say you've crossed the pond for nothing. Call me tomorrow, we might have more. This storm's mighty slow, forward movement only six miles an hour, if that. There are thirty-five-miles-an-hour sustained winds on the surface, but no eye yet."

To Robin I said, "It's a toss-up."

"Heads it's a hurricane?"

"Do you *want* it to be a hurricane?" I asked curiously.

It seemed to me that in fact he did, but he shook his bespectacled head and said, "No, I definitely don't. I've lived here in Florida for forty years, and I've gone inland from the coast every time evacuation's been advised. We've been lucky with water surge too. There's a reef parallel with the coast here about half a mile out and in some way it lowers the storm surge and inhibits the formation of large waves. Where there's no reef, it's the water, not the wind, that kills most people."

One couldn't live so long in a hurricane alley, I supposed, without learning a few deadly statistics, and on my second (glorious) evening in his house, Robin switched on the Weather Channel for us all to see how Odin was coming along.

Dramatically well, was the answer.

The pressure in the circling center of the tropical depression Odin, a happy television voice announced, had dropped 20 millibars in the past two hours. Almost unheard of! Now officially designated a vigorous tropical storm, Odin, generating winds around sixty-five m.p.h., lay more than two hundred miles south of Jamaica and was traveling due north at seven miles an hour.

Robin absorbed the information thoughtfully and announced that on the next day we would all take a flight to Grand Cayman Island for a few days in the sun.

As we had spent the whole of that day swimming in the Darcy pool, drinking Darcy revivers and lying in the Florida sun, Robin had only one possible intention: to move, if not directly into the eye of Odin, at least to where it could see us.

Kris stalked with huge elastic strides around the sunny pool deck and the half-shaded terrace above. Odin, tracked by radar and satellites, was too small for his taste, too slow, and too far from land. Robin said dryly that he was sorry not to have been able to fix a better display.

Evelyn thought hurricane-chasing a dangerous and juvenile sport and said she wasn't going to Grand Cayman, she was staying comfortably at home: and Robin reminded her that *if* Odin intensified, and *if* Odin changed course, as hurricanes were liable to do from one minute to the next, it might be *she* who found the monster roaring on her doorstep, not us.

"What is more," she continued firmly, ignoring the threat, "tonight for dinner we're having stone crabs, Florida's pride, and after that Kris can repeat to us the poem he's been muttering to himself all day, and after that you can watch hours of Weather Channel if you like, but don't wake me in the morning, I'm not catching any flight to anywhere."

"What poem?" Robin asked.

"There's no poem. I'm going for a swim," Kris said immediately, and was still in the pool at sunset.

"He did recite a poem," Evelyn complained, "why does he pretend he didn't?"

I said from experience, "Give him time."

In time he would either repeat his verses or tear them up. It would depend on how he felt.

The stone crabs for dinner, with mustard sauce and green salad, beat fish pie with parsley sauce out of sight, and over coffee out on the terrace in soft silhouetting light, Kris said, without preliminaries, "I went to Cape Canaveral, you know."

We nodded.

"I'll fly through a hurricane, but those first astronauts sat on countless tons of rocket fuel and lit a match. So . . . well . . . I wrote for them. I wrote about Cape Canaveral, about the past . . . about the future."

He stood up abruptly and carried his coffee cup to the end of the terrace. His voice came matter-of-factly out of the dark.

"There are lonely concrete launch pads there, deep set in dusty grass,
They are circles scarcely fire-marked, barely twenty feet across,
Rockets stood there, waiting, men inside with trusting courage,
For the lift-off to the stars."

No one spoke.

Kris said,

"Now shuttles roar routinely to a station
up in orbit,
  Soon they'll print a cosmic schedule, issue a
boarding pass,
  And who will spare a memory or even a
passing thank-you,
  To those circles in the grass?"

More silence.
With a sigh, Kris said,

"Many a windy year will blow across the
Cape abandoned.
  Ghosts of fear and bumpy hearts will thin
and fade and pass.
  Weeds green the concrete circles. It's from a
launch pad out in orbit
  That men have gone to Mars."

Kris walked over and put his coffee cup on the
table.

"So you see," he said, a near-laugh lightening
his concept, "I'm no John Keats."

Robin said judiciously, "An interesting aperçu,
all the same."

Kris left Robin explaining an aperçu to Evelyn and walked me to the edge of the terrace to look at the moon reflected in the pool.

"Robin's arranged a Piper in Cayman," he said. "I've checked that I can fly it. Are you on?"

"I can't afford much."

"Don't fuss about the money. Are you spiritually on?"

"Yes."

"Great." My unqualified agreement excited him. "I was sure that's why you came."

"Why is Robin so keen on us going to Odin?"

Kris wrinkled his tall pale forehead. "Understanding why people do things, that's your sort of work, not mine."

"I liked your poem."

He grimaced. "You should go to the Cape. You'd never believe that the moon walks were spawned from those concrete slabs."

There were times, there were days, when the extremes of Kris's seesaw nature fell into balance, not just as always for his solo two-minute onscreen weather forecasts, but also for a lasting peace. It was as if the careful pilot took over even after the wheels had landed. On the evening of the Cape Canaveral verses he sounded more levelheaded than I'd ever known him out of an airplane.

"Did you see Bell?" he asked.

"I talked to her on the telephone."

"Will she marry me, do you think?"

I blew a breath of exasperation down my nose.

"First," I said, "you'd better ask her."

"And next?"

"Both of you practice keeping your temper. Count ten before you yell."

He thought it over and nodded. "You tell her, and I'll do it."

I nodded. I doubted that either would manage it, but an attempt was an advance.

In a typical non sequitur he conversationally asked, "What do you know of Trox Island?"

"Er." I thought without result. "Does Bell like it, or something?"

"Bell? It's nothing to do with Bell. It's to do with Robin and Evelyn."

I said "Oh?" vaguely. "I've never heard of it."

"It seems that most people have never heard of it," Kris said, "but suppose Robin wants you and me to fly to Trox Island, never mind through Odin's eye."

I said, puzzled, "Whyever should he?"

"I think it's something to do with mushrooms."

"Oh no, Kris," I protested. "I'm not risking my life for mushrooms."

"You won't be risking your life. In the past, dozens of planes have flown through hurricanes to gather essential and helpful information, and almost none has been lost."

Almost none, I thought, wasn't enormously reassuring.

"So why mushrooms?" I asked.

"Robin was talking on the phone soon after I came," Kris explained, "and I accidentally overheard him, and it was something about me and possibly my friend, that's you, and Odin and mushrooms on Trox Island."

"And you haven't asked him about it?"

"Well . . . not yet. I mean . . . I don't want to upset him . . . he says he's paying for us to go to Cayman, and he's paying the cost of the aircraft . . ."

"I'll ask him," I said, and later, peacefully, nightcap glass of cognac to hand, I mentioned Bell's account of the Darcy mushroom and sod farm business and wondered where he found fungus and grass to grow best.

"Florida," he promptly said. "I grow my grass in swampland up near Lake Okeechobee. Best wet agricultural conditions for sod in the States."

"And someone mentioned Trox Island too. Where's that?" I put no force into an ultra-calm inquiry, but even so I sensed a tightening, and then a deliberate loosening in my host.

"Trox?" He took his time answering. He opened a heavy gleaming wood thermidor and fiddled lengthily with cutting and lighting a cigar. Internal debate came out in punctuating puffs of smoke. I sat placidly, looking out from the terrace to the vast untroubled sea.

"Trox," Robin said pleasantly at length, sure he had the whole tobacco tip redly glowing, "is one of the many little islands sticking up in the Caribbean Sea. I believe Trox is chiefly constructed of guano—that's bird droppings, of course."

"Fertilizer," I agreed.

He nodded. "So I understand, but I've never been there myself." He inhaled smoke and blew it out, and said how much Evelyn and he were enjoying having Kris and me as houseguests, and how interesting he had found Kris's view of the future of space travel, and how much he looked forward to Kris's reports on shaking hands with Odin. He had dropped Trox Island as if of no interest. I tried again to mention it and he cut me off immediately, saying flatly, "Think about Odin. Forget Trox Island. Let me fill your glass."

Evelyn drew me away, wanting me to identify the stars, turning aside as boring our engrossment with shifting winds.

At the end of the evening Kris and I each returned to our colorful basic tropical bedrooms; brilliant fabrics, wicker furniture, white tiled floor, ceiling fan circling, bright bathroom adjacent, all an ultimate comfort. I fell asleep as easily as on the previous evening, but half-woke hours later in the dark wondering why the London streetlights weren't throwing familiar shadows on the ceiling.

Miami . . . I drifted to full consciousness . . . I was in Sand Dollar Beach, named for the flat round decorative shells sometimes found on the shoreline. They were a sort of sea urchins of the order Clypeasteroida . . . I'd looked them up.

I switched on the bedside light, felt restless, got up, padded in and out of the bathroom, and finally, with a towel and in swimming shorts made my way through the dark house, across the terrace and down into the soothing pool.

Robin Darcy, friendly but secretive, generous beyond normal, had given us too much and told us too little. So what the devil were Kris and I set on? And could it be a one-way trip?

Mrs. Mevagissey relied on my earnings, as I for twenty past years had lived on hers. I had no right to risk the money that paid the nurses. They alone made her existence bearable. My priority was to fly through a hurricane and to return home safely. Kris's plans came second, Robin's third.

Odin, my own knowledge and forward-looking perception told me, could grow quite quickly from Category 3 to Category 5 on the Saffir-Simpson scale, which meant that the speeds of its winds would destroy every instrument put out to measure them. Category 5 meant Odin would deliver catastrophic damage in storm surge wherever it touched on shore; it could sustain incredible winds of around 180 miles an hour in its eye wall . . . and little islands, with or without mushrooms, could be flooded and disappear.

I relaxed in the semi-cool water and swam lengths with economic strokes, covering distance without concentrating. All my life swimming had been the one competitive sport my grandmother and I had been comfortably able to afford for me, though from sixteen onwards I'd deserted municipal pools and Olympic-type racing for longer endurance trials and surfing. By the time Kris and I went to Florida I was growing out also of the urge to race at all, but I still had the shoulders and movements of long practice.

Thinking only of Hurricane Odin and Trox Island, I slid out of the pool in a while and stood, toweling, with my back to the house.

A voice behind me said with goose-bumpy menace, "Stand still and raise your hands."

I nearly swung round thoughtlessly and would doubtless have been shot, but after a moment of reconsideration I dropped the towel and did as I'd been told.

"Now turn round slowly."

I turned round, realizing that I, on the pool deck, was in unlit shadow to anyone up on the terrace.

Robin stood up there, lit from behind by a glow in the house. Round cozy Robin held a handgun pointing motionlessly where it could do me terminal damage.

"I'm Perry," I said. "I was swimming."

"Come forward where I can see you. And come slowly, or I'll shoot."

If he hadn't so obviously been speaking the simple truth, I might have joked; instead I slowly stepped forward until the house lights shone into my eyes.

"What are you doing out here?" Robin asked blankly, lowering the gun to point at my feet.

"I couldn't sleep. Can I put my hands down now?"

He shook himself slightly as if waking up, opening his mouth and nodding, but in the second before life returned to normal the pool area was suddenly full of blinding lights, blue uniforms, shouting voices and horribly purposeful black guns. The wish—the willingness—to kill reached me like shock waves. I felt battered by noise. I was told to kneel and did so, and was held down by a ruthless hand on my neck.

Robin was ineffectually speaking. The blue-uniformed police, not listening, continued with their rough mission, which was if not to put a bullet in him, at least to immobilize the intruder and shout garbled words into his befuddled ear, words Robin later identified as my "rights."

For what seemed ages I went on kneeling ignominiously on the pool deck, feeling stupid in my swimming shorts, gripped by unfriendly hands, with wrists clicked into handcuffs behind my back (always behind one's back in Florida, Robin said, and in most other states). My protests got nowhere against their loud-voiced and fulfilling abuse until Robin finally reached the chief uniform's attention. The intruder, he apologized, was a houseguest.

A houseguest swimming at three-thirty in the morning?

Very sorry, Robin said. Very sorry.

Unwillingly deprived of their prey, the blue uniforms with surliness holstered their guns and rested their lightbulbs. They reported back by radio to their home base, produced forms for Robin to sign, treated both of us with continuing suspicion, retrieved their handcuffs and finally disappeared as fast as they had come.

I stood up stiffly, picked up the towel, crossed the terrace and followed Robin into the house.

He wasn't pleased with me, nor inclined to realize that he hadn't warned me about any alarms.

"I had no idea," he said crossly, "that you would swim in the middle of the night. There are burglar alarms round the terrace which alert a security firm to the presence of an intruder. There's a direct line to the police and a warning buzzer in my bedroom. I suppose you'd better have a drink."

"No . . . I'm sorry for the trouble."

I wound and tied the towel round my hips like a loincloth and Robin assessed me with thoughtfulness, crossing his wrists below his stomach to hold his gun.

"I must say," he said judiciously, "that you behaved very coolly under fire."

I hadn't felt cool. My heart rate had been of Cape Canaveral speed.

I asked, "How far off were they from actually shooting?"

"The distance of a trigger's travel," Robin said. He put his handgun into a pocket in his robe. "Go back to bed. I hope you sleep."

Before I could move, however, the telephone rang, and without surprise at this early-morning summons, Robin answered.

"Yes," he said into the receiver. "A false alarm. My houseguest . . . midnight swim . . . yes, everything's fine . . . yes . . . yes . . . it's Hereford . . . yes, that's right, Hereford. No, the police weren't happy, but I assure you all is well." He put down the receiver and briefly explained to me that the security firm had been checking. "They always do, after the police radio in that it's a false alarm."

Robin accompanied me to my bedroom door, recovering his milder manner on the way.

"I should have told you about the alarm," he murmured. "But never mind, no harm done."

"No." I smiled goodnight, and he with a laugh said he hoped I would be as unruffled when I met Odin.

LEAVING EVELYN AT home, Robin, Kris and I flew on Cayman Airways from Miami to Grand Cayman in the morning, Robin with still good humor telling Kris about our adventures in the night. Kris, on the far side of the house, had slept soundly through the din.

It was after we'd cleared immigration that trickles of decent information slowly reached me, but without flowing together to make a stream.

Robin and Kris, collected by car outside the airport, were driven away, telling me transport was there for me as well but otherwise leaving me standing in unexpectedly hot air temperature wondering what to do next.

"Next" turned out to be a thin woman in bleached often-washed cotton trousers and a white sleeveless top who walked straight up to me and said, "Dr. Stuart, I presume."

Her voice was crisply grand-house-in-the-country English. She'd seen a lot of British weather forecasts and she knew me by sight, she said. She told me to get into the front cab of her orange pickup truck, standing not far ahead. She sounded accustomed to being in charge.

"Robin Darcy . . . Kris . . ." I began.

She interrupted, "Kris Ironside has gone for familiarization flights in the aircraft he'll be flying. Get in the pickup, do."

I sat in the cab and roasted in the heat, which allowed no respite, even with the windows open. It was the second half of October south of the Tropic of Cancer. I took off my too conventional tie and thought of a tepid shower.

"I'm Amy Ford," the woman said, identifying herself as she drove out of the airport. "How do you do?"

"Could I ask where are we going?"

"I have an errand to run in George Town. Then to my house."

She drove a short distance into a compact and prosperous-looking small town, its streets lined with shade trees and alive with camera-clicking tourists.

"This is the island's capital, George Town," Amy said, and added, "It's the only real town, actually."

"All these people . . ."

"They come off the cruise ships," Amy said, and

pointed, as we rounded a corner, to the broad open sea where three huge passenger ships rode at anchor, and imitation pirate galleons popped off imitation cannonballs, and container ships edged into the quayside bringing food and bulldozers.

Amy parked within running distance of the public library to return a book; then, after passing important-looking bank buildings, she drove back along the harborfront, where friendly drivers amazingly gave way with smiles.

"Nice place," I said, meaning it.

Amy took the comment as natural. "My house next," she said. "Not far."

Her house, not far, as she'd said, must have covered eight thousand square feet of the oceanfront paradise it was set in; a clone of Robin Darcy's easy opulence but magnified by two.

She led the way into a sitting room, small by the house's overall standard, but blessedly cool with air-conditioning and a rotating ceiling fan. There was a view through heavy sliding glass doors of intensely blue sea, there were chairs and china figures in tropically exuberant colors, and there was a man in white shorts who said "Michael Ford" and shook my hand.

"You look bigger than on the screen." His comment was without offense and said in roughly the same accent as his wife, though I would have placed him a shade lower in the social hierarchy, however bulging the coffers.

In between my basic weather work (and frankly to earn more in order to pay Jett van Els and her sisters), I lectured freelance and after-dinner talked, and, from a natural aptitude for mimicry, I'd learned to recognize the origins of many accents. Not nearly in such incredible detail as Shaw's Professor Higgins, of course, but enough in the right places to amuse.

I would have put Michael Ford's vocal roots, like my own, as somewhere in western rural Berkshire, but in his case the basic material had been polished by studied layers of gloss.

Scarcely taller than Robin Darcy, Michael Ford, with his tanned bare broad-shouldered torso and his strong shoe-and-sockless slightly bowed brown legs, looked like the useful muscle that the rounded Robin lacked.

Amy Ford said, "Cold drink?" to me and poured orange juice lavishly onto ice cubes, and it wasn't until I tasted it that I realized there was a good deal of something like Bacardi in its kick.

I said, "Would you mind awfully telling me

who you are and why I'm here?" And I heard Amy's tones in my own; slightly shocking.

Amy, however, appearing not to notice, did in part explain.

"I sold Robin my airplane. As I understand it, your friend is going to fly it through this hurricane Odin, and you are here to navigate."

I thought blankly, whyever would Robin buy a doubtless expensive airplane for Kris—someone he'd casually met at a lunch party—to fly through a violent storm?

"Robin bought my airplane for Nicky, actually," Amy said, seeing nothing odd in it, "but of course Nicky went away."

"Hurricane Nicky?" I asked.

"Naturally. Of course. But this new storm was brewing more or less on Nicky's heels, one might say, and Robin said he'd met Kris, who was a good pilot, and Kris wanted to fly through a hurricane, so . . . well . . . here you are."

As an explanation it raised more questions than it answered.

I said over my strongly laced juice, "Where is Odin this morning, do you know?"

As of two hours earlier, Odin, according to my helpful pal at the Miami Hurricane Center, had been intensifying south of Jamaica and causing the population of that island to contemplate safety in the hills.

"If you're going towards Odin," my pal warned, "remember that on Grand Cayman Island there aren't any hills to go to."

"Is Odin likely to hit Cayman?"

"Look, Perry, you know damned well that not even Odin knows where it's going. But the report just coming in puts Odin high in Category Three, that's a fierce hurricane, Perry, you get out of there. Disregard what I said before, and go."

"What about Trox Island?" I asked.

He said, "Where?" and after a pause added, "If that's one of that scatter of little islands in the western Caribbean, then don't go there, Perry, don't. If Odin goes on developing it could hit any of those islands head on and wipe them out."

"Wind or storm surge?"

"Both." He hesitated. "We can easily be wrong, so it's better not to guess. At the moment I'd put my money on Odin veering northwest to miss Jamaica; and as Grand Cayman," he finally assured me, "would then be straight ahead of Odin . . . it's a place to leave, not play around in, if you have any sense."

I suppose I had no sense.

I asked, "Where exactly is Trox Island?"

"Is it important? I'll look it up." There was a rustling of paper. "Here we are. Islands in the West Caribbean . . . Roncador Cay . . . Swan . . . Thunder Knoll. Here it is . . . Trox. Number of inhabitants, anything from zero to twenty, mostly fishermen. Size, one mile long, half a mile wide. Highest point above sea level, two hundred feet. Volcanic? No. Constructed of bird droppings, guano, coral and limestone rock. Map coordinates, 17.50 degrees north, 81.44 west." Another rustle of paper. "There you are, then, it's just a peak of guano-covered rock sticking up from undersea mountains."

"Any farming? Any mushrooms?"

"Why mushrooms? No, if anything, you might find coconuts. It says here there are palm trees."

"Who does Trox belong to?"

"It doesn't say in this list. All it says is 'Ownership Disputed.'"

"And is that the absolute lot?"

"Yes, except that it says there's a landing for boats and an old grass strip for aircraft, but no fuel and no maintenance. Nothing. Forget it."

He was busy at work and could talk no longer.

His final advice was "Go home": and he meant by home, England.

Michael Ford looked at the heavy gold watch weighing down his left wrist and pushed buttons on a vast television set until he reached a noisy channel giving alarmist details of the development of Odin.

Odin had become organized into a full-grown hurricane with a central area where the winds were circling ever faster, leaving a calm small round quiet center like a hub. Odin, with this well-developed "eye," was now circling with winds of a hundred and twenty miles an hour or more, but was still going forwards slowly at seven. The low-pressure center of winds aloft had weakened and allowed a stronger circling in the central dense overcast, resulting in the distinct formation of the eye.

Kris, at least, would be pleased to hear the development was official.

Odin was seven hundred and fifty miles south of where Evelyn peacefully sunned herself on the Sand Dollar pool deck, and even from where I stood on Grand Cayman Island, the view through the windows of sand and palm trees, two hundred miles from a major storm, was calm, sunny and without a breeze. It seemed impossible that any speed of wind could blow away a town as thoroughly as Hurricane Andrew had, or that any ocean surge could drown three hundred thousand people as in Bangladesh. I knew pretty thoroughly the paths of the winds of the world and had studied most of the devilments of nature, but like many a volcanologist I'd warmed my hands from afar without walking round an erupting rim.

As a committed fly-through prospect the satellite picture of Odin was soul-shrink daunting. Did I really intend to fly with Kris into the center of *that?*

I had brought with me by habit my small accurate camera, but even given the best lens in the world, I was not going to see any satellite's-eye view. The circling top of a great hurricane, where the winds were coldest, rose to maybe fifty or sixty thousand feet. Kris and I, without oxygen, couldn't go much higher than ten thousand: and we would fly into the quiet central hub, read and note the air pressure there, ditto the wind speeds in the eye wall, and fly out on the other side to make our way back to the home field. For most of the way, might we not be buffeted about in rain cloud? But we would be traveling faster than the wind.

How the hell, I thought privately, did one *find* the eye? How was I supposed to navigate? I'd had no rehearsals. Who would give me a quick course in hurricane dead reckoning? Who would distract me from the word "dead"?

Why did I, all the same, want to do that flight more than anything else?

The Weather Channel went on chattering in civilized tones about the downward march of millibars, those useful measurements of low air pressure and forthcoming disaster.

The television screen in the Ford house looked out from a clearly expensive wall fitment, and Amy, Michael and I sat around in lush armchairs glancing occasionally at the image of the wide white swirling mass while they told me that historically Grand Cayman had suffered few major direct hits, but that of course there was always a first time. Their blithe voices, though, said they didn't believe it.

I'd heard jockeys describe the atmosphere in the changing room before they'd gone out to partner half a ton of horse in the Grand National Steeplechase over the biggest, most demanding jumps in the sport. They were going into breakneck para-

plegic country, and they did it for love. I'd wondered why they felt compelled; and in the Fords'
clean bright wealthy sitting room, I found I knew.

DURING THE SEVERAL idle hours before Robin
and Kris reappeared, I learned among other
things that in the United States Amy had owned,
managed and sold a string of video rental stores,
while Michael had equipped gymnasiums and
collected membership money.

They were both proud of their achievements, also
proud of each other, and in those areas talked freely.

I learned that neither Amy nor Michael were
themselves licensed pilots, though Amy had been
taking instruction before she sold her aircraft to
Robin.

"Why did you sell it to Robin?" I asked Amy
without pressure, more as time-filling chitchat
than as a purposeful inquiry.

Michael made a damping movement of his
hand as if urging caution, but Amy answered
limpidly, "He wanted it. He made a good offer,
so I agreed." She finished her tall glass of orange
mixture. "If you want to know *why* he bought it,
you'll have to ask him."

Robin and Kris came back at that moment in
good spirits, so I did ask him straight out, lightly,

there and then, as if it were merely again a conversational opening without purpose.

Robin blinked, paused, smiled, and in the same misleading way answered, "Amy wouldn't want me to tell you that she could buy a diamond necklace if she sold me her airplane."

"And more besides," Michael heartily said, relieved.

I smiled warmly. They were all capable liars. Amy gave Kris a tall glass tinkling with ice and I told him neutrally, "Mine has rum in it."

He was halfway up to a manic high, but non-alcoholic, as usual. He looked piercingly at the almost full glass standing beside me on a small table, then he tasted his own, set it down, and with sizzling enthusiasm told me the news.

"It's a terrific plane. Two engines. I had an instructor put me through its paces. Passed with O.K. O.K., Robin's happy. Everyone's happy. Mind you, most people think amateurs should stay strictly away from storms, but they'll take account of what we'll measure, even if we don't have a fully equipped flying laboratory . . ."

"When are we going?" I asked.

Everyone looked at the Weather Channel's update. Odin by that moment had dropped another couple of frightening millibars and had moved one minute northwest. A bright-mannered elderly studio visitor with—I guessed—a payoff from the tourist trade rejoiced that Odin was circling over water and doing no harm to holiday makers or people vacationing ashore. Kris looked at me cynically and shrugged, as in circling over a warm sea Odin was strengthening all the time.

"Tomorrow morning," Kris said. "Oh-eight hundred. Eight o'clock. Before it gets too hot."

Michael and Amy insisted on having Robin, Kris and me all stay overnight in their house. They gave us unending drinks, more rather than less alcoholic, to Kris's embarrassment, and Michael grilled steaks on a brick-built barbecue with a flourish of proprietorial strength inside a shiny vinyl apron.

Kris and I were given small tasks to do, like folding napkins and filling a tub with ice cubes; small tasks that kept us close to Amy's side. It became somehow understood that neither of us should wander away, and with Robin's alarm system in mind, I stayed where my hosts wanted. It felt to me a shade like luxurious imprisonment, but I had little money and no good excuse for insisting on a hotel instead.

Michael, besides, though on the surface all friendly, a genial cook, had also, I slowly realized, an agility with all those muscles that spoke of combat rather than the exercise machines he had dealt in.

Odin on the television moved slowly, dangerously, northwest.

Amy, pleasantly, with my help, laying plates at a dining table in an insect-screened porch near the barbecue, exclaimed suddenly to the rest of us, "How good-looking Kris is! And you too, of course, Perry. Does the BBC choose the forecasters for their ultra-attractive faces?"

Kris grinned. "All the time."

I was used to the way Kris looked, but it was true, I knew, that at one time he'd clung onto his job in the aftermath of one of his more outrageous statements only because of the swoon factor in women viewers. Unusually, though, for such a handsome person, he was equally liked by men, and that, I thought, lay somewhere in his manic-depressive spectrum, from which he offered a friendship that could be wildly scatty but had no sex in it. His reliance on me was in the nature of an expedition leader being certain that whatever the catastrophe, he could absolutely rely on base camp being there for him.

He brought zany lightheartedness to that strange evening in Cayman, but he refused Robin's request for a repeat recital of the Cape Canaveral verses; asked why not, he replied that the genesis of the verses had lain in depression and should stay there.

I watched Robin thoughtfully contemplate Kris. Robin had got himself more than a good amateur pilot, he'd got a British national celebrity, and I wondered if in his so-far-unexplained planning, this celebrity factor had been intentional or unforeseen.

By six-thirty the next morning, Odin had been firmly declared a Category 4 hurricane, traveling northwest at less than seven miles an hour.

Straight ahead, if it continued on that path, it would in a day or two smash into the house of Michael and Amy, blowing away its opulence, sweeping through the bright little room with a hundred tons of sand-heavy water.

Kris came to stand beside me, watching the deadly drama on the screen and being pleased at the sharp definition of the eye.

"Come on then," he said, "we might as well go." His eyes shone like a child's ready for a party. "We're not the only people flying," he added. "And I'd better file a flight plan."

We went back to the airfield in the orange pickup truck, with directions from Amy, and among a surprising number of light aircraft standing in a separated area designated "general aviation," Kris singled out and patted approvingly the twin-engine propeller-driven Piper that Robin had bought.

"Why don't you sit in this little beauty while I go and file the flight plan?" Kris suggested. "I won't be long."

"How about a map?" I asked.

He fiddled about unlocking the door with his back to me and after a while turned and said, "What we really need is a direction to Odin's eye, not a regular map."

"Can they give you that direction from here?"

"They sure can."

He more or less trotted off eagerly, leaving me behind.

He and I, I thought, had been friends for years and I'd seen him through enough suicidally bad times to know when he was avoiding telling me the truth. That morning in Cayman's airport, he wouldn't meet my eyes.

He came back from the offices waving a sheet of paper, which he thrust into my hands for me

to read while he went through his external
checks. Those checks, for that aircraft, only semi-
familiar to Kris, were in stapled sections of instructions, a small heap of them lying on the
captain's seat. Kris checked the exterior of the airplane with the appropriate section of instructions
in hand to refer to, and I read the flight information sheet he'd filed with the Air Traffic Service.

Most of it was to me double Dutch. When he'd
finished the external checks, I asked him what
was meant by the addresses given for instance as
MWCRZTZX and MKJKZOZYX.

"Don't worry about it," he said.

"I'm not going unless you tell me."

He stared, astonished, at my mild mutiny.
"Well, then," he said, "the first lot of letters is the
address of Grand Cayman Tower, in this airport,
and the second is Kingston Airspace, Jamaica,
where we'll find Odin, probably. Satisfied?"

He pointed lower down the form to our "destination airfield," which was listed as ZZZZ, because we weren't sure where we were going.
"Odin," he said.

"And how about a map?" I asked. "I'm really
not going with you without a map."

In England he would never have flown any-where without a map. To set off into the wide Caribbean without one was madness.

"I know where I'm going," he said mulishly.

"Then you don't need a navigator."

"Perry!"

"A radio map," I said. "One with Trox Island on it."

His half-awakened sense of shock came fully alive.

He frowned. He said, "Robin will be livid."

"Robin's using us," I answered him.

"How?" He didn't want to believe it. "He's been the tops for us. He's paying everything for us, don't forget. He even bought this airplane from Amy."

I said, "What if he bought himself an aircraft so that he could do what he liked with it? What if he got himself a good amateur pilot, little known in this area, and one, what's more, who's an expert meteorologist, who can deal with and understand cyclonic winds?"

"But he's just an enthusiast," Kris protested.

I said, "I'll bet he's got you to include the island in our flight . . . and perhaps it's ZZZZ on the flight plan . . . and I'll bet he persuaded you not to tell me where we're going."

"Perry . . ." He looked shattered, but denied nothing.

"So did he tell you *why?*" I asked. "Did he tell you what to do on Trox Island if we got there? Did he say why he wasn't going himself? And, chief of the difficult questions, what is so odd about the destination or the purpose for going there, that it has to be camouflaged in a hurricane?"

4

KRIS AND I climbed through the rear door of Amy's/Robin's truly terrific little airplane and sat in executive-style seats facing each other across a table. It had been designed originally for ten narrow people with only emergency male toilet facilities, but Amy (I guessed) had rearranged things to two flight-deck seats for pilots, four for passengers in comfort in a cabin and, at the rear, a reasonable privy with a lockable door.

Kris confessed without shame that Robin had indeed persuaded him to leave me out of the flight planning. "Robin was afraid you wouldn't agree to go to Trox Island," he said, "but I told him I would persuade you. And of course you will go, won't you? I can't do it all without help."

"What would we be going there for?"

"To report back on the state of the mush-rooms."

"*Mushrooms!*" I didn't believe him, and disliked the feeling.

"It's on the way to Odin," Kris said, cajoling. "Just a dogleg, and a brief stop." He was trying to rationalize it. "And of course this super airplane has been fitted by Robin with extra instruments which will register air pressure in millibars and record it on tape from second to second, and wind-speed gauges too. They're easy for you to operate from your seat. All you do is press but-tons to activate the radio altimeter and it calcu-lates everything by itself and displays the air pressure at sea level. I'll show you."

"And these special altimeter and wind-speed–measuring instruments are expensive?"

"Very. They were installed with storms in mind, I think, in time for Hurricane Nicky. That's when Robin bought the airplane from Amy. And as you see, Robin's put so much money into our trip," Kris said plaintively. "I sort of had to agree to do what he asked."

"Why isn't he going himself?"

"You're strong, he isn't." Kris rethought this and added, "He has an appointment back in Miami that he can't avoid."

"And what he wanted," I suggested, "was for us to go to Trox, while I thought we were heading straight for Odin, because I had no map?"

Kris nodded without embarrassment. "We filled in most of the flight plan yesterday afternoon."

The secrecy appalled me, but I did very much want to fly through a hurricane, and I was unlikely ever to have another chance. I settled for Trox, with or without lies and mushrooms, as the payment for Odin.

Kris, sensing it, and clearly relieved, pointed to various filled-in spaces on the form. "That's the probable overall mileage. That's fuel—we're taking full tanks. That's our cruising speed. That's our flight level. Then, lower down, there's our endurance, that's the time we can stay airborne on full tanks. All of those figures allow for a dogleg to the island. Then we circled M, which means maritime because we're going over water, and the circle round J says we're carrying life jackets, and F means the life jackets are fluorescent."

"And are they?" I asked. "And do we in fact have life jackets on board?"

"Perry! Of course we do. You're so suspicious."

"No," I sighed. "Just checking, like you do."

"Well . . ." He hesitated, but pointed again. "To set your mind at rest, that D stands for Dinghy, and we do have one of those too, and it says on this form that it has a cover for shelter, and it's bright orange, and will accommodate ten people."

"Where is it?" I asked, and Kris, still slightly hurt, pointed to a wrapped gray bundle occupying one of the passenger seats.

"Robin bought a new one," Kris said. "He's made a point of doing everything right. Everyone around us knew he was giving us the best equipment."

"Bully for him," I said dryly, but Kris was oblivious to sarcasm.

"Then down near the bottom," he said, continuing to point at the form, "there's the color of this airplane, white, and Robin's name and address as operator, that means owner in this case, and of course my own name as pilot, and my signature, and that's the lot."

"Great," I said, though halfheartedly, with reservations. "But we still need a map."

Kris surrendered. "All right. All right. We'll take a bloody map. I'll go and get one."

I went with him this time, across the tarmac to a small building set apart from the main passenger areas and into a busy private pilots' room filled with tables, chairs, a rudimentary cafeteria selling coffee and Danish pastries and eight or nine amateur aviators with strung-up nerves pretending icy calm in face of the cross-hurricane adventure.

Odin in all its terror claimed maximum attention, an update of its position and composition being displayed continuously on a television-type screen. Hurricane Odin, with winds now reported at 155 m.p.h. in the eye wall, had just about reached Category 5 on the Saffir-Simpson scale. The eye was currently located at 17.0 degrees north, 78.3 degrees west, and was moving northwest at six miles an hour. Pressure in the eye had last been measured at 930 millibars, having dropped from 967 overnight. The eye at present measured eleven miles across.

Two steps at a time, Kris went up the stairs, which apparently led to the desk receiving flight plans and to a kiosk selling small necessities for pathfinding, including topographical and radio maps. Kris bought both, carrying them down like trophies.

While he was gone, one of the other pilots, following Kris with his gaze, said regretfully, "Sad about Bob Farraday, wasn't it?"

I said, "Er . . ." and was told Bob Farraday, Amy Ford's instructor, had been killed in a car crash a month ago. "She sold her plane then, the one you and your friend are flying in. I thought you knew."

I shook my head: but it explained why she'd sold such a gem.

The consensus among the earnest hurricane hunters all around us put the true direction of the eye at 152 degrees from Grand Cayman's Owen Roberts airport; but that figure had to be modified by the awkward facts that compass needles didn't point to true north, and that the cyclonic winds would change the aircraft's heading from minute to minute. Naturally the whole eye, also, was on the move.

Listening to the knowledgeable chatter of the others, I thought that Kris and I were attempting an impossible task, but Kris himself, bouncing with energy and grinning with joy, simply took me and the maps back to Robin's Piper and spread the maps out on the table.

"The eye to Odin is *there,*"he said firmly, drawing in pencil a small circle on the radio map, and, with the dexterity I was used to in him, he worked out, with the aid of a pocket calculator, the heading and speed at which he should travel to reach his target. It was, to do him justice, almost exactly the course he'd been going to fly even if I hadn't insisted on the maps. He'd written his chosen headings on half a postcard, which at that point he produced with satisfaction from his shirt pocket: and there were other numbers written below the way to the eye, which after a pause he explained.

"I suppose you'd better know. . . . Well, this figure, this second one, is the magnetic heading from Cayman to Trox Island. The next one is from Trox Island to Odin's eye, and the fourth one is from the eye back to Cayman. If we go right *now,* these headings will take us round, you'll see."

I stared at him, thinking him halfway to insane. This Piper airplane, though, unlike Kris's own Cherokee at White Waltham, this luxurious little transport did have all sorts of electronic capabilities, so while Kris did all his remaining checks meticulously, I read the slim instruction booklet on how to navigate by radio transmissions.

The whole enterprise, I reckoned, would degenerate into a jolly little flip far away from Odin, from which calm corner we could return to Grand Cayman safely, thanks to various land-based transmitters called non-directional beacons, or NDBs for short.

I learned much later that low-level navigation over the western Caribbean had once been easy, thanks to three strong directional beacons positioned at Panama, Swan Island and Bimini (in the Bahamas), but that with the advent of the global positioning system used by commercial aircraft, the amateurs' standbys had been dismantled. Kris and I, the day we set off in blithe ignorance to Trox Island, could have benefited hugely from cross references from beacons at Panama, Swan Island and Bimini.

With Kris's basic navigating kit containing always a set of plastic measuring pieces, I ruled a straight track line from Grand Cayman to Trox on both maps and, having squeezed the information out of Kris, who was still inclined to look backward to his feeling of obligation and to his new alliance with Robin, wrote in the airspeed, and consequently the time, that should deliver us to Trox.

My arrival time and heading weren't much different from Kris's own calculations, and "I told you so," he said.

I sat back in my chair. "What does Robin want us to do on Trox Island? You keep avoiding any details. He's spent a lot of money, as you've said, but we still don't know *why.*"

"He wants you to take photographs." He—and Robin also—who'd come out of the Ford house in his sleeping pajamas to wave us off in the truck, had checked that I hadn't forgotten my camera.

"Photographs? What of?"

Kris shifted in his seat. "He just said photographs . . . as if you would know what he wanted when you saw it." But Kris, I knew later, was concocting again.

The enterprise looked less and less sensible to me, but in a stab at normal procedures I suggested we put on the life jackets at that point, leaving them of course uninflated, but ready if necessary.

Kris, having won the bigger battle, meekly strapped himself into the flat orange life vest and ignored it.

Along the row of parked light aircraft two or three were on the move. With a sharp inspection of his watch, and a grumble about a lot of time wasted, Kris climbed forward into the captain's seat and, looking relieved not to have to answer more questions, finished his pre-takeoff checks by winding his altimeter needle to zero to give the home airfield's present air pressure, which at sea level read 1002 on the millibar scale. Then he started the engines and asked the tower for permission to taxi.

I put on headphones, like Kris, and from the co-pilot's seat, asked for permission for takeoff.

Permission was granted laconically, the tower on the whole preferring only authorized military aircraft to chase a hurricane's eye. Kris, though, with determination and skill roared down the runway, soared out over water, and steered straight for Odin.

My surprise lasted about as far as the line-of-sight horizon from Grand Cayman, and then with the ground's attention on the next plane after us, and the next after that, Kris altered course abruptly and headed instead for the mushrooms of Trox.

Kris was busy with hands on switches, and

when everything had settled I found that we were no longer in radio contact with anyone, as the pilot had systematically turned the tuning dials to indicate out-of-area frequencies. We were, as no doubt he and Robin had planned, alone in the wide sky: and the wide sky was developing rough gusty patches, even though the outer edges of the hurricane lay by forecast a long way ahead.

Through the headsets which we both still wore, Kris said, "Flight time to Trox should now be twenty minutes, but the winds are stronger than I planned for. Start looking ahead in ten minutes. Robin said the island's sometimes difficult to see."

I said I thought our radio silence was madness. Kris merely grinned.

Ten minutes passed, and twenty. The wave crests multiplied over the gray water below us, the cloud shreds were thickening and the aircraft bumped heavily in increasingly unstable air.

No island. No small insignificant guano-covered rock. I redid all the navigational calculations, and they put us still on course.

Trox Island, when to my vast relief it at last appeared visibly on our starboard bow, looked at first only like a straighter, longer, white-breaking wave crest. I shook Kris's arm and pointed ahead and downwards, and saw the unacknowledged anxiety clear in a flash from his forehead.

He grinned again, vindicated. He lowered the aircraft from two thousand feet down to a few hundred, circling the narrow strip of dark-looking land carefully so as not to lose sight of it in the increasing cloud. He'd been told by Robin of the existence of the landing strip, but, look as we might, neither Kris nor I could distinguish it until he made an almost despairing pass across the narrowest width of land at no higher than three hundred feet, and again, as all my attention was looking for it, it was I who first spotted the indistinct flat roadlike line along the center length of the otherwise rocky strip. The runway, disconcertingly, was greenish-gray, not tarmac, and was made of flattened, consolidated earth, overgrown with grass.

Kris, seeing the rudimentary strip also, swung closely round and flew the whole length of it at barely more than a hundred feet off the ground, but neither to his eyes nor mine were there any rocks or any other obstructions along its length.

"Robin swore we could land here." Kris's voice through the headphones sounded more brave than convinced.

I thought that Robin hadn't taken the fierce crosswind into account. Had Robin ever landed on the strip himself at all? Robin wasn't a flier. But then, nor was I . . . but I did at least understand wind.

Hands gripping the control yoke, Kris with tension in his whole body increased the engines' power to near maximum and flew round the island again, gaining height and coming in finally to land from the other end of the runway, still in a crosswind but at least this time with a passable on-the-nose component.

Fighting the gusts, Kris forgot to lower the wheels—his Cherokee at White Waltham had a fixed undercarriage—and he looked horrified for all of five seconds while I pointed silently at the three lights that should have been green, but weren't. Three green lights, I'd once read in a flying book, meant that all three landing wheels were down and locked in the landing position.

"God," Kris shouted, "I've forgotten the downwind checks . . . I've *forgotten* them *all* . . . Brakes off, undercarriage down, fuel mixture rich, propellers fully fine . . ." His busy fingers set everything right . . . all, I guessed, except his self-respect. "Harness buckled, hatches closed and locked, autopilot disengaged, as if I'd engaged the bloody thing in the first place, hold on, Perry, hold on, here we go . . ."

He made, in the circumstances, a commendably adequate landing; and I'd been in some commercial tooth-rattlers that had shaken one's spine a great deal worse.

"Sorry," he said, which was unlike him. He stretched his fingers, loosening the muscles. "I forgot those bloody checks!" He sounded tragedy-stricken. "How *could* I?"

"We got down. Stop fussing," I said. "What do we do next?"

"Um . . ." In an absentminded trance he could think of nothing but his oversights.

I tried again. "Kris, we landed safely, didn't we? So here we are, safe."

"Well . . . yes. Have you looked at the altimeter?"

I hadn't, but I did then. The millibar scale still read 1002, but the needle gave our altitude at sea level as minus 360 feet. When Kris wound the needle again to zero, the millibars had dropped to 990, and he gazed at this result as if mesmerized.

"Well, we're not staying here at the end of the runway forever, are we?" I asked. "So how about snapping out of it? There's Odin, don't forget."

His awareness seemed to click at once back to normal and as if I were stupid to ask, he said, "We flew over some buildings when we came into land, didn't you notice? So that's obviously the place to start."

He turned the airplane and taxied back the length of the grass-grown strip, ending on the edge of what looked like a small model village consisting of three or four white-painted wooden houses, several long low sheds fashioned from hemispherical corrugated iron, a tiny church with a spire and two large solid-looking concrete huts.

"Robin said the mushrooms grow in the corrugated iron sheds," Kris announced, jumping down to the ground, "so we'd better take a look."

Unexpectedly, there were no locked doors. Also, as surprising, there were no people.

Final astonishment . . . no mushrooms.

I took a few photographs of no mushrooms.

There were long waist-height trays in the sheds full of compost containing oak-wood chips; and chanterelles at least, I knew, flourished in oak forests, their natural habitat. The air smelled musty and full of fungus spores. Nothing

I could see or smell was worth the trouble of our travels.

Kris wandered about on his own, and we met at length in one of the thick concrete huts to compare notes.

No fungi of any kind.

"Not even a bloody toadstool," Kris said in disgust. "And very little else."

The houses were empty of people and were untidily furnished with clutter due for discarding. The church had had tablets on the white internal walls, but they had been unscrewed and removed, leaving rectangular darker patches. Water came supplied, not in the pipes provided, but in buckets lifted by ropes from underground rainwater tanks.

The hut we stood in, cool owing to windowless concrete walls about four feet thick, had once, we guessed, been living quarters of sorts: there were four plank bunk beds but no bedding, and there had once been electric lighting, but all that remained were wires coming out of the walls.

"There's another hut that looks as if it once held a generator," Kris said, and I nodded.

"The mushroom sheds had climate control once," I said, "and an efficient-looking pumped sprinkler system."

"The whole place has been stripped," Kris sighed. "We're wasting our time."

"Let's look at the landing stage," I suggested, and we walked down a hill of dried mud from the village to a wood and concrete dock long enough for a merchant ship's mooring.

Again, no people and precious little else. No ropes, no chains, no crane. It was as if the last boat out of there had cleared up everything behind it.

As for living things, apart from humans, there were hundreds of big dark blue birds with brown legs, thousands of all sizes of iguanas and a large slow-moving mixed herd of cattle that wandered free, ate grass and paid us no attention.

I photographed the lot, but by the end was no nearer understanding what Robin intended us to do there or see, and was still a light-year from the answer to why.

We'd landed on the island at fourteen minutes after eleven, and by the time we'd concluded our comprehensive but fairly fruitless wander around, it was more than two hours later.

The wind, which had been intermittently gusty since our arrival, suddenly strengthened into a steady gale from the north, alarming us both, as it meant the outer winds of Odin, cycling counterclockwise, would be buffeting not only us mortals soon, but would be threatening also the airplane, which could look after itself in the air, but might be blown onto its back on the ground.

We ran, the wind strengthening all the time, and Kris, scrambling into his seat, made only sketchy checks for once before starting the engines, and the briefest of gauge inspections afterwards. Then he pointed the airplane's nose more or less straight up the runway and opened the throttles to maximum.

The airplane shook with protest but at a low ground speed leapt into the air so fiercely that Kris was fighting with quivering wrists to keep the climbing attitude within safe limits: and although it was the worst minute for it, I thought of the hurricane hunters who had in the past disappeared without trace . . . and understood how it could have happened.

Kris, sweating, pushed the nose down and let the airplane rise like a hawk, and within a minute we were at three thousand feet and climbing, and Trox Island had disappeared into the murk behind us.

It wasn't until that moment that I realized that

in our urgent race to be airborne I had somehow dropped my camera. All those careful pictures of nothing! I searched all my pockets and all round my right-hand flight deck seat, but without success.

Cursing, I told Kris.

"Well, we're not going back to look for it." He sounded annoyed, but found this idea preposterous, as I did. It was all he could do to hold the plane steady, but he was also happy to be back in the air, and with visible relief fished in his shirt pocket for his lunatic flight plan.

"Steer zero eight zero, just north of east," he shouted, giving me instructions while he fished around for his headset and settled the microphone near his mouth. "That should take us to the eye."

"The eye isn't where it was yesterday," I yelled back, handing over the controls and putting on my own headset, in my turn.

"I thought of that," Kris said, "and factored it in."

What he hadn't factored in, though we didn't know it at the moment, was that Odin, as hurricanes were likely to do, had thoroughly and suddenly changed course. The whole circulating mass was now heading due west, which would, within twenty-four hours, take it inexorably over the island we'd left.

At Trox we'd taken off our life jackets and left them lying in the cabin, and I went back there, once Kris looked more in control, and put mine on again. I took Kris's forward and against his inclination made him put his on also.

"We're not going to ditch," he protested.

"All the same . . ."

With reluctance he let me put the flat orange jacket over his head and fasten the tapes round his waist.

Our progress towards the center of Odin wasn't in the least orderly or controlled. Clouds whipped past the window and gradually grew thicker and darker until we were frankly flying in a hundred percent humidity, or in other words, rain.

Though with his own furrowed forehead and tight mouth giving every physical impression of justifiable worry, Kris told me truculently that we weren't giving up, however adverse the weather. The airplane, he insisted, was tough enough for the job and if I wanted to chicken out I should have done so back in Newmarket.

"Are you talking to yourself?" I asked. It was, indeed, hard to hear each other even through the headsets. "How fast are we going?"

Kris didn't reply. I reckoned that we had had the wind in its fury sweeping us sideways and we were now flying very fast in and through the circulatory pattern. I couldn't even guess at our position on either map and with force insisted that we should join the world again by setting bona-fide frequencies on the radio. Kris tacitly gave in, but I harvested only shrieks and whistles and for human contact, weak and far away, a woman's voice speaking Spanish.

The reawakened radio, however, prodded me into clearer thought, and so, despite the bumping tumult all around us, I switched on both of Robin's special measuring instruments, ignoring Kris's yelled protests that they were for use only in the eye and eye wall. He shut up, though, and his eyes widened in incredulity when he saw the millibar indicator on the modified radio altimeter descend from the 990 we'd set on Trox down through 980 and 970 and 960 and waver on 950 before shaking there and falling towards 940.

If we followed the descent of the millibars, surely we would find that they bottomed out in the eye? The air pressure was at its lowest in the eye. Kris, converted by the sliding figures, began slowly and progressively steering left, going round with the winds.

Regular altimeters measured the outside pressure. Pilots set the sea-level pressure on the instrument and the change between the two was displayed as the altitude in feet. The radio altimeter measured our height by bouncing a radio wave back from the surface of the sea like radar. Without it we would have been in real trouble as we wouldn't have known the sea-level pressure even if the sea had been level. If we flew too low, we could hit the waves. It would have helped if I'd been given hours of instruction instead of simply pressing "Start" buttons when I felt like it.

The millibar count went on shrinking fast from 940 to 935 . . . 930 . . . 924. Too low, I thought. The new instrument had to be wrong. *Had* to be . . . or I was misreading it . . . yet 880 had been clocked in a storm in the past. 924 wasn't impossible, but 923? 921? We were lost, I thought. My theory was destroying us . . . 920 . . . 919 . . . it was over . . . The eye's pressure had stood at 930 at Cayman that morning . . . it couldn't possibly have dropped so fast . . . But 919 . . . 919

and still falling . . . I glanced at the regular altimeter and tried to do the mental arithmetic. We were almost down at sea level . . . dangerous . . . "Don't go lower," I told Kris urgently. "We're in cloud just above the water . . . Go up, go up, we'll hit . . ."

Kris was a good pilot for a lunch trip to Newmarket. Neither of us had imagined the standard of skill a hurricane demanded. With a stubbornly locked jaw he made a slow left turn at 919 millibars, inching lower . . . lower . . . Then 919 steadied on the nose, and I held my breath . . .

At just touching 918 millibars on the scale we burst out of cloud into bright sunlight.

We had hit the eye! We had actually *done* it! We were at the very heart of Odin. It was in a way our Everest, our lives' peak, the summit we would never see again. To fly through the eye of a hurricane . . . I had wanted to, but only at that moment did I realize how much.

We were scraping the limits at 918 millibars. Huge waves like mountains moved close below us, smoothly powerful but not licking upward to swallow our remarkable world.

There were tears on Kris's pale cheeks and I daresay on mine also.

In that amazing moment of revelation and fulfillment I felt overwhelmingly and unconditionally grateful to Robin Darcy. Never mind that I didn't trust him across a peanut, never mind that he'd persuaded Kris to lie to me, never mind that the escapade to Trox had seriously endangered us, if it hadn't been for his money, his airplane, his instruments, his enthusiasm and—yes—his hidden and possibly criminal purposes, we would both have been keeping our feet on the ground and following Odin's progress from afar on a television screen, and we could never have said, like my grandmother, "Been there. Done that."

According to the airspeed indicator we were traveling fast enough to give us barely three minutes of calm before we flew into the fearsome winds in the eye wall opposite, and Kris, making the same calculations, immediately began to hold us in a tight circle, so that we stayed in Odin's calm hub long enough to get used to it.

Below us—perhaps only two hundred feet below us—the moving sea was blue from the amazing sunshine that shone brightly also on the airplane, and threw angled shadows on our faces. Above us, the funnel, with only soft spirals of cloud in it, led far upwards to brief glimpses of blue sky. Kris kept the airplane circling in a slow climb until we were at, perhaps, four or five thousand feet above sea level, and had become accustomed to our extraordinary situation, and would remember it.

We were alone in the eye. Down to blue sea, up to blue sky, no one else shared our strange revolving world.

"Stadium effect," Kris noted happily.

I nodded. The stadium effect meant that the eye was wider at the top, and narrower at the water's surface; like a sports stadium, in fact.

All around the calm hub the terrifying winds in the whirling wall looked impenetrable. It was one thing to reach the golden sun in the center, but now we had to calculate the way home. Kris again produced the card with the headings, though even he admitted that the fourth set was no longer right.

"Work it out," he told me. "You can do it."

We hadn't even tried to follow the professional hurricane hunters' flight pattern of three passes straight through the eye at ten thousand feet. We were, in effect, on our own.

I reckoned by computer that if we headed north we would make a landfall, if not in Cay-

man, actually a small target, then in Jamaica, or
as a last resort, Cuba. We just had time and gas to
stay aloft for that, and with luck, long before then
we would be alive on the radio again and could
ask for directions. Embarrassing, but better than
crashing.

Kris agreed to fly north in general but to head
east to enter the eye wall, as the counterclockwise
winds that were at their maximum there would
tend to sweep us round to the north anyway, until
we were clear of the first sixty miles or so and had
reached the outer areas of the hurricane.

The second wind of a hurricane on the ground
came when the eye had passed, taking with it the
illusion that the storm was over. The second wind
of a hurricane hit from the southwest like a moving wall of concrete, catastrophically destroying
everything that had survived the first onslaught.

The second wind of a Category 5 hurricane
screamed and shrieked and traveled faster than a
champion could serve a tennis ace. The second
wind brought inches, torrents, of mud-liquefying
rain. It brought misery and homelessness and
washed away bridges—and to get back safe to
Grand Cayman we had to fly again through the
storm's fury.

"Work out our height," Kris said. His voice sounded unsteady and his eyes were alarmed. I made the simple calculation that air pressure normally fell by one millibar every thirty feet of height . . . but mental concentration always fell with altitude . . . and neither Kris nor I were any longer razor sharp because of the by-then buffeting noisy leap-around world enveloping us.

Kris headed east and, at eight thousand feet on the altimeter, resolutely set course for land. Even with full power thundering in the engines we were both sure that we'd underestimated drift and that the rotating wind system was blowing us anywhere but where we wanted to go.

Blue sky had vanished. The sea tumbled and raced, gray and brown.

Cloud and rain closed around us. We were blind, and couldn't measure our forward progress. Kris was giving up trying. His thoughts were a straight line.

For minutes I lived with the certainty that Kris and I and the airplane weren't up to the job. My grandmother's heebie-jeebies raised my skin in bumps. Kris, visibly losing his nerve, said, "Mayday, Mayday, Mayday" repeatedly into the headset, broadcasting a plea that no one heard.

We might have made it, even then, if we'd held

to the northerly course and if nothing had gone wrong: but from one second to the next, with the speed of most disasters, a simple mechanical change tossed us straight into the realms of chaos, to the turbulent territory of all the demons.

The right-hand engine stopped.

Immediately the whole aircraft lost its balance, tipped sideways, spun in a circle, put its nose up, put it down again . . . Kris was shouting, "Full opposite rudder, stick forward, full opposite rudder," and stamping hard down with his left foot, and I remembered that "stick forward, full opposite rudder" brought a single-engined airplane out of a spin, and I didn't know if it made the asymmetric wildness of a dead twin-engine better or worse. I tried the radio again, to broadcast Kris's voice, and heard only Spanish, very faint.

Space and time got jumbled. Thought became reduced for both of us to one idea at a time. My own mind clamped down onto the one reassurance that there was a life raft dinghy behind me in the passenger cabin, and that as airplanes didn't float, we would need it.

Bashing around in the restricted tumbling spaces I somehow got my hands onto the big bundle and clutched it, holding on even when any sort of steering became doubtful and Kris, still hauling rightly or wrongly at the control column, began chanting again over and over, "Mayday, Mayday, stick forward, full opposite rudder . . . Mayday . . ." and in desperation, "I'm heading back to Trox Island. Back to Trox."

Though his voice chattered on uselessly he nevertheless successfully muscled a lopsided control of the bucking, twisting, rocking aircraft while it dropped against his will from about eight thousand feet, and only when I yelled at him to be ready to jump did he seem to realize that having only one embattled and hard-worked engine overheating in that tempest meant that we were losing the fight. He could see the galloping waves, but even then would have denied their inevitability . . . except that seawater splashed on the windshield.

With a screech of awakening terror he stretched out stiff fingers to the switches and pulled the nose up crookedly, with the port engine and propeller still racing at full power, and somehow we met the water flat on the belly on a frightful accelerating wave. At first contact the Piper skipped back up into the air, twisting violently to the left and dropping its nose. The second strike was heavier and, in that strange way that the mind wanders even in emergencies, I thought of the exam question, set long ago, which discussed the best material for a seat belt and how it had to stretch and absorb the kinetic energy to protect the occupant in a sudden collision. As the airplane buried itself into the near vertical face of the next towering whitecap, our seat belts fulfilled their purpose, absorbed our energy and brought us to a teeth-rattling halt.

Almost in the second of impact I kicked open the rear door and jumped into the raging water, clutching the dinghy with me for precious survival and yanking at the cord that inflated it. It swelled hugely at once and as it unfolded the weight of it tore it out of my arms, all except a narrow rope circling it, for people in the water to hang onto. I did hang on for a very short while, but the screaming gale made a farce of any strength I might have thought I had, and I devastatingly knew I couldn't hold it in place while Kris too unbuckled himself and left the sinking ship.

He came very fast indeed out of the front door, though, and by luck jumped first with one foot onto the already flooded wing and then fell straight into the almost fully inflated dinghy, at the moment it tore itself out of my hands. The wind and waves seized the expanding craft instantly and blew it a great way from the sinking airplane, and for a moment I could see Kris's long horror-filled face looking back at me. Then clouds and rain enveloped and parted us violently into invisibility and for only a brief time longer could I see even the waterlogged airplane until it completed a fast wing-down sliding disappearance into oblivion and was gone forever.

Without much hope I pulled the inflation cords of the life jacket that represented my only chance of survival, and the fact that the jacket inflated swiftly in the designed manner seemed truly the only faint shred of possible security, and not much of that, anyway.

My shoes came off, and I slid also out of my pants, so that I wore only underpants and a once-white shirt and the orange fluorescent life jacket. The Caribbean water, comparatively warm, might throw me about, but I wasn't going to die of hypothermia. There were comforting stories of lost sailors being picked up after days at sea. Disregard, I thought, the awkward info that they hadn't been battling hurricane-size waves.

It was daylight, and my watch had stopped,

water-filled, at 2:15 P.M., when we had ditched. At home I kept a cheap waterproof watch for swimming: idiotic that I hadn't brought it. Such silly thoughts. Time had no meaning in the sea.

Yet when Kris and I didn't reappear at the Cayman airport, Robin Darcy would surely send out rescuers. Kris's orange dinghy could be seen for miles, and my life jacket, though a smaller dot in the ocean, was purposely bright. I shut my mind to the driving rain and fearsome colossal waves that would keep a life-jacket-seeking helicopter safe on the ground at home.

Odin was a slow-moving hurricane, but even the slow ones eventually passed. I, to live, had first to outlast Odin, and then to be visible, and then to be preferably visible on a regular cross-Caribbean air route.

Thoughts came slowly, none of them joyful. For instance, a thought unwelcome: the Caribbean was a very big sea. For another instance, another thought: I might be a practiced surf rider, but first, I didn't have a surfboard handy, and second, no surfboard ever could realistically ride a thirty-foot storm surge.

With useless jumbled thought, then, and no constructive decisions, I struggled simply to stay afloat with my head up out of the water. The life jacket was at least one of those with the main flotation collar in front supporting one's chin, so that even when overwhelmed by the curling crest of a towering wave, the life jacket slowly righted its wearer—like a saturated cork rising.

One could swallow saltwater and gasp painfully for air. One could claw oneself constantly upright into surface-whipping winds and stay there for a while, just able to breathe, but after the late afternoon had passed miserably into darkness, one could begin, in the endless heavy battering of racing waves, to feel that nothing, now, could grant deliverance, or reprieve.

One could pass into delirium, and one could drown.

5

A LONG TIME after coherent thought of any kind had stopped . . . when flashes of illusion still made me believe my grandmother in silver was swimming in the waves not far ahead . . . a long time after the apparitions of Robin and Kris, holding hands, had dissolved from beckoning me wetly towards them to be shot . . . in the roaring nonhuman severity of Odin, while the remains of instinct flickered still in heart valves and groped for life in brain stem, a monstrous wave picked me up and lifted me high and flung the rag doll I'd become against an impossibly towering peak.

The peak wasn't water . . . it was rock.

Far from giving me joy, it knocked me out.

This gift of a spared life, I gleaned a fair time later, came from the rock wall forming one end of the deserted jetty where ships had once docked to unload the life-blood stores for Trox Island.

There were the remains of scrubby bushes and sticklike saplings still growing indomitably from cracks and ledges, and it was among them, and gripped by them against an uneven and abrasive rock face, that I had come to rest.

Held fast there, I slowly seeped back to consciousness, and it seemed at first natural, and then with woozy reflection, extremely *unnatural,* that I should know where I was.

The knowledge came without strength or desire to do anything about it. I turned myself slightly to look along to the end of the dock and found that more than half of the structure, though built of very heavy timber and rooted in concrete, had been torn away as if made of cardboard.

Consciousness drifted away again into a troubled bad-dream-filled utterly exhausted state that was as much daze as sleep.

Several centuries or so later I noticed it had been raining ever since I'd opened my saltwater-swollen eyes. Rain washed the salt from my limbs but all my skin was crinkled from too long an immersion, and in spite of water water everywhere nor any drop to drink, I had like any ancient mariner a scorchingly painful salt-induced thirst.

Rain . . . I opened my mouth to it hungrily. It filled my throat; it filled my mind. I realized that my grandmother wasn't really out there in silver, swimming. Robin Darcy's gun was back in Sand Dollar Beach, scaring the shit out of intruders.

Weakness went on, however, encouraging me to lie still. On the other hand, I was halfway up a low cliff, lying among roots that the constant rain was loosening: and as if on cue, some of the bushes slid out of their anchorage and sent me tumbling and slithering with a lot of scratches down and down until I reached the hard surface of the dock itself.

By good luck the dock, though now smashed, had originally been built for the mooring of merchant ships, which meant the surface of the dock itself was above the turgid water. Brown rough waves sped threateningly along beside its length now, but only a few slapped heavily over its surface, as if searching for things to suck back into their grasp. The height and vigor of the waves that had managed my arrival had died down by nearly half. Seas of the present weight couldn't have ripped up something as heavy as the dock.

So I lay a bit longer in the rain and thought of Kris and the eye of Odin, and the whole day seemed unreal.

The whole day . . . The light was gray . . . but it wasn't *night,* and it had been night when I'd been on the edge of drowning.

Yesterday, I thought with incredulity . . . Kris and I had come here yesterday . . . and I'd spent all night in the black water, and I'd seen the shape of the cliff I'd crashed onto because the tired old world was spinning slowly towards the return of gray morning.

Turning over again on the shattered dock, I realized that it hadn't been so much damaged on the day before. There hadn't been any damage at all. I simply hadn't the energy to do more than conclude that the destructive winds of Odin had crossed the island since we'd left. Soon, I told myself, soon I would go back up the hill to the little village. Soon I would get on with living. I had actually never before felt so weak.

As if to prod my flagging spirits, the heavy rain abruptly stopped.

To make some sort of start, I fiddled with the

clips fastening the life jacket and managed only to tie the tapes into more difficult knots. Undoing them took ages. It was stupid how much my arms ached.

I still had no impression of hours. Day was light, night was dark. When day began fading again I finally put some resolution into things and with more effort than normal struggled to my bare feet and very slowly trudged up from sea level to the village, which sat on the cliff top at a height of roughly two hundred feet. Storm surge waves might not wash away whole communities at such a height, but hurricane winds came with no such inhibitions. The little village of the day gone by, the houses, the church and the mushroom sheds, all had been blown to destruction.

I stood stock still, the life jacket dangling from my hand.

The concrete rectangles where the houses had stood were still in place; the roofs had vanished and the timbers of their walls were heaped and scattered with broken window frames twisted, glass gone. The water-catching cisterns were full of debris and mud, with no buckets to be seen.

The church had no roof. The spire and two

walls had collapsed. All the mushroom sheds had vanished, though on the ground in outline one could see where they had been.

The only structures still standing were the two ultra-thick-walled concrete huts, and even they showed marks of battery from other flying debris.

Without shoes—and with socks sea-lost also—I found the village area made for even more uncomfortable progress than the hill, but I trod my way gingerly to the nearest of the thick-walled huts, the one that had contained the bunk beds, and went inside.

The doorway—with no door—led through the four-foot-thick wall into deepening gloom, where my eyes took time to adjust. The entrance, I reckoned at length, had been almost face-on to the wind, in view of the chaotic results. A good quantity of wood was still inside the hut, even though no longer neatly organized into bunks. Hefty planks seemed to have been hurtled across the interior space to crash like battering rams into the walls. The force needed for the holes they had dug in the plastered walls gave me the thankful shivers: Kris and I might have thought we would find safe shelter in there if the storm had caught us on land.

Shelter . . . It occurred to me that the roof hadn't blown off, as it had off everything else, except perhaps off the other hut. The tangled planks, and the concrete floor, were mostly dry. Outside it was still not raining, though the light was fading against a heavy sky.

No one would come now before night. No one could have seen little Trox earlier in blinding rain. Accept it, I thought with tiredness; in twelve hours, but not before, someone would come.

Believe it.

Someone will come.

In the remains of light I laid several planks side by side on the dank inhospitable concrete, and with the flotation collar for a pillow I lay down on my back . . . and couldn't sleep.

Thirst had passed, but hunger burrowed like a screw in my stomach. I'd eaten nothing since the barbecue dinner in the Ford house, and I hadn't wanted breakfast in the run up to the Odin hunt. The uneaten Danish pastries of Owen Roberts airfield tantalized my emptiness until I could almost smell them. In the morning I'd find food and drink, I told myself, but without shoes I wasn't going foraging in the dark.

The island air, at least, was sweetly warm; and

if it rained again, I would be dry. Hurricanes, particularly those like Odin, that formed and gained their strength in the Caribbean, not the Atlantic, were notoriously unpredictable in their travel, but they seldom turned right round one hundred and eighty degrees and retraced their former path. If it had happened, the occurrences had been so rare that it wasn't worth worrying about.

I closed my eyes, but after its sluggish day my brain accelerated and relentlessly reviewed, remembered and relived all the steps to my present troubles. There were still whole prairies of unanswered questions defeating the simplest speculations, like why grow mushrooms on a tiny island in the Caribbean Sea? Like why send two meteorologists to race a hurricane to see what state the mushrooms were in? But surely Robin Darcy wouldn't have bought an airplane just for that . . . and he'd bought it for Nicky, not Odin.

I supposed that someone, somewhere, might make sense of it. Robin had to know . . . didn't he?

I spent a long time imagining Kris in the orange dinghy, his face looking back at me in horror as the screaming elements seized his future. If he managed to stay in the dinghy he would whirl across the face of the waters faster than racing speedboats. According to the instructions I'd followed too carelessly about how to open the dinghy (I should have climbed in to start with) there were a rudder and two paddles to steer with, but the calm sea they needed lay long hours ahead.

I switched off at the possibility that the gales had sucked the dinghy airborne. I balked at the probability that the canvas inflated shell had gone somersaulting over and over across the seas until Kris fell out into the water and met no Trox cliffs to scoop him to land.

I shifted restlessly on my hard plank bed, and long before dawn went outside to sit with my back against the hut's exterior wall, my sight filled unexpectedly with stars.

The hurricane had gone over. The night was cloudless and still. Only the waves, heavily hurrying along the ruined mooring stage with a distant slap and hiss, spoke of the terrible force unleashed a day earlier on the little wrecked hamlet.

Hunger set me moving as soon as I could see where I was treading, but I already knew all the cupboards were bare, even if any were still standing. When the people of Trox Island had left they'd packed their lives to go with them. I looked in vain for a container that would hold liquids, and ended by sucking up spoonfuls of rainwater from any sort of hollow I came across.

There was nothing to eat except muddy grass.

I navigated carefully over to the second thick-walled hut, which had been empty anyway on our first visit, and stood inside looking in puzzlement at the change high winds had wrought.

For a start, the inner surface of two of the walls had been peeled away, leaving bare cinderblocks in view. The two huts, though appearing the same from outside, were constructed differently within. The hut I'd passed the night in had been built of solid concrete with a plaster facing. The second hut's thick walls had been lined with pre-fabricated panels of plasterlike walling, and it was several of these that had been torn off their fastenings and broken in pieces.

Because I was expecting to see nothing but destruction, it took me a while to notice that there were differences in these ripped-off walls, and that, in particular, one panel, dangling half off its fixings, was half-hiding a door of sorts underneath.

I went over for a closer look and found that the inner door, behind the loose bit of walling, was fastened shut by a combination lock and was the front, in fact, of a safe.

If the thoroughness of the rest of the exodus was anything to go by, that safe too would be as bare as Mother Hubbard's. I tried to pull it open, on the basis that the wind had weakened or destroyed everything it reached, but this one barrier stood obstinately fast and, giving it up, I returned to my hunt for food.

The big blue birds with brown legs looked tantalizing, but without shoes I couldn't catch one, and without fire I'd have to eat one raw, and I wasn't yet desperate enough to try it. I could perhaps catch one of the larger iguanas, which moved more slowly than the little ones, but again the lack of cooking deterred me.

But where were the cows?

Cows gave milk, and milk was food. There had been a large free-roaming herd of cattle on the island two days ago, and surely some of them had had calves, and calves needed milk . . .

As long as the whole herd hadn't been blasted

into the sea, as long as I could get a cow to stand still, as long as I could find any decent container such as an empty Coca-Cola can to drink from, my worst and most immediate predicament would be solved.

Problem: I couldn't see the herd.

Trox was a mile long, with the village at one end and the consolidated grass airstrip extending from it to the other. I carefully walked to the beginning of the strip, from where we'd raced to get off in the airplane, but search as I could for cows, I saw not so much as a tail swishing.

What I did find, though, to my delight, was my dropped camera. Second thoughts cooled the enthusiasm somewhat as although it was supposed to be waterproof and was still in its protective leather slipcover, it had been lying deep in mud as if I'd also stamped on it when I'd dropped it. I picked it up sadly and held it dangling with its straps entwined in the tapes of the life jacket.

With hunger still a priority I set off along one side of the runway, seeing a rocky fringe of land sloping down between the flat grass and the tossing sea. There was room for a herd there, but not a cow in sight. Depressed, I left that side of the runway and crossed over it to the other, and on the way thought that although that landing strip had been fabricated of earth and grass, it had been quite a feat of engineering, as its dimensions were wide and long enough to accommodate full-sized cargo and passenger aircraft, not just small twin-engined toys.

On the other side of the runway there was a much wider extent of rocky land, much of it scraped bare by abrasive winds. Palm trees lay on their sides, roots helpless in the air, palm crowns like sodden mopheads on the ground. Palm trees . . . coconuts . . . I diverged from cows to coconut milk and lost a bit more skin from legs and feet in descending from runway height down nearer to sea level.

Before I found a coconut, I found the cows.

They were lying in a long dark group, their stomachs on the ground. A low cliff beyond them had given shelter of sorts against the gales, and I supposed their own weight and mass had done the rest.

Many of them turned their heads as I approached, and a few lumbered to their feet, at which point I took note of bulls among the cows and wondered if the milking expedition wasn't after all a bad idea.

Three of the bulls were heavy-shouldered Brahmans. Two were cream-colored Charolais. Four were brownish red-and-white Herefords. Four more were what in horse circles would have been called chestnut in color, but were outside my rudimentary agriculture. Several were black-and-white Friesians.

Satisfied that I meant no harm, the gentlemen of the herd lost interest, moved their great heads around without menace and settled down again in peace.

As Friesians, I distantly remembered, were lavish milk producers, I inched a wincingly careful way round the vast throng of big animals until I came to a large docile-looking Friesian cow with a satisfied calf lying beside her. I hadn't actually ever milked a cow before, and as soon as I touched her the big creature lumbered to her feet and looked at me balefully with mournful off-putting eyes. If hunger hadn't been so pressingly painful I would have stopped right there, particularly when she stretched her neck and issued a long, hollow comment, which brought a whole lot of her companions to their feet.

The only container I had was the slipcover of my camera, a filthy, muddy, soaking-wet soft black leather pouch.

I went down on my knees to the Friesian lady,

who looked round in manifest surprise at my attempt to use her milk as dish-washing liquid, and although my best efforts yielded little, by the fourth filling, rubbing and emptying, the contents of the pouch looked whiter and cleaner and getting on for drinkable.

I sipped the sixth pouchful. The milk was warm, rich and frothy, and tasted faintly of mud. I tested the next few amounts with increasing confidence, and I drank the pretty clean tenth pouchful entirely, before the cow ran out of patience, swished her tail in my face and with dignity swayed conclusively away.

With a stomach quietened for the moment I walked back to the ruined village and by one of the mud-laden rainwater cisterns rinsed the pouch as best I could. Using a damp shirttail, I wiped mud from my now-dry camera until when I pressed the shutter release button for a third try, it actually worked, and not only clicked but automatically wound on the film.

I used two more exposures taking views of the village's destruction. I would probably then have snapped the cattle, most of whom had followed me slowly up the island and were now standing around watching me in curiosity, except that of the roll of thirty-six exposures I'd begun with, there were only a few left. Cows were cows were cows anywhere. Cows were as interesting as no mushrooms.

SUNSHINE RETURNED TO the Caribbean.

By midday, judging time according to the sun's height in the sky, no one had come.

Two days had passed since Kris and I had left Grand Cayman. We would surely be missed.

Someone would come.

I WANDERED INTO the second of the thick-walled huts merely for something to do, and in the same aimless fashion pulled the loose flapping panels of off-white walling entirely away from the concrete underneath. Minus its cover, the safe was revealed as a square gray metal box of about two feet by two, let bodily into the wall at waist height. I frowned. If it hadn't been for the hurricane, the safe would have remained out of general sight: and it wasn't unusual, I thought, to find some way of camouflaging the very existence of a cache.

I tried again to open its door, but it seemed a hurricane-proof steel box could easily deny access to the soft hands of meteorologists.

The way in consisted most obviously of a short flat lever, but to allow the lever to be moved there was an electronic key pad—letters as well as numbers—like that of a touch telephone. It seemed a complicated lock to find on a mushroom farm; just one more mystery, in the whole series of unanswerable questions.

Sighing, I strolled outside again, where the cattle now populated what was left of the village's foundations and were behaving with aversion round the uncovered parts of the muddy cisterns. If they stretched their necks down far enough they might just be able to drink the filthy water, but thirst hadn't yet driven them to such lengths.

It was interesting, I thought, that the cattle mostly hadn't sorted themselves into separate breeds but stood in haphazard groups, Charolais mixed with Friesians, a Brahman bull from sacred-cow India in a clump of beef-producing Herefords, and on the fringes there were a few hulking dark shapes that I hadn't noticed before, of black Aberdeen Angus.

The brain plays odd tricks, and besides, taught by my grandmother, I'd always given brain-cell room to random connections of apparently unconnected thoughts.

I'd had a friend called Angus when we were both about ten, and he had had very large stick-out ears. Teasing, people laughed at him and called him Aberdeen because his stick-out ears looked like a cow's, and he had cried about it, and sank so deep in depression that his parents had let him have cosmetic surgery, and then other boys had teased him about "pinning back his lugholes" until he cried about that too. My grandmother had told "Aberdeen" Angus to his sad little face to be glad he had ears at all, it was better than being deaf.

Trox Island was a ridiculous place to be remembering stick-out-ears Angus. My grandmother would be admonishing me that I might not have food better than milk, nor shoes, nor comfort, but I did have life.

I went back into the concrete hut and without hesitation tapped out ANGUS in numbers— 26487—on the touch pad of the combination lock of the safe.

Nothing happened. No clicks, no encouraging blips. Stick-out-ears Angus didn't work the lever to open the box, and of course there was no reason to suppose it would.

With nothing much else to do to pass the time

I walked across what might have been a sort of village square and looked again at the damaged interior of the hut I'd spent half the night in.

Why did a mushroom farm need a hut with walls four feet thick and a hurricane-proof roof? A mushroom farm didn't, was the concise answer; but a meteorological or seismic station might. The instruments and the records would have left with the general inhabitants, but a building that housed a seismograph, for instance, would need to be constructed to be of extreme inertia in itself before it could measure earthquake tremors far away. The concrete floor, I guessed, would be at least as thick as the walls.

Outside again, I looked up at the clear blue sky and listened to the subsiding march of the waves, but what I really needed was a rescuing aircraft, and of that there was no sign.

Evelyn, perhaps, was lying in the sun on Sand Dollar Beach wondering where Kris and Perry had got to. But Odin was still on the rampage *somewhere,* and Evelyn, perhaps, had taken to the hills . . . of which Florida had few.

Thoughts dribbled on. In Robin's house the police came waving guns at houseguests who swam at three in the morning, and the security checked by telephone to make sure all was well. "Yes," Robin had said easily, "yes, it's Hereford."

Hereford? I stood on Trox looking at a red and white cow, a Hereford. So what if Robin's Hereford was to the Sand Dollar Beach security firm a sort of password. Hereford . . . Hereford . . . All is well.

Why not?

People used the same password over and over in many different configurations, because it was easier to remember one password than many.

With still all the time in the world, I was simply playing games. I went back to the touchpad of the safe and tapped 4373 (HERE) and 3673 (FORD) and instantly there was a loud click.

Astonished, I grasped the lever by its flat handle and tried lifting it upwards, and without the slightest stiffness in its travel the lever rose upward and the door silently opened.

Treasure there was none, or at least not to my eyes at that first meeting. Two objects only lay on the cloth-covered lining of the gray metal safe. One of them was a yellow box, an electronic-looking instrument complete with a dial with a pointer and a short rod on the end of a curled cable like that on a telephone. It seemed to me from much past acquaintance that the box was probably a Geiger counter, and when I lifted it out and pressed an on-off switch, it rewarded me with slow irregular unurgent clicks. A Geiger counter indeed, with few Geigers to count. Technically, a Geiger counter counted high-speed particles emitted by the decay of radioactive material. The short rod contained a tube invented long ago by physicists Geiger and Müller. A high-energy particle, entering the tube, ionized the gas inside, which allowed the gas to conduct electricity, thus creating a pulse of current, which in turn caused the click.

Lying beside the Geiger counter, the only other thing hidden away was a single fawn folder, the sort used universally in offices to help with filing.

The folder, when I lifted it out in its turn, contained roughly twenty sheets of paper, nearly all in different sizes, with and without formal headings, and all in foreign scripts, most of which I didn't recognize. There were combinations of letters-with-numbers on almost every page, whatever the language, and it was those that I recognized positively and with alarm. A few sheets were stapled together in pairs and two seemed to be lists of addresses, though as they were written in a script I thought might be Arabic, I couldn't read any of them.

I put the folder back in the safe, but left the door open, and went thoughtfully outside again into the sun. The cattle turned their heads to watch me. Several of them mooed, several more made slopping pats of steaming waste. As a day's entertainment, they were hardly a riot.

Counting, I found I had four exposures left on my reel of film. I changed my mind and took one view of the cattle, including in it as many different breeds as I could find grouped in one place. Then I went back to the safe, to sort out which three of the papers in the folder were most worth immortality.

Trying to assess them all carefully out in bright daylight made the choice no easier, but in the end I settled on four of them, photographing two separately, and the last two side by side. The film ran out after that last exposure, and to my frustration the automatic rewind stopped and stuck at the place where I had cleaned off the mud. There was no way of knowing if any pictures at all had survived, though I didn't think it mattered enormously if they were ruined. However, to save it from any further rain, I tied the camera by its strap to a convenient beam near the safe, high up and out of reach of cows.

I wondered, as I put the papers back in the folder and the folder back in the safe, whether or not I should leave everything locked in as I had found it; and I did so chiefly to keep the papers too away from the cows, some of whom had come after me with so much curiosity that they were crowding the doorway and trying to push themselves and their big heads inside. I shooed them out again, but in a strange way I was glad of their company, and not as lonely as I would have been without them.

The day seemed endless, and nobody came.

TWELVE HOURS OF darkness. A long time until dawn.

I slept in brief patches, uncomfortably, and woke finally in the early gray light to the sole comfort that in the setting sun's rays the evening before, I had seen a gleam which had proved to be an empty soup can wedged into the ruins of one of the houses; and although it was misshapen and filled with dusty debris, it made a better milk-carton than the camera case.

The cows had given me supper, and also an

early breakfast, and then they moved off in a herd as if of one mind towards the runway, where they put their heads down to the grass, and kept it both fertilized and short.

When the sun rose it was three days since Kris and I had flown out of Grand Cayman Island.

The eye of Hurricane Odin, after traveling northwest for three days at seven miles an hour, might at that moment, I thought, be raising gales and storm surges along the Cayman shores. It wasn't reasonable, I told myself, to expect anyone in those circumstances to come looking for fool-hardy aviators who had most certainly crashed at sea.

I put together a rough low seat of timbers in a place that would afford shadow when the sun was highest, and sat there to give my still bare feet a respite. Cuts, scratches and insect bites round my ankles itched abominably and refused to heal. I went through a long morning of self-pitying depression, unable to believe I would have to spend much more time there and un-willing in consequence to start building a bear-able way to live.

I thought of my grandmother, who, apart from any anxiety she might have had if anyone had told her I was missing, would certainly have issued brisk and bracing instructions along the lines of, "Perry, build yourself a house, filter some drinking water, weave some sandals, look for coconuts, keep a log of the days, go for a swim . . . don't mope."

She had never complained, neither when her legs stopped working, nor ever since. She had taught me always simply to bear as best I could whatever could not possibly be put right; and in that category she had included my lack of father or mother.

She wouldn't have thought much of my spinelessness on Trox. Her presence sat with me at midday in the patch of shade, sympathetic but unforgiving. It was my grandmother therefore who prodded me that afternoon into walking to the other end of the runway, shoes or no shoes, and I came across a way down to a white-sandy beach there, from which I swam, pitting my diminished strength against still heavy rough surf, but feeling clean and refreshed afterwards.

Down that end of the island there was a veritable forest of snapped-off hardwood trees as well as uprooted coconut palms and the stripped remains of what I guessed were broad-leaved banana trees. By scavenging I found two viable coconuts and, still attached to its stalk, a full-grown ripe mango: a feast.

But the blue sky remained empty, and no one came.

BY THE NEXT morning even the gray tossing sea had returned to Caribbean blue.

To pass the dragging time, I took the folder of papers out of the safe, and in the sun sat staring at each one separately, trying to make even the smallest sense of languages I couldn't read. The nearest I came to recognition was a paper I guessed to be in Greek, on account of the symbols Ω and π, omega and pi.

All of the papers were scattered with numbers, and where numbers occurred they were written in the script known as Latin, or otherwise ordinary English.

Eventually, letting ideas drift, I thought that some of the bunch might be an inventory, a stock-taking, of round-the-world species and quantities, possibly of the mushrooms that had once grown in the now blown-away sheds.

Fine, I thought; but why the Geiger counter?

I replaced the folder and spent an idle hour listening to irregular but fairly frequent clicks as I walked around the dead village raising live evidence of radiation.

I expected the counter to count, as background radiation was all around us all the time, a combination from naturally occurring radioactive material in the earth's crust and "cosmic rays," high-energy particles arriving from outer space emitted by the sun about ten minutes and ninety-three million miles ago.

But there seemed to be rather a high count rate, especially near to the bases of the blown-away houses. High count rates were not unusual. Residents of Aberdeen, the Granite City of Scotland, experienced a higher background than normal, as granite contained many radioactive atoms. I looked around me and tried to remember what my pal in Miami had said—"Constructed of bird droppings, guano, coral and limestone rock." Were bird droppings radioactive? No, I thought not.

Putting the rod near the cracks in the concrete floors raised an endless stream of clicks; clicks so fast that they coalesced into one sound.

I thought of radon. Radon gas could be a problem the world over as it was produced by the decay of naturally occurring uranium in rocks and seeped unseen and unsmelled into people's homes, giving them cancer. But, I thought, radon needed an enclosed space to congregate and the hurricane had ensured there were no enclosed spaces left. And besides, limestone had little radioactive uranium in it to decay.

So what was causing the count? Was this perhaps why the islanders had left: not because of Nicky, still less because of Odin, but because they feared the radioactivity under their feet?

If the Geiger counter was energized round the houses, it practically took off over the outlined remnants of the foundations of the mushroom sheds. Frowning, I made a long detour down and off the runway to see if the cattle en masse were emitting strong radioactivity too, but to my relief they weren't. I hadn't, it seemed, drunk quantities of radioactive milk.

Eventually the Geiger counter lost its attraction as entertainment and I restored it to the safe. The folder lay there also, each sheet familiar but reproaching my lack of scholarship.

I closed the safe and locked it, and again in the idyllic air I added one more piece of wood to a growing line. Each piece of wood represented a day, and at that moment there were four of them. Four long days and longer nights.

Despair was too strong a word for it.

Perhaps despondency was better.

WHEN THEY CAME for me, they came with guns.

6

I N THE LATE afternoon of my fifth day on the island while I swam in the sea off the small sandy beach at the far end of the landing strip, a twin-engined airplane droned in, dropped down neatly over the distant village and rolled nearly halfway down the strip before pausing, turning and taxiing back to what, before Odin, had been habitation.

Every day I had lain the bright yellow-orange life jacket conspicuously on the runway and weighted it with stones in the hope that it would be visible from any passing low-flying aircraft, and although the cattle had thoroughly dirtied it a couple of times I had washed it well enough for the purpose in one of the filthy cisterns. With absolute joy then, I reckoned that the jacket had successfully delivered its intended message, and I scrambled with haste up the winding rocky path from the little beach, aiming, sore feet or not, to run towards my rescuers so they should see me before believing the island to be deserted and flying off again.

In my anxiety to be seen I gave no thought at all to the possibility that the newcomers might not be friendly. They had come in an aircraft that would take eighteen or so passengers comfortably: the sort of aircraft regularly used for flying people to and from small islands. The sort of aircraft sensibly sent out to survey small islands for hurricane survivors. A workhorse aircraft, unremarkable.

I was surprised but not disturbed that no one emerged from it as I shuffled and ran and struggled up the runway. It was a scorching hot day and I thought only that they would have air-conditioning and glorious cold drinks on board. I was about twenty yards away when the rear door opened and unfolded to enable five figures to walk down a short stairway to the ground.

They all wore the same thing—shiny metallic

coveralls with great hoods coming down over their shoulders, with smoked plastic rectangles instead of faces: more like space suits than suitable wear for a stifling Caribbean afternoon. I'd seen those outfits before—radiation protection suits. I'd seen what they were carrying before too—deadly black assault rifles, which they aimed like a firing squad at my chest.

I stopped. I found it less than amusing to be a target again, but at least no one this time read me my "rights." No one told me I could remain silent but if I said anything it would be held against me in court. No one mentioned a court of any description. Silence, however, agreed with me fine.

One of the suits took a hand off his weapon long enough to beckon to me to walk forward and, seeing no advantage in trying to run, I slowly advanced until signaled to stop.

I must have looked a bit primitive. I wore only what Odin had left me: underpants and torn shirt. My chin was dark with unshaven beard and my feet were bruised and swollen. The television audience back home, used to my well-brushed tidy screen self, would have been affronted and disbelieving.

The five suits talked to each other for a while but were too far away for me to hear what they said. I hopefully guessed in the end that they weren't so much concerned about their exposure to radioactivity as about preventing me from recognizing them if I saw them anywhere again in future. This helpfully implied that they'd voted against killing me casually and chucking my corpse into the sea—from where it might wash up again inconveniently—and also, I thought, it meant that they hadn't known I would be on the island at all.

I'd had four long days and nights for thinking, and many things in that time had grown clearer. If they gave me a reasonable chance to act, they could report me to be as ignorant when they found me as I'd been when I got lost.

Three of the suits peeled off and headed for the village area, leaving only two with their unamiable black machinery pointing my way. These two in fact looked nervous more than murderous, shuffling uncertainly from foot to foot; but nervous gunmen frightened me more than those who knew their business. I stood very still and didn't speak, and was glad not to be sweltering inside heavy protective gear.

When eventually the other three returned from their walkabout, they were carrying in plain sight both the Geiger counter and the folder of papers. If they'd found my camera in its new out-of-cow-reach perch near the top of a high tangle of timbers, they weren't telling.

All five conferred near the aircraft, then a different group of three walked up the entry stairs and pulled the door shut behind them.

My spirits sank to zero when they started both of the engines, but as the two left to guard me continued unemotionally to do so, I waited as patiently as I could manage, even if screaming inside. Food, sleep and shoes, I needed all of those. On that island paradise I'd had a surfeit of hunger, thirst, heat, insects and general deprivation, and I was perilously near to begging.

Turn your mind, I told myself, to something else.

A gentle wind was blowing steadily up the runway towards the village, but the aircraft, though traveling the right way for takeoff, was going far too slowly to achieve lift. Eventually it stopped altogether, disgorging one figure who walked to an edge of the runway to survey the rocky terrain between landing strip and sea. The figure returned

and reboarded, and the travel-stop-search procedure was repeated again and again.

They were looking for the cattle, I realized, and
although I could have saved them time, I didn't.
I let them stop and search, stop and search, stop
and search until they came across the peaceful
beasts lying and chewing the cud down at the far
end of the island, where there was a patch of
more succulent grass.

The airplane turned back after a lengthy herd
inspection and stopped where it had been before.

Another general discussion took place, which
resulted in two of my longtime guards advancing
on me nervously, one with gun held ready, the
other to tie first a blindfolding scarf around my
head and next a thinner uncomfortable restraint
round my wrists, behind my back.

I thought of several protests, both verbal and
physical, but saw no point in any of them, and
nor did I complain when roughly prodded,
blindly stumbling, up the stairs into the body of
the aircraft to be pushed into a rear seat. The engines roared immediately as if in a hurry to be
gone and the aircraft lifted easily into the blue.

I consequently didn't see Trox Island or its familiar ruins when I was leaving it; but if three of

my captors thought I didn't know who they were, they were wrong.

BY THE TIME we touched down, at a guess thirty-five to forty minutes later, I'd added cramp to my woes, a minor inconvenience compared to not having been flung overboard into the deep Caribbean. The aircraft taxied a good way after it landed, and then waited, with the engines ticking over, until the rear door was lowered and some of the passengers left through it. Then the door closed again and the aircraft taxied lengthily again, and again it stopped with the engines still running. Again I heard the rear door being lowered, and with sweat and rapid heartbeat I thought that if death were on its way to me it would be here at the end of a long taxi ride to nowhere.

Prods and pushes propelled me stumbling down the steps onto stony ground. This exit wasn't followed immediately by a bullet through the brain, but by a blind walk through a squeaking gate in a rattling fence. Rough hands gave me an overbalancing final thrust forward, and while I tottered to stand upright I heard the squeaky gate slam shut behind me and with immense thankfulness understood I'd been unmistakably shoved free into the living present.

I swallowed, shuddered, felt sick. The aircraft taxied away into limbo. I thought with banality that it's remarkable how stupid one feels standing half naked and blindfolded with one's wrists tied, in the middle of God knows where.

After a while, in which I tried unsuccessfully to free my hands, a voice at my shoulder asked in puzzlement, "What you doing out here, mon?" and I answered with husky, out-of-use vocal cords, but endless gratitude, "If you untie me, I'll tell you."

He was big, black and laughing at my predicament, and he held the white cotton triangular bandage that had been wrapped round my head.

"You got bandages where you don't need them, mon," he said happily. "Who trussed you up like a chicken, eh? Your woman, eh?" He tore and untied with strong fingers the bandages round my wrists. "Where are your shoes, mon?" he asked. "Your feet have been bleeding." He saw the whole thing as a joke.

I smiled stiffly in return and asked where I was. It was evening, on the edge of night. Lights everywhere in the distance.

"On Crewe Road, of course. Where've you been?"

I said neutrally, "On Trox Island."

A frown replaced the laugh. "The hurricane wiped out that place, they say."

I was standing on a grass verge of a road beside a wire mesh fence that skirted a medium-sized commercial airport. When I asked my laughing helper if it were Jamaica or Grand Cayman, he told me with more good humor than ever that it was Owen Roberts, mon, Cayman. Of course Hurricane Odin had passed south of here, praise the Lord. He himself, now, he was from Jamaica, mon, but Crewe Road was in George Town, Grand Cayman.

He was naturally and endlessly curious about the state he'd found me in, but accepted that if I'd been set upon and robbed of my clothes and money and everything else I was mainly in need of transport, and cheerfully offered me a ride in his brother-in-law's Jeep, which he was driving along Crewe Road when he saw me standing there helpless . . . and where did I want to go?

To Michael Ford's house, I said, if he knew it, and he shrugged and drove me there with much less warmth if not with outright disapproval, and he merely nodded when at the Fords' front gate I thanked him profoundly for his kindness. He thrust the bandages into my hands, said, "Not good people" and drove off as if he were sorry he had stopped for me at all.

MICHAEL AND AMY Ford greeted me with extreme astonishment.

"We thought you were dead . . . !"

"Kris said . . ."

Kris said.

Michael and Amy warmly gestured me to come in, and led the way to the same sitting room as before.

"Kris is alive?" I asked. "Is it true?"

Michael said heartily, "Of course he's alive." He looked me up and down in the sitting-room lights. "My dear man, what a state you're in."

With a grimace I asked if my clothes and passport were still in their house and was relieved when Amy said she hadn't yet sent them to England.

"And my grandmother . . ." I said. "Can I pay you for a call to her?"

"My dear man, be our guest." He pushed a telephone my way. "She'll be asleep, though. It's midnight in London."

I pressed the buttons. "She'll want to know I'm alive."

The voice that answered was predictably that of a nurse. Less predictably, it was the voice of Jett van Els, who exclaimed, "We were told you were dead . . ."

My grandmother, awakened, remarked toughly that she'd known all along that I was still alive and then rather spoiled the effect by sobbing.

"I said . . ." She swallowed and paused. "I told them you could outswim any hurricane. I said it, even if it isn't true."

"Who is them?" I asked.

"The BBC. They wanted to put a tribute to you on the weather forecast and I told them to wait."

I smiled, wished her a peaceful sleep, promised to call the next day and, as I put down the receiver, asked Michael and Amy if they knew where to find Kris.

"There's no search-and-rescue facility on Cayman," Amy said. "Robin called and said he felt responsible for letting Kris and you set off on such a risky flight and he organized a helicopter from Florida when you didn't return and sent it out looking for both of you, after the worst of the storm had passed; and it did find Kris in

the life raft, which was pretty amazing considering . . ."

"But . . ." Michael continued as Amy paused.
"Kris told me the airplane had sunk in terrible
waves and he saw you being swept away and all
you had was a life jacket and he said not even a
very good swimmer like you could have lived
through waves more than thirty feet high."

"I was lucky," I said. "When was he found?"

"Don't you want to get dressed?" Amy interrupted sympathetically. "And your poor
feet . . . !"

I was being careful to stand on her tiles so as
not to dirty her rugs. "My feet are O.K. . . . when
did the helicopter find Kris?"

Michael, frowning, answered vaguely, "Not yesterday . . . the day before, I think." He looked for
confirmation to Amy, who indecisively nodded.

"And, er . . ." I asked without pressure, "where
is he now?"

Amy answered, but after thought. "He went
home to England. He said he was due back at
work. Now, do put better clothes on. All your
things are still in the room you used here."

I gave in to her housekeeperly urging and in
deep luxury showered, got rid of the stubbly be-

ginnings of beard, and dressed in clean soap-smelling shirt, cotton trousers and flip-flop sandals. Amy greeted the result with hands held high and multiple compliments, and Michael said he had lit the barbecue fire and was baking potatoes to go with the steak.

It wasn't until after the food that they asked where I'd been and how I'd survived, and they showed shock and interest in suitable intensities at my account.

I explained that Kris in the last minute of control before the aircraft crashed into the sea had said that he was going to try to reach Trox Island, and that by some miracle the currents had actually swept me back there, where we had landed earlier on some errand for Robin.

"What errand?" Michael asked intently.

I said I didn't know. I said I didn't think Kris was clear about it either. I looked blankly puzzled. I told them that most extraordinarily I'd been brought back to Cayman in some sort of semi-military aircraft with a crew wearing radiation suits and carrying assault weapons. The crew hadn't spoken to me or done anything I understood. It was all very odd, but anyway they'd blindfolded me, tied my wrists with bandages

from—I supposed—the first-aid box every aircraft had to carry, and when they'd landed here
on Cayman, they let me go. A Jamaican man
who was passing had kindly untied me and
driven me to the Fords' door.

"Good heavens!" Amy exclaimed. "How dreadful!"

"Are you going to the police?" Michael asked,
frowning.

"I shouldn't think so," I confessed. "I don't
want to get that crew into trouble. I don't think
they were pleased I was on the island, but, even
if they tied me up to do it, they did bring me
back here safely. Whatever they were doing there,
it's none of my business."

Michael and Amy smiled broadly with evident
approval. I didn't tell them I knew for a certainty
that three of my captors/rescuers had been
Michael and Amy themselves, and Robin Darcy
too.

I didn't thank them for working out how to get
me back to civilization without my seeing their
faces, though I was pleased they had done it.

I didn't say that I'd had ages to memorize the
aircraft's registration letters and numbers—which
began with N, and were therefore American.

I certainly didn't tell them I'd opened their safe and had had little else to do for lengthy days but try to decipher the messages of the foreign-language letters.

Amy crossed the sitting room, raised her arms again, stood on tiptoes and kissed my cheek. She smelled sweetly of the same scent as one of the crew, the slender guard who had had to stretch up high to tie the blindfold tightly round my head.

Robin, rotund round Robin, had had to wear his just visible heavily framed eyeglasses inside his silver helmet to see what he was doing, and also, in the sort of unconscious mannerism every-one has, he had stood with his wrists crossed below his stomach, as he had done both in New-market and on his own terrace when the police had come to deal with his "intruder."

Amy, short and slender, and Michael, broad-shouldered and bow-legged, had completed and revealed the trio's back view unmistakably as they walked away from the aircraft towards the thick-walled huts.

Identifying them, in view of their intention *not* to be known, had sent the severe flutter of fear through my gut that had kept me silent, passive and concentrated in front of their guns.

With excuses of real tiredness I put an early end to the smiling artificiality of the evening, and, to my hosts' perceptible relief, went to bed.

ODIN, AS I discovered heavy-eyed from the television after another night of bad dreams, had changed direction yet again since Kris and I had left Trox Island to search for the eye.

Michael having waved me permissively towards his telephone, I reached my meteorological colleague in Miami and shocked him into believing that Lazarus had nothing on P. Stuart.

When I asked if he could spare the time to have me call on him in his office on my way back to England he said with enthusiasm that he'd leave word at the front desk; and later that day, after the friendliest of farewells from Michael and Amy, who drove me to Owen Roberts airport in their orange truck, I landed in Miami, sought out my so far unseen good telephone pal, and was shown into the tracking heart of the hurricane center.

My pal, Will, turned out to be about twenty-five, tall, thin, dedicated and full of welcome.

"You're in here only because you're *you,*" he said. "Your BBC employers gave you the thumbs-up."

"Good of them."

He looked sharply at my face, correctly interpreted my mild cynicism and took me to meet the team of meteorologists dealing with Odin. So it was I who was the other damn fool, they said, who'd flown through Odin's eye and ditched near the eye wall? I was.

It was crazy to have attempted a fly-through, they said. Amateur hurricane hunters were a pest. The U.S. Air Force's 53rd Weather Reconnaissance Flight alone had enough experience and instrumentation.

I meekly agreed. My pal Will returned my cynicism doubled, accepted my contrition and showed me how the storm trackers were still worried about Odin, which had changed direction yet again and was now very slowly passing from the Caribbean into the Gulf of Mexico, where it at present distantly threatened Galveston in Texas. The warm Gulf waters were again strengthening the circulation dangerously. Neither Will nor I could understand how I'd survived the weight of the towering seas.

When I suggested a thank-you drink at the end of his shift Will looked at his watch and said he'd already arranged for me to meet someone I might find interesting, and when we were settled at a small sidewalk table under a red-and-blue sun umbrella, we were joined by a lanky bearded sixtyish eccentric who slapped Will vigorously on the back, told me his name was Unwin and demanded, "What exactly do you want to know about Trox Island?"

Taken by surprise I said "Er . . ." irresolutely, and then with gratitude, "More or less anything you can tell me."

He could tell me about forty minutes' worth, he said. He'd done the research for a book on Trox, but couldn't find a publisher interested. He had been to the island many times himself as pilot of the weekly Dakota, an ancient DC-3 that had flown in with perishable supplies for the thirty or more people who lived there.

He said those residents were mostly meteorologists and seismologists—who employed him— and mushroom growers and timber and coconut merchants, and in the past there had been a great trade in guano. He said there were thousands of booby birds making the guano and hundreds of thousands of iguanas doing nothing. He said the island had once been used as a communications post by undercover agents from the United

States, but the C.I.A. was now denying it. They had built the runway, though, and they once had a radio transmitter there, but it had been dismantled years ago.

I asked to whom the island belonged, and Unwin took a long time over his reply. "Once it was British, then American," he said eventually. "Then a whole bunch of South American countries claimed it, but no one wanted to keep it longer than for their own purposes because there's no running water there, only rain caught in cisterns, and no electricity, since one group who took it over looted the generator. So when they've finished with it each group just abandons it, it seems to me. Long before Hurricane Nicky, let alone Odin, a company called the Unified Trading Company were running things, but about a month ago they suddenly slammed down the shutters on harmless people like me." He grinned, unexpectedly showing large yellow teeth. "If you want to own the island yourself, just go and live there, say it's yours, and fight off all boarders."

He interrupted his saga to attend to the cold Heineken ordered for us all by Will, and then, as if delighted to open the floodgates, went on.

"There was something funny about those mushrooms. I mean, a couple of real mushroom farmers I talked to said you'd never try to grow even exotic mushrooms on a commercial basis on such a small scale. They were experimental mushrooms, people said, but the Unified Trading Company brought in their own workers, from Europe, so no one local even knew what was really going on. And it was the same for the cows."

"Cows?" Will asked, mystified. "What cows?"

Unwin the Trox specialist showed his teeth again. "One day when I was there a whole shipload of bulls and cows was disembarked and they walked up from the jetty, and through the village, and spread out all over the island. There was a heck of a fuss about it with the residents, but the bulls never chased or gored any humans. They just gored each other and rogered the cows, and bit by bit they grew tamer and had calves and spent most of their time keeping the runway grass short. Hell knows what Odin did to them. I should think they all died."

Will reminded him I'd been on the island since Odin, and I told him how the cattle survived by huddling flat on their stomachs all together like a carpet. And why were they there in the first place? I asked, but the expert said he didn't know.

He changed the subject to the scientists who had built both of the thick-walled huts and measured earthquakes on seismographs there and sent up radiosonde balloons to measure air pressure and temperature aloft each day. He knew them all by name as he worked for them, flying the Dakota.

The Unified Trading Company had taken over the second hut, and Unwin, frowning, said that towards the end the residents had told him the second hut had had a man guarding it with a rifle all the time, so that no one except the top men in the company could go in there. Those top men had said that as long as they were there as caretakers, the island belonged to *them*.

"A right muddle," I commented. "Why did the caretakers leave?"

Unwin leaned back in the wrought-iron café chair and assessed me from under lowered lids.

"Something frightened the residents," he slowly said.

I asked, "Do you know what it was?"

Unwin hesitated, then said they were told the mushroom sheds had become radioactive and the houses were unsafe, with radon gas coming up from their foundations. "A boat came for everyone, though, and they loaded all their belongings onto it and sailed to Cayman, where most of them have relatives. But everybody left Trox at least a month ago, and no one's developed radiation sickness, as far as I know."

I let a minute or two pass, and asked, "Did you see any of the top men of Unified Trading guarding the hut when you were there?"

Unwin nodded and finished his beer. I waited with stifled impatience while he arranged for refills, but at length the source of all explanations agreed that yes, the top men, about five of them, had taken it in turns to stand guard over the hut, only actually they had sat on a chair in the doorway with a gun across their knees, and that had gone on for about a week, until the fishing boat arrived and took everyone to Cayman.

"Did the Unified Trading men come from Cayman?" I asked.

After deliberation he answered, "Some of them did."

"And the others?"

Unwin answered straightforwardly, "I don't know. First of all before they started the evacuation they brought a big heavy cardboard box in off the boat and rolled it up to the second hut, on a sort of cart with wheels they used there; and don't ask me what was in the box. I don't know." He paused. "Everyone watched."

The safe had been in the box, I thought.

"Did you go into the hut afterwards?" I asked.

"Everyone went in. The Traders didn't stop people anymore but no one knew what they'd brought in the box, and there was nothing to see except the seismograph, which had been there before."

"And . . . um . . . what did the top men look like?"

Unwin pondered and sighed. "They were all forty or fifty. They wore baseball caps, but they weren't young. It was three or four weeks ago. I can't remember." He swallowed half a pint of beer, stood up and flapped a hand in a forty-minute farewell. "I'm going back to Trox next week," he said. "I'm supposed to be taking people and things to help to rebuild the meteorological station."

"What was all that about radioactivity?" Will asked, still mystified, watching Unwin's vanishing back.

I looked at Will vaguely. "I don't really know. Where does he live?"

"Over a hippie tee-shirt store, next road to the right. Unwin's a funny fish. I thought he'd be more interesting. Sorry."

I said, "He knew a lot about the place."

Will nodded ruefully and said, "I'd hardly heard of Trox Island before you asked me about it."

"That makes two of us. Let's just forget it."

His fast agreement to this shuffling-off suggestion was the basis of all our future friendship: he didn't want to have to take anything seriously— except the weather, of course.

So I didn't tell him I'd been sucked into some sort of conspiracy, and now the conspirators regretted it and would like to spit me out again, so to speak, but they wanted to be sure first that I hadn't recognized them or understood why they needed to blindfold me to rescue me. All of that was more likely to alienate Will than engage his further help.

We finished our beers in easy accord, and he invited me without hangups to go on sharing his world wind news; while I offered him, as we parted, tours of the meteorological headquarters, back home at Bracknell, Berkshire.

Unwin, when I went looking for him, was sitting under another sun umbrella, drinking another beer.

I sat beside him. He shrugged and said, "Trox used to be a pretty place, you know."

"Will you get back there by DC-3?"

"Sure."

"Did the Unified Trading Company, too, use a regular airplane of their own to service their staff?"

Unwin, bored, drank his beer, yawned, and said that mostly they rented one, it was cheaper.

Did he know *which* airplane they rented?

He knew the type. When I wrote out the registration number, he nodded positively with recognition and awakening interest. "That's the one. It belongs to Downsouth Air Rentals. You can charter it with or without pilot by the hour, day, week, whatever you like."

He accepted another refill.

"If anything much happens on Trox," I suggested, "anything odd, I mean, would you pass the info to Will, to forward it to me?" I gave him some money I could hardly afford and he counted it without enthusiasm.

"All right," he agreed.

"I left my camera there, in one of the thick-walled huts, tied up by its strap to a beam near the roof, out of the cows' reach. The camera's useless. It's all stuck up with mud. But I'd quite like it back, if you find it. If you send it to me, mud and all, how about a full case of Heineken?"

"Two cases," he said. We shook on it, and I wrote for him my grandmother's address.

I touched the small paper with the aircraft registration number on it and asked without hope, "I don't suppose you know where I would find the fishing boat that did Trox Island's evacuation?"

Unwin's yellow teeth spread wide in a grin and he jerked a thumb over his shoulder.

"You walk a bit lame," he observed, "and you have a long way to go. She's the *Darnwell Rose,* down to the end of the road, turn left, third . . . no, fourth dock along. It's not really a fishing boat. It's an all-purpose offshore merchantman."

I thanked him sincerely and started down the long road, and presently found him catching me up.

"I know the master. He's sailing tonight. I owe him a beer," he said, and I was glad of his company and his introduction.

The master of the *Darnwell Rose,* bulky, with gold sleeve rings, bushily bearded, went below with Unwin to more beer in his cabin, and sent up a fearsomely tough-looking second-in-command to unbutton to me about Trox.

"A trading company, Unified Traders, had chartered the *Darnwell Rose* to ship a whole load of household goods from Trox Island to Grand Cayman," he said, "and there had been a question about clearing everything from regulations about radon gas, but they'd had no problem in the end. None of the furniture was radioactive, so we did the job."

I asked, "Do you remember taking to Trox Island a heavy cardboard container?"

"The safe, do you mean?"

"Yes." I nodded.

"Look," he said. "If I tell you what happened, I'll deny it."

"I would expect nothing less."

He sniffed and wiped his nose with the back of his hand.

"So," he said, "to stop it getting damaged on the journey the safe door was wedged open with a lot of screwed-up paper and there was a folder type of thing lying in a drawer in a desk nearby, and as we were to take all the furniture, one of the deckhands put the folder in the safe and took the desk, and when everything had been cleared by the Geiger counter they put that too in the safe, meaning both things only to be there for a minute or two, but a seaman shut the safe door and they couldn't open it again—so they just put the whole safe into the slot in the wall that was ready for it, and left it there, and no one ever complained. The master reckoned the trading company that chartered us knew how to get the door open again. Is that what you wanted to know?"

"That's fine, thank you."

I gave him the rest of my dollar bills, thanked Unwin and the master and gratefully accepted their offer of a ride to the airport.

Deciding, before I caught the night flight to London, that helping the conspirators to get rid of me neatly involved a polite goodbye to Robin Darcy (who'd lost his airplane to our foolhardiness, after all), I called his number but heard only Evelyn's voice saying, "Please leave a message."

"I'll write," I said, grateful for the let-off, and traveled home, knees-under-chin, trying to sleep, but with the reality of sore feet and the memory of guns and hurricanes keeping me awake.

7

WHEN I REACHED her in the morning my grandmother sat with her mouth open, disapproving of my appearance.

"Hi, Gran," I said mildly. "How's things?"

She shed her shock briefly. "You do know you're due on the screen today? You look awful, Perry."

"Thanks so much."

"And you've got all those extra Fireworks Night shows."

"It will rain," I said. "Can I sleep tonight on your sofa?"

She agreed at once without question.

"And I want to talk to you about what I should do."

She looked with seriousness into my face. The few times I'd asked her for help in that way had meant an adult-to-adult evaluation of the known facts with no gender or generation gap involved. The one rule we'd kept so far had been to give any life-altering decisions a chance to mature, which meant never acting on impulse.

Her decision to go on travel-writing through her later seventies had had input from a whole parade of specialists, and for my abandonment of a career in physics for the presentation of the vagaries of wind and temperature over the British Isles she had called in a casting agency expert in assessing personality.

She had taken days to agree to the ongoing expense of having a private nurse, but, once it was decided, she had sold her precious diamonds, gifts from her husband (my grandfather), to refurbish the whole shabby apartment and to buy a runabout for me and a customized car for herself, to take her and her motor wheelchair on expeditions for her travel firm. We would live, she persuaded me, in style.

The nurse came out of the kitchen and offered me coffee. Coffee, I thought, was nowhere near enough.

"Go for an hour's walk, my dear," my grand-mother said sweetly to her, and smiled with age-old wiles.

Jett van Els, working beyond her week-on, week-off schedule, asked if I would still be there if she returned in an hour. I could have said I would be there *whenever* . . . but after she'd gone out into the chilly damp all-too-English November day I called a different young woman first.

Tentatively, I spoke to Belladonna, who replied in an ear-drum shattering shriek.

"Perry! Dad told me yesterday you were alive. I can't believe it! We all thought you'd drowned."

"Well . . . no," I assured her calmingly, and asked where I could find Kris.

"I'm supposed to be marrying him, did you know?"

"Congratulations."

"He asked me when I'd thought him dead all day. It's not fair."

"Your true feelings came out." I smiled. "Where is he?"

"Here. He drove to see Oliver Quigley, heaven knows why, that poor man's a frightful wreck even though Dad's not going to sue him over the filly after all, and then Kris is going to work, he's on his way now, actually, he spent the night here . . . with me. Not the first time . . . why am I telling you."

I sorted out her meanings and inquired about the filly. Alive or dead?

"Alive," Bell said. "Sick to death but not dying, except that her mane and tail are thinning out; and now the equine research place are talking about what's wrong with her isn't ragwort in her hay, which they thought had been fed to her to nobble her, but, and you'll never believe it, they think it may be due to *radiation sickness,* I ask you!"

I sat on my grandmother's sofa as if punched breathless.

I said "Uh?" uselessly.

"Radiation sickness," Bell repeated disgustedly. "They say, in the filly it's very mild, if it can ever be said to have a *mild,* but probably terminal, complaint. They say she's probably been exposed to radium or something similar. And where did she get it? Dad's absolutely furious. Kris said *you* would have known where to get radium. He said you'd have known about uranium and plutonium too because you were a physicist as well as a weather forecaster."

"Mm," I said. "Well, it's very difficult to get hold of radium but not impossible. Marie Curie isolated it from pitchblende a hundred years or more ago in Paris. But the others . . ." I stopped abruptly, and then said, "Did Kris talk about me as if I were dead?"

"I'm so sorry, Perry, we all did."

I said not to worry, learned where Kris would be when and sent good wishes to her father. Then I sat in the armchair beside my grandmother's wheels, and told her everything significant I had seen and felt and thought since Caspar Harvey's invitation to lunch at Newmarket.

She listened as if she'd been everywhere with me, as if her eyes and ears had duplicated my own.

At the end, she said in great alarm, "You need to ask someone for information, Perry, and for help."

"Yes," I agreed, "but *who?*"

That corny old phrase "going to the authorities" raised its banal head. Who, exactly, was an authority? Could I walk into the local nick and expect to be believed? No, I couldn't.

"Maybe," I said after thought, "I'll try the Health and Safety Executive."

"Who are they?"

"They inspect factories."

My grandmother shook her head, but I looked them up under civil service departments in the phone book and got them to agree to a meeting in an hour. Being Perry Stuart, weatherman and widely known TV face, had its uses.

Jett van Els returned to the minute with the warmth of Eve in her brown eyes and the chill of November on her cheeks. There had been other nurses in my life with generous and willing impulses as temporary as their employment, but my all-seeing grandparent, while Jett made coffee in the kitchen, unexpectedly warned me this time not to awaken what I couldn't later put back to sleep. In amusement I promised, but a promise wasn't enough.

"I mean it," my grandmother said. "When you want to be, you're too powerful for your own good."

Powerful wasn't the word for my impact on the motherly fiftyish official I at length met as my first true "authority." I was not, she pointed out, a factory.

"I'm talking about a trading company," I said.

She pursed her mouth. "Has it anything to do with weather?"

"No."

She looked aimlessly for a while into the distance, sighed, then wrote a few words on a slip of paper and handed it to me.

"Try here," she said. "You never know."

The "here" of the instruction was an office high in the premises of a textbook publishing house in Kensington. I rode an elevator as directed by an entrance-hall name-taker, and was met when the doors slid open by a young female general assistant with long untidy brownish hair and a long creased brownish skirt.

"I'm Melanie," she announced, and then exclaimed, "I *say!* Aren't you Perry Stuart? Good heavens! Come this way."

The office she led me into was small and its occupant, large. Four bare walls and a skylight housed a desk, two chairs of so-so comfort and a gray metal filing cabinet. The tall man who rose to a sketchy handshake and an introduction of himself as John Rupert could easily have filled the part of textbook publisher downstairs.

"My colleague at the Health and Safety Executive," he said without preliminaries, "informs me you may have something to tell me about the Unified Trading Company—and while we are at this stage, do you find your appearance a hindrance on occasion?"

I said, "I couldn't come to your office, for instance, without someone remarking that I'd been here."

"Melanie, for instance?"

"I'm afraid so."

"Mm." He thought briefly; so briefly that I was pretty certain he'd thought before my arrival. "If you were to publish a textbook, Dr. Stuart, what subject would you choose?"

I gave him not the instinctive answer of "Wind and rain," but the more oblique thought "Depression."

His eyes narrowed. He nodded briefly. He said, "I was told you might be a player." A contemplative silence lengthened. "There appears to exist," he said finally, "a small packet of extremely sensitive information. I myself think it's very unlikely you've seen it, but I'm told that if you have, you may have understood what you were looking at." He left another extended pause. "Can you help us?"

Who, I wondered, was us? Us, I concluded, were "the authorities" I'd come looking for. "Us" had to be trusted . . . for now.

I asked, "Where would you look for your sensitive package?"

"It could be anywhere in the world." John Rupert pinched the thin bridge of his nose. "We had a man in Mexico, near the northern border. He'd had a sight of a sensitive package, he'd reported its existence, he'd heard it was for sale and on its way to Miami. He asked us whether he should steal it if he could, or buy it." John Rupert grimaced. "He let the wrong people know that he had seen it, and he was found floating facedown in the Florida Everglades with a bullet in his head and his legs half eaten away by alligators."

I'd got myself into a right pickle, I thought, and telling anyone anything at all was asking for more trouble, if not a bullet. I didn't know if what I'd learned was worth dying for, and yet I found I couldn't, from some obscure instinct towards justice and order, simply walk away and forget it.

"Suppose," I said at length, "as a result of too many cooks trying to keep a sensitive package safe, it gets too thoroughly hidden away on an island and has to be retrieved so that it can be used. It's no good to anyone if it's not in use." I stopped.

"Go on, go on," John Rupert urged.

"To collect the package there's a suitable light airplane available, but no suitable pilot to fly it, until along comes a meteorologist, a private pilot with a hankering to fly through the eye of a hurricane. The pilot agrees to make a detour flight to pick up the package, in return for his hurricane adventure."

John Rupert, understanding, gave me a nod.

"That simple errand fails," I said. "The hurricane crashes the aircraft into the sea. Collecting the package, still essential, now involves more certain measures, such as a calmer sky, and a much larger aircraft with a bigger crew equipped and ready to do actual battle if necessary."

"Battle for the package?"

"More like battle for the repossession of the whole island, whose ownership is in dispute. The crew, I think, are the Unified Trading Company, who ruled the place before they frightened the residents away by growing exotic mushrooms in containers that gave off radioactivity . . ." I stopped talking. His face was smoothing to disbelief.

"Goodbye," I said briefly, standing up. "Children in school can make more or less anything appear to give off radioactive alpha particles. Just scatter a little powdered uranium ore around." I gave him a small card with my grandmother's phone number on it. "Phone if you're interested in any more."

"Stop," he said, his interest growing already.

"People aren't wrong to be frightened," I said from the doorway. "If you swallow a pea-sized alpha particle source, it will kill you, but you can carry it safely for a long time in a paper bag. I expect I'm telling you what you already know."

"Don't go yet."

"I have to take the bad news from Aix to Ghent."

John Rupert laughed.

KRIS IN THE end was easy to find as he was back at the BBC Weather Centre at Wood Lane, preparing to share with me the bad-weather broadcast ahead for the run-up to Guy Fawkes Night.

He greeted me with a yelp and a crushing hug, and I suffered similar warm squeezing all round the office. Comment on thinness and gauntness could last only minutes when, to the relief of the forecaster standing by to give the kids the damp news for squibs, reliable old Stuart had returned from the dead and popped up on time.

Kris himself looked spectacularly tanned with sun-brightened hair and mustache, and he rose at the sight of me from gloom to stratosphere as fast as any of his rocket lift-off poems.

"I can't believe it!" His voice could probably be heard all down Wood Lane. "How come you're here? We all thought your gran a bit touched yesterday, insisting you'd have got a message to her if you'd drowned!"

We walked along a quiet passage towards the room we all shared between appearances—all except the guru, who had a retreat to himself—and Kris, with small skips and jumps like a young boy, told me that he in the life raft had scudded with the wind across the western edge of Odin for days until Robin's hired helicopter operators had spotted him and winched him up. The description of his rescue poured out of him like an uncorked flood, as if to prevent any other subject surfacing, but in the end I put an anchoring hand on his arm and congratulated him on his engagement to Bell.

"Don't tell her father," he said in alarm. "Old Caspar wouldn't exactly have wept if he'd had to get someone else to tell him it was hay-cutting time."

There was too much truth in that to be funny.
I let it go without contradiction and asked instead, "What did Robin Darcy say about losing
his airplane?"

"I haven't talked to him since that morning we
set off. If I call his home in Sand Dollar Beach I
just get Evelyn's voice on an answering machine.
But poor old Robin, what *can* he say? It was he
who urged us to go."

"Well . . ." I frowned. "What did he really want
you to do on that island?"

"Trox?"

"Yes, of course, Trox."

"How should I know?" Kris shrugged absentmindedly, then suddenly looked wary.

"Perhaps," I mildly suggested, "because he himself told you."

Kris slowed and stopped in two paces as if he
had just remembered he'd given me two different
answers already to that question.

"I'm so *glad,*" he said explosively. "I'm really so
pleased you're alive."

"So am I that you are." We beamed at each
other, and whatever else was said, that was the
truth.

We shouldered through a swinging door into a

change-clothes and brush-hair environment, where shiny foreheads and noses were dusted to matte by a lady dragon of twenty-three who tended to follow one into camera range waving a powder puff. Kris fell into flirtatious chat with her, but kept glancing my way from under his eyelids as if half hoping that I would after all disappear.

Instead I asked, but lightheartedly, as if it were a joke, "What did Robin say about our 'wheels-up' approach to Trox Island?"

"Nothing. I haven't talked to him. I told you."

The dragoness had been darkening his almost white eyebrows. Kris, irritated by my tactlessness in reminding him of his imperfection, pushed her hand away sharply and snappily told me no one was perfect all the time. It wasn't exactly the moment, I decided, to tell him I knew the right-hand—starboard—engine had stopped only because the pilot had forgotten to flip the switch from the empty fuel tank to the full one.

Flying though a hurricane had been stress enough. Kris had forgotten the switch until too late and dealing with the unbalancing weight of a dead engine as well had been beyond his limits.

The Cayman Trench was one of the deepest

valleys in the world's ocean floor, and unless Robin went to the unlikely and expensive trouble of finding and raising the wreckage, Kris's last-second panicked too late wild yell and stretch-out-toward-the-switch would remain forever his secret.

I did, though, want him to tell me truthfully why we'd gone to Trox at all, and in the end, in exasperation, he moodily gave in.

"It's no big deal," he said. "All Robin wanted me to do on Trox Island was to collect a folder of papers that had been left behind by mistake, and bring them back to him without you having a good look at them first. Don't ask me why he didn't want you to, I don't know, but, like I said before, you and I both owed him a lot, so I agreed. He said his folder was in a desk in one of the thick-walled huts, and he wanted me to collect it safely before it was blown away by Hurricane Odin. But when we got there I couldn't even find the desk. All the furniture had gone already."

"And . . . um . . ." I pondered. "You didn't tell Robin . . ."

"No, I didn't. Apparently when we didn't return according to our flight plan the control tower people in Grand Cayman got in touch with Evelyn on the Darcy answering machine, and it was Evelyn, that pearly old duck, who paid for the search helicopter to go out looking for me and you as soon as the weather was possible."

I asked wryly, "Will she send us a bill?"

"Which would you rather be," Kris asked, "broke or dead?"

I DRIFTED ROUND the Weather Centre all afternoon catching up on the past two weeks of wind and gossip and preparing and presenting at six-thirty and nine-thirty the shape of things to come.

Friday, the next day, the Fifth of November, Gunpowder, Treason, and Plot, looked like being a groan again for dads and children alike. A band of rain would cross the whole British area between lunch and bedtime the next day, starting in the west of Scotland and traveling south and counterclockwise, with veering winds later in the day bringing clouds and drizzle across southern England to mess up the Catherine wheels of Essex. Light the sodden blue touch-paper and retire to bed.

I spent a quiet late evening with my grandmother and Jett van Els, a muscle and mind respite, a doze-

on, doze-off breathing spell split only twice; first by
Kris on a high at ten-thirty, giving a long TV funny
overview of November fog banks.

Second, when Jett had begun the slow tough
task of my grandmother's Tarzan act from wheelchair to nighttime comfort, the telephone rang
clamorously and Jett briskly answered it, but instead of a reply to the usual type of magazine
question like, "How does one paint one's toenails
if one can't feel one's toes," we had Jett's no-
nonsense inquiry, "I'll ask when he'll be available. Who shall I say called? John Rupert?" She
lifted her eyebrows comically, and I stretched out
a hand to the receiver and said, "Hello?"

He had a ghostwriter for me, he said straightforwardly, and I agreed to meet the ghost between broadcasts in the morning.

Later, with my grandmother as always only fit-
fully asleep in her airy room, Jett and I took a
couple of cushions and sat, well wrapped in
Edwardian-type fur-lined car rugs, on a stone seat
for two in a small glass-windowed entrance porch
built to keep nineteen-o-eight ladies dry from
carriage to gentlemen's beds.

The night air felt fresh and smelled of low-tide
mud. We sat close to each other for warmth and

didn't talk much. If the whole of life were simple like this, I thought, there would be peace among seagulls and no wind to speak of. I kissed Jett van Els without heeding my grandmother's fears, and got kissed cheerfully back, and many things became understood between us in an oasis of tranquillity.

But there's a calm spell at the center of every hurricane. The fury of the second wind was as always round the corner.

IN THE VERY early morning I shed my grandmother's comfortable sofa in time to appear on her screen at breakfast, and did my best to soften the rainy news for the nation. The celebration night of the brave traitor and his low-grade explosive was going to pass as unsatisfactorily as the first, whatever I said.

During the morning, between rueful appearances steering short of apology, I made a quick trip by bus to Kensington and rode the elevator to the seventh floor to discuss a book on depression with a ghost.

I accepted a so-so chair and coffee with ginger snaps, listening to John Rupert's rational plans for a book not about depressions, but about storms, which he said would sell better.

Was he *serious* about a book? I asked, and he said civilly why not? Books had been written about shark's teeth before now.

"And incidentally," he murmured, eating the ginger cookie set out for me, "it was 'How they brought the *good* news *from* Ghent *to* Aix.'"

"Whatever," I said.

"Robert Browning," he added.

The door quietly opened, admitting an unmistakable ghost, a feeble-looking grandfather with thin white hair and strong sinews for shaking hands.

They introduced him to me without melodrama by name as "Ghost," no Mr. . . . no first name, just Ghost, and John Rupert calmly asked me to repeat what I'd told him the day before.

"Say it all again?" I protested.

"Say it again, but different, so while Ghost understands it for the first time, I see things more clearly."

I sighed. "Well then . . . Say that by mistake a folder of papers has been left on a Caribbean island, and the island has no radio, no telephone, no mail service and no people . . . but it does have a usable airstrip."

I continued with breaks for thought, and for Ghost's assimilation of what had happened.

"Say it is essential to retrieve the folder."

A break . . .

"Say there is a suitable aircraft available, but no discreet pilot, as yours has been killed in a car crash."

Another break . . .

"Then at a lunch party in England a pilot appears who longs to fly through the eye of a hurricane. He's a meteorologist, and there's a hurricane in the offing in the Caribbean—Nicky—and it is hurricane season in general. A flight through a hurricane is offered in return for a simple side trip to collect the folder of papers."

"Reasonable," Ghost said.

"Mm. The pilot took along another meteorologist friend as a navigator and general helper . . ."

"And the friend was you?" John Rupert said.

I nodded. "Our flight through the hurricane ended in the sea. The pilot was saved by helicopter, and I was thrown back onto the island by the currents. I came across the folder of letters, but I didn't know they were important, or at least not to begin with . . . They were written in many different scripts and languages."

"And you have them?" The ghost showed great excitement, a matter of twitches and shivers very like Oliver Quigley.

"No." I disappointed him. "I did read everything as best I could, but I didn't speak any of the
languages . . ." I picked absentmindedly at my
fingers, but I was certain about what I said: "One
of the languages was Russian."

John Rupert, sitting on a corner of the desk
and swinging a leg, interestedly asked, "So why
was it Russian? And how did you know?"

I explained, "There's a letter and a number
combination that jumps off the page at anyone
with the slightest bit of scientific knowledge, and
it is U-235. On one of those foreign language
pages, that combination was written Y-235, and
that symbol Y is Russian for uranium."

I drew Y-235 to show them and said, "That
sort of uranium has been enriched and con-
densed from U-238 by a process called sieving
or gas diffusion. Pu-239 is enriched plutonium
Pu-240. They are the materials for nuclear
weapons."

They asked with frowns for more.

"Starting from U-235 as a fact"—I smiled
faintly—"either that same letter and numbers
combination, or that of Pu-239, reappeared
somewhere in different scripts on every page in
the folder. If I could guess at understanding, I'd
say that what I've thought of as correspondence

were definitely also lists. Lists in Greek and German and Arabic and Russian, and probably Hebrew. As for the others . . . I didn't know enough, but some of the other numbers had different appearances and might have been dates or prices."

"Lists . . . Lists of what, exactly?"

"Lists of ingredients of nuclear explosive devices. They are, aren't they, the ultrasensitive package you were talking about?"

They were unready to commit themselves.

I said, "As far as I could understand those pages, I could see they were a sort of shopping list. Some of them stated what fissile material was available, and where. And some of them stated what was wanted. If those pages are lists of goods wanted and goods for sale, it means the Unified Trading Company are in essence *middlemen.*"

There was a short silence. Neither Ghost nor John Rupert ridiculed the notion, so I went on. "There's a world shortage of many types of fissile material—that is, the wherewithal of making nuclear bombs. And there's a world glut of legitimate sovereign states and general brutish terrorists who know how to make them. They're not extraordinarily difficult to construct. Only there's—thank God—not enough enriched uranium and plutonium to go round. There's a world shortage, as I said.

"Those letters in that package, I'm as sure as one can be, are notes of what's now out on the market. A high proportion of the world's bomb-making capacity has been locked up in Russia since the end of the Cold War. The old Soviet bloc don't want the dangerous makings scattered about any more than we do, and they guard them carefully, but there are thieves and schemers everywhere. I'd guess if anyone like you managed to put the Unified Trading Company out of business there would soon be someone else taking their place."

"One less is always significant," Ghost said primly.

He had pale gray eyes reflecting gray threatening cloud from the skylight. He hadn't the vigor, I reckoned, to write a bounce-you-out-of-your-seat book about storms.

"Are you saying," John Rupert inquired, "that you believe there will be uncountable outfits similar to the Unified Trading Company, acting as middlemen, and I suppose raking off a huge commission?"

"I've no idea how many," I said. "I forecast the

weather. I got involved in the uranium business by accident, and I want out."

My protest fell on stony ground and was ignored.

"All those letters in the folder will soon be out of date," I pointed out. "If they were inventories, if they were putting people who had access to U-235 in touch with people who could afford it . . . well, things will change in six months' time."

Ghost thinly smiled. "We are satisfied you saw the prime up-to-date collection of—shall we say—goods available. I think, although we usually operate on the 'need to know' principle, we sometimes don't tell people things it turns out they vitally *did* need to know, so what I am going to ask you, and perhaps tell you, may or may not be of help to you. Am I clear?"

As mud, I thought. I looked at my watch. Buses were erratic anyway on busy shopping mornings, and it was raining. I would just run, I thought. Poor old feet.

"Don't worry about the time," John Rupert said. "I'll send you back to the BBC in a car."

Ghost said, "Think. Please concentrate. What we quite urgently need most from that package are the names of those who *want* and those who *have*. Can you remember *any* of them?"

I was afraid I could remember only a part of one.

Anything, it seemed, would be better than nothing.

"Then," I said, "one of the headings contained the word *Hippostat.*" I spelled it for them. "It might mean racecourse, and it might not."

"It might." Ghost nodded. "Have you any idea where that whole package is now?"

Clear and bright in my memory was an image of Michael Ford walking back from the second thick-walled hut carrying the Geiger counter in one hand and the folder in the other. He had taken them into the aircraft, and there they stayed.

Equally sharp was the awareness of the care Michael Ford had taken not to put an early end to my days. Or maybe it had been Amy, who'd kept me alive with the bandages. Or maybe even Robin, the round one with brains.

I was behaving ambivalently when I answered Ghost truthfully, and felt guilty for it.

"I don't know," I said, "where the package is now."

I had some sort of fumbling idea of persuading the group members to give up their habit—a bit like smoking—just more deadly. I hadn't thought everything through beyond my own salvation.

John Rupert, vaguely disappointed with what he rightly judged, I saw, to be a last-minute with-drawal of wholeheartedness, kept his own prom-ise and beckoned up a car and driver to return me to Wood Lane.

In between afternoon forecasts I got through to him on the phone and found him polite but minus his earlier zeal.

He said, "Ghost believes you changed sides in midstream. I'd like to know why."

"Some of the Traders could easily have put me in a coffin. I remembered that they didn't."

"It's an old dilemma," he said in a tired voice. "If you believe in a cause, do you kill your friend who doesn't?"

I said slowly, "No."

"Remember our man from Mexico. Remember the alligators. He got no mercy. When you're ready, call me again . . . and don't leave it too late."

"I'll tell you now . . ." I began, stopped, began again, "If you're interested yet . . . about the radioactivity. The alpha particles on Trox Island."

His voice came to life a bit. He said, "I did ask my children about that yesterday evening, and of course you were right, they had studied radioac-tivity in school."

"Mm," I said. "But the thirty or so people who lived on Trox Island didn't know you can safely make a Geiger counter sound as if it's busting its guts. They heard the frantically fast clicks and they were told the appropriate story . . . *panic, everyone, those fancy mushrooms are radioactive and there's radon gas pouring out of the ground beneath the houses, but we, your benefactors, the Unified Trading Company, will guarantee you won't be contaminated yourselves by radiation, only the actual buildings and the mushrooms, and we will send an excellent boat to take you all to safety.*"

"Do you mean the Trading Company deliberately persuaded everyone into leaving the island?"

I smiled. "They couldn't leave fast enough. Radioactivity is scary because you can't see it or feel it. That's why people tend to think it's more dangerous than it really is. But they all in the end will be reassured, as none of them will show any signs of radiation sickness."

John Rupert thanked me, but still coolly, for the Geiger-Müller road show. "And I suppose you know," he said, "the big question it still leaves unanswered?"

I nodded over the phone. *"Why,"* I inquired, "did the Traders want the island to themselves?"

8

THE TIRING EVENING ended at last in clearing skies, and devoted enduring fireworks fanatics let off rainbow-colored pop-pop sparkling starbursts in soggily dripping back gardens.

I knew my grandmother and Jett would both be asleep when I finally left work. I couldn't ask refuge for a second night on the sofa, anyway. One night was succor; a second, indulgence. My grandmother had never believed in lengthy bouts of bleeding heart.

I walked the half mile from the BBC towards my home, towards attic, telescope, chronometer and futon, deeply breathing the damp night air and promising myself an absence of November fifth on future calendars.

When I neared my doorstep, midnight or not, there was agitation on my pager, which buzzed in the waist pocket of my pants; a tremor rather than a noise, owing to my frequent presence in silence-demanding places. Late hour regardless, Belladonna answered my call-back with relief and my "Where are you?" inquiry with a giggle.

"In George Loricroft's bedroom. Don't tell Kris."

"Is there a *Mrs.* Loricroft there, perhaps?"

"You're such a spoilsport, Perry," Bell grumbled. "Her name is Glenda and she wants to talk to you."

Glenda Loricroft, dimly remembered from that fateful Sunday lunch as a shiny blonde in a pale blue sweater that stretched across the front, had a voice that Lancashire lasses would have felt at home with. Her George, she told me, had gone off to Baden-Baden, or so he said, and she wanted to know what the weather was like there, please luv.

"Give me Bell," I asked, and wanted to know why I should go back into the Weather Center on such a hunt on such a night.

"Perry, be your age!" Bell said. "Glenda thinks George is having it off with an undeclared fräulein. If I give you date and time and place, could you tell her whether the *actual* meshed with what her lover-boy declared?"

"No, Bell, it's a nonstarter. Impossible. All he has to say is that he doesn't remember or was fast asleep."

"Glenda says he's never where he says he will be. Tonight he's supposed to be in Baden-Baden for the races, but tomorrow he won't know it's been snowing."

I said, "Stop it, Bell. Get Kris to do it. I'm asleep on my feet."

"Kris won't do a thing. He just talks about trains."

In alarm I said, "Where is he? Why is he talking about trains?"

"Something about fuel switches," Bell said lightly. "I don't understand him. You're the only one who follows his mind."

"Well . . . find him."

The urgency in my voice got through to her suddenly.

"He's not lost!" she exclaimed.

"Then where is he?"

"He said he was up on your roof."

I went through the house in dismay and out into the cold little patch of wintry grass at the back and looked up, and there he was, sitting astride the vaulted roof of slates and leaning against a dead chimney of crumbling brick.

"Climb down," I called. "I can't catch you."

"You can see fireworks all over London from up here," he yelled. "Come up."

"I'm going to bed."

"George Loricroft isn't in Baden-Baden," Kris intoned, "and Oliver Quigley didn't turn up in Berlin or Hamburg, and I bet my future father-in-law chickened out of Cologne."

"What are you talking about?" I shouted up.

"Robin Darcy is in Newmarket."

I could still hear Bell's voice distantly on the telephone, so I put the receiver to my mouth and asked her if she'd heard what Kris said.

"He said Robin Darcy is here in Newmarket, and yes, he is, he's staying at the Bedford Arms. What of it? When he's in England on business he often comes here to see Dad. They'll be going to Doncaster races tomorrow. It's the last meeting of the main Flat season. Half Newmarket will be going. My boss George has a runner for my father in the November Handicap, the big race of the day, and there aren't any races tomorrow at Baden-Baden, the whole thing's rubbish."

"He'll be home for breakfast," I said soothingly, which raised a wail from Glenda and an accusation of heartlessness from Bell.

Enough, I thought. I said, "Bell and Glenda, please get off my phone and Kris, please get off my roof, and I'll see you all tomorrow."

Incredibly, there was silence. I went indoors and up to my attic for hours of solid sleep and woke early to find Kris yawning in my kitchen alcove and pouring Thai curry sauce onto tofu, his latest disgusting obsession.

"Morning," he said.

"How did you get in?"

He looked pained. "You gave me a key last Christmas."

I thought back. "That was for waiting for the refrigerator repair man."

"Do you want it back?" Kris read labels on bottles of chili oil he took from a paper carrier. He'd been Thai-food shopping yesterday for that and lemon grass and dried spices, he said.

I said I supposed he could keep the key. Also he could use my shower (he had done so: my towels were wet) and watch my TV (now on, but mute). Making the usual dash to the door on the way to put together the Saturday morning program—

including a summing up of the weather prospects for Saturday sport (dry, cold and sunny for racing at Doncaster, blustery showers for a soccer match at Wembley)—I caught a glimpse of Kris marking his choices on my newspaper's racing pages and starting to fill in my crossword.

I shrugged into my warm padded jacket and with temporary benevolence, as I opened my front door to depart, I asked him with restraint merely to lock up when he left.

"By the way," he said, "I looked up your schedule. You're free today after the sports forecast. I'm flying to Doncaster races. There's an airfield next to the racecourse. Will you come?"

I closed my door on his question mark and started down the stairs. If I didn't go he would believe it was because of wheels up and an empty fuel tank and, given his seesaw psyche, that imagined adverse judgment would convince him I despised him and that he had no friends. The answer to "Am I my brother's keeper?" was yes, unfortunately, all too often.

Two floors down I reversed, though already late. When I opened my front door again Kris was standing waiting, expecting me.

"Pick me up in Wood Lane at ten-fifteen," I

said. "Don't forget Bell said Robin Darcy will be at the races with her father."

Kris gave no sign of alarm. "Ten-fifteen," I repeated, and ran. Well . . . hobbled, though things were getting better from the ankle down.

OUR FLIGHT FROM White Waltham to Doncaster went impeccably, with Kris overmeticulous at getting every check perfect. He had actually no need to, if he wanted to impress, as I now believed (and was never going to tell him) that he was a great pilot up to a fine line on a panic scale and a lethal danger above that. Without Trox and Odin, I reckoned, there was no one safer. After that I would learn and pay attention, and know what to look for.

Doncaster took the weather that would have smiled on poor Guy F.

Kris and I almost missed the first race owing to the program's early start in the short daylight, but watched the second under the bright yellow-gray sky that itself brought out smiles, good humor and the favorites as winners.

Kris and Bell advanced and retreated all afternoon in a complicated mating dance. Caspar Harvey watched them with a scowl. George Loricroft strode past, head in air, his wife, Glenda, scuttling after him with endless complaints of "Baden-Baden."

Oliver Quigley trembled from owner to owner, excusing his losers before they'd lined up to run.

People in clusters asked Kris for his autograph. "Don't you *mind,*" Bell asked me, "that they're asking him more than you?"

"He's welcome." As so often on November sixth, I'd collected more of a mournful battery of young reproachful eyes than an onslaught of enthusiastic name collectors. The day it worried me, I would resign.

I looked around and said to Bell, "Did you come with your father and Robin Darcy? I haven't seen Robin anywhere."

"They came by car together," Bell said briefly. "They said they wanted to talk. I came with Glenda and she's driving me mad. Of *course* George didn't go to Baden-Baden, whyever should he when the races are here? And as for all the other places! She never stops."

"What other places?" I asked her absentmindedly, watching horses walk round the parade ring and admiring as always their loose-limbed natural beauty.

Bell dug a roughly torn memo square of pink paper out of her green coat pocket and squinted at it in the bright light.

"Glenda says George has excuses for Budapest, where he says it was snowing, ditto heavy snow at Pardubice in the Czech Republic, more snow in Berlin, and it was freezing in Warsaw and Hamburg, and he wasn't at any of those places, she's sure of it. So what's going on?"

"I have absolutely no idea."

"If Glenda comes this way," Bell said, "don't leave me."

Bell's pink eyelids fluttered over a thoroughly enticing smile. Kris finished signing autographs instantly and edged his long spine between me and his (possibly) future wife.

They went off contentedly, for once, for a sandwich, nicely asking me to join them, but relaxed that I didn't. I stayed near the weighing room looking out unhurriedly for Robin the Round. I wished after all I'd gone for the sandwich when Glenda and her loud Lancashire voice advanced like a storm surge and smothered me with her theories.

Her dyed-blonde shiny hair was of Andy Warhol explicit brashness. Forty-eight identical

Glendas haunted one's nightmare of an art gallery.

Oliver Quigley, of all people, came to my aid, or seemed to, stuttering at my shoulder while giving Glenda a stare of quite extraordinary ill will.

I'd seldom paid Oliver's quivering voice or problems much genuinely caring attention, and it was with similar make-believe that I asked earnestly after the sick filly's health. Glenda suspended her animation suddenly and stood with her mouth open wide, as if waiting for Oliver's answer; and suddenly it was as if this encounter were between two much deeper personalities than I'd superficially seen earlier. There were glints in the Lancashire eyes that were far from funny, and I began to wonder whether all the Quigley shivering was a way of camouflaging the stronger inner man, of hiding the iron foundations that he didn't want recognized.

I looked back to the lunch party, to the day I'd met all these Newmarket people, those strangers who now seemed familiar. Perhaps they'd showed to the world that day only their outsides, and perhaps, as with Robin Darcy, it was the inside that mattered.

"It's because of *you*," Glenda said suddenly with

venom, closing her lips together with pinching force. "It's *you* that's taking George to Baden-Baden, and don't you deny it." She was accusing Oliver. She seemed oblivious of me.

Oliver Quigley certainly looked blank, but not, to my fresh vision, from ignorance, but rather from the shock of having Glenda put into public words what should have lived in secrecy and silence.

"And," continued Glenda spitefully, "it's no good trying to tell me you didn't go with him to Poland and Germany and all those places, it was snowing a lot of the time and Perry could prove it if he could only be bothered . . ."

"Glenda!" Oliver interrupted with straightforward warning and oblivious menace, wiping out in one word all the dithery presentation of ages.

"Yeah, yeah," Glenda said dismissively, "you're all angry because of the filly."

She swiveled on her high-heeled shiny boots and marched away, her weight forward on her toes, leaving Oliver Quigley speechless and aghast, as if he'd lost both his sword and his shield at one stroke.

He switched his gaze back to me, and although it was far too late in reality, he chose to believe I'd seen and heard nothing. The quakes came back into his manner. He stuttered a good deal, but no intelligible words came out. After a while, as if he'd resumed his habitual role, he nodded vaguely in my direction, and as his own personal quiver counter was more or less back to normal he unglued himself from my vicinity and was soon to be seen talking with jerkily disturbed hand movements to the filly's owner, Caspar Harvey. Neither man looked even reasonably calm, let alone happy.

Kris, further away, bent his height down to accommodate the size of a short plump man that I with a faint shock saw to be Robin Darcy. Though I knew he had arrived at Doncaster with Caspar Harvey, Robin Darcy in actual living presence was somehow disturbing.

The last time I'd seen him had been on Trox Island, when he'd been dressed in disguising overalls and helmet, and had watched Michael carry the folder from hut to aircraft, when Michael had transported before my eyes the same sort of ultrasensitive package that I'd been told had brought finis to a careless man from Mexico.

I watched Robin Darcy amiably pat Kris on the arm without in any way being repulsed. Normally Kris jerked away from any affectionate touch, even from Bell, though if he himself was the toucher, that was different.

Kris, I reflected without excitement, had been determined to please Robin by having us detour to Trox. Kris liked pleasing Robin, and I would do well not to forget it.

The two of them spoke intensely for a short while with Kris nodding assent. When they parted, they shook hands. I watched and wondered if Kris would tell me what they'd said. On past form, I supposed with a shrug, quite probably not.

I leaned against the rails round the weighing room and the winners' unsaddling enclosure and did my best to pretend that the comings and goings of other trainers and jockeys were of far greater interest than anything Glenda had said. I stood with laziness in the bright air and, as quite often, simply let random thoughts drift with disorganization, until "Baden-Baden" and "Poland" and "snow" announced themselves to me insistently as somehow meaningful, and meaningful because of Glenda and the filly.

Glenda was tit-tupping away in the distance. Glenda was jealous of Quigley and of Harvey . . .

Nonsense, I thought. As a result of the filly's illness, Harvey had transferred his other horses from Quigley to her own husband, Loricroft, and I doubted if that outcome was what she'd intended.

Unexpectedly, with one of those inexplicable shifts in the drifting brain that delivers a revelation to a vacuum, a word arrived in my mind with such clarity that I couldn't understand why I hadn't thought of it earlier. The word had been part of the heading on one of the letters in the folder on Trox. I'd thought I could remember only Hippostat, but now I knew there was another—and probably more significant—address, though it still lacked pinpoint direction.

Rennbahn.

Baden-Baden Rennbahn.

Tum titty tum tum.

Rennbahn, in German script.

I did what half an hour earlier I would have classed as impossible, and deliberately moved into Glenda's path. Her own thoughts were elsewhere. She tripped over my foot with her fancy boots.

She said, "Baden-Baden," under her breath, not paying me any attention, a view of life that changed rapidly when I offered after all to look up for her the weather, past, present and anywhere, and any time she wanted.

"Do you mean it?" she demanded, eyes, voice and mind all sharpening fast to an acute awareness quite at odds with her glittery hair.

"I can't do it until Monday," I said. "I can't use the necessary computer until then."

She objected, "Bell says you're the head of home forecasting. I'd have thought you could do what you like as such." I said I was only the deputy head, and to myself I added that I wasn't going to use up any favors on results I thought of as highly speculative. I smiled my best apologetic excuse to Glenda and truthfully explained that the mainframe computer ran on Sundays for strictly necessary reasons. Tracing errant husbands wasn't classed as essential or necessary.

"And why," I asked without pressure, "does he go to Baden-Baden and those other places?"

"Girls, of course! I'll give you the list." Glitzy Glenda wasn't quite a fool. "All those places are racecourses," she said. "I suppose you don't know."

"No," I agreed. "All in Germany?"

"What a clever boy! Not all, but most."

"And does your husband have runners there?"

"Haven't I told you, he says so? He says the races are abandoned because of snow, but I'm telling you, it doesn't snow when he says it does."

"I'll look it up for you," I promised.

She gave me from her handbag a copy of the list she'd given to Bell, and I glanced at it briefly before stowing it in a pocket.

"Baden-Baden," she said. "It's rubbish."

I was so close to her at that moment that I could smell alcohol on her breath and see little black beads on the ends of her rigid eyelashes. The shiny blonde hair had minuscule black roots.

"I'll divorce George," she said with sudden and vicious intent. "And it will serve him right."

I suddenly couldn't be bothered to try any more at that moment to unwind any of Newmarket's twisted and destructive personalities. I spent the hour round the November Handicap simply watching the mechanics of the different, bewitching, wider world of racing, and winning a tiny amount when Harvey's runner, the second favorite, came in third.

I wasn't sure whether or not Robin Darcy was actively avoiding me, but in the end the meeting certainly looked accidental: one of those times when two people turn together and find themselves face to face.

We must both have had hours to prepare. We said to each other everything appropriate. I bewailed the loss of his beautiful aircraft, he rejoiced in the survival of Kris and myself. He thanked me for the letter I'd sent him from Miami airport half an hour before I left to fly home. I hoped he'd had a good journey himself: he had arrived at Newmarket yesterday, he confided.

He was friendly. He shook hands. He invited me anytime to visit again with himself and Evelyn. I wanted to say to him, "Where's the folder? For whom will you fix the sale of the next bargaining chip, the next bit of bomb?"

In the brown eyes behind the big black frames there was the same sort of question and answer: "Did Perry Stuart read those lists in the folder? He can't have done. He couldn't have opened the safe. He certainly heard my password, Hereford, but it would have meant nothing."

I wanted to say, "Whichever of you thought of the blindfold, thank you"; and I read, "You don't know how close you came to a bullet."

I wondered what he had said to Kris . . . wondered what he wanted Kris to do.

I wished Robin Darcy had been an ally, not an enemy. Born clever . . . why should such a man trade in death?

Too many clever men chose to trade in death.

He gave me a nod and moved off to where, not far away, Caspar Harvey, able but not brilliant, received lukewarm plaudits for his horse's third place in the November Handicap. Nothing but winning would have pleased his bullish attitude to racing, and I thought Oliver Quigley literally to be inviting trouble when in Caspar's hearing he said that given *his* training methods and *his* instructions to the jockey, the horse would have won.

By the end of six races, when Kris and I went back to the airfield to fly home, the extra physical demands of the past ten days had drained my normally perceptive self to the equivalent of a worn-out battery. We spent long minutes on farewells to most of the Newmarket contingent in the car park nearest to the landing ground, and I was dozing even when Kris was taxiing down the field for takeoff. He changed fuel tanks ostentatiously. I pretended not to notice.

On this Saturday, late in the year for daylight landings, Kris had arranged with his friend in the control tower at White Waltham to put car-battery-powered lamps down the runway to shine a path for his quiet approach and arrival at about five o'clock, half past toast and teatime.

We were in the air and a long way south of Doncaster when Kris shook me awake.

"Sorry," I said, yawning and reaching for the map. "Where are we?" It was still just light enough to see the three Rs, roads, rivers and railways. "No problem with those," I said. He always flew a straight heading.

Kris however wasn't worrying about being lost but about oil on the windshield, he said.

"What?" I asked blankly.

"Oil. On the windshield. Perry, wake up."

It was the urgency of those last three words that sharply reached my senses. I did wake up. My heart lurched.

There were dark gold threadlike lines on the windshield, which as I watched were joined by more lines, which were running and spreading *upwards* over the glass.

Horrified, we both understood what was happening. The hot oil that should have been circulating *inside* the engine case, lubricating the four thundering pistons, was somehow coming out into the engine compartment itself, and from there it was sliding upwards and backwards in droplets through the engine cowling's cracklike edges to hit the glass of the windshield . . . and from there, gradually to spread and cover the whole windshield with oil . . . and so, effectively, blind the pilot.

The oil itself wasn't the dirty brown-black old stuff that had been cleansing inner engine surfaces for many hours of flight. Kris always looked after his pride and joy, and he had changed his oil regularly. The disaster on the windshield had been clean for the Newmarket lunch.

"God Almighty," Kris said. "What the hell do we do now?"

"Keep straight on our course," I said automatically, "so we know where we are."

"That's the *easiest*. What if *all* the oil comes out? The engine will go dry and seize up." Kris suddenly sounded comically unconcerned. "And how do we land, if we can't see where we're going?"

"Can we *break* the windshield?" I suggested.

"Get with it, Perry." He was both sarcastic and fatalistic. "The windshield's made of toughened glass to withstand birdstrike. And even if we could break it—and what with—we'd have our faces cut to ribbons, and we'd need goggles as in the old Tiger Moth days, and even then we'd be going too fast, it would be like facing a Category 3 hurricane wind, it can't be done."

"Forget it," I said, "keep our course and height. We'll have to find a large public commercial airport open late on a Saturday afternoon."

"Oh great." He glanced across at me. "How do we find one of those?"

"It's a doddle." With immense thankfulness I took note that this time we were sensibly in contact by radio with the outside world, as we did have an aeronautical map giving the radio frequencies of airports. We didn't have parachutes or ejector seats—couldn't have everything.

"You keep straight," I told Kris. "I'll get us down to an airfield."

"You get us down," he repeated, making a joke of it, "and I'll crash."

Such a damned stupid way to die, I thought. Blinded by oil . . . the only thing worse would be to switch on the windshield wipers, which would fatally smear the oil into a thick continuous curtain, whereas now it was just possible to see through the thread lines to the ground far beneath.

Far . . . Kris was giving in to the temptation of losing height so as to see the ground better, but height gave us a better chance of clear radio reception by any airfield.

"Go back up," I said coaxingly.

"It's my bloody airplane."

"It's my bloody life."

We needed a big airport as soon as possible, and fortune smiled on us for once. I asked Kris dryly if he had any objection to Luton, almost dead ahead.

"You're joking! A real live airport? Not so much of the dead."

I told the area radio controller about the oil and said we would aim for Luton, approximately only thirty miles away. There was an incredulous silence at Luton at our lack of any radio aid except radio itself, and we got only a laid-back assessment of our chances (slim) from a useful man in Luton's control tower, who said he could put us over the runway and clear everything else off it, and after that it was up to us.

He gave us a private frequency for talking to him direct, so as not to clutter other air traffic.

"On second thoughts, better than trains, perhaps," Kris yelled to me, grinning, manic spirits ascendant in the actual face of mortal danger.

I said, "A suicidal pilot is the last thing I need!"

"It may be the last thing you get."

"I'll never forgive you . . ."

The man at Luton said in our ears, "We've an old D/F machine here. Do you know how to fly a QDM?"

Kris said, "Sure," and I said, "Yes," but we should both have correctly said, "Affirmative," which would still not, in my case, have been the truth. D/F meant Direction Finding and QDM was an air code asking for a direction to steer, and that was the extent of my own knowledge. Kris, I thanked the fates, muttered that he had done a QDM approach once, years before, when he had got lost.

Did he remember the procedure?

Not clearly, he said. A joke, he thought it. He typically *would*.

Our helper at Luton resignedly told Kris to press the "transmit" button and say nothing, then turn left and after two minutes transmit again, and he told us he now knew which blip we were on his dial, and he knew what we should steer to reach him, but he couldn't tell how far away we were from him, and he wouldn't know until he could see us on his doorstep.

He might see *us,* we told him, but we couldn't see *him.* Oil seemed to be coming out faster. Forward visibility had reduced pretty much to zero. The side windows were starting to fog, with droplets blowing backwards in streaks.

We traveled straight to Luton airport with his expert help, Kris again flying on instruments as if born to it and telling weak jokes all the way. Lights were starting to show on the ground in the still see-through bit of glass along the lower edge of the side windows. Kris's stream of jokes dried as the radio operator carefully steered him round in a pear-shaped sky pattern that ended with the Cherokee lined up with the single wide runway that now lay a mile straight ahead.

The runway ran from west to east. We were to land towards the west, into the prevailing wind.

To my private dismay, landing to the west meant also facing into the setting sun. The last rays of sunset hit the oil and made the windshield a glowing golden enclosing glory, exciting and beautiful and more deadly than ever.

"Jeez," Kris said, "I'll write a poem."

"Not just now."

"Say your prayers."

"You keep your mind on getting us down."

"We'll get down anyway."

"Safely," I said.

He grinned.

The voice from the control tower said in our ears, "I see you clearly. Lower flaps . . . descend to two hundred feet . . . maintain heading . . . allow for a ten-knot cross wind from the left . . ."

Kris checked that I'd set the altimeter to match the height of Luton's airfield above sea level and lowered the flaps, the wing sections that gave greater lift at slow speed.

"This isn't Odin," he said. "Pity really. We could do with a nice warm sea here for a splash-down landing."

I'd thought the same. The oil was thicker on the windows, and getting progressively worse.

"You're about a hundred feet up," the radio said in my ear. "The runway's straight ahead. Can you see the ground at all?"

"Can I, shit," Kris said, which wasn't in the air manual.

He throttled back the power to settle onto his normal landing speed and held the heading straight.

The tower said, "Stay straight . . . good . . . reduce power . . . no, *increase* power . . . hold it steady . . . reduce power . . . sink . . . straighten the rudder. I said *straighten . . . straighten.*"

Traveling at landing speed we hit the ground extremely hard and bounced back into the air with every bone shaking, with even our eyes insecure in their sockets.

Our airspeed read eighty miles an hour on the

dial and was now dropping too fast. At sixty we'd be going too slowly for the wings to keep us aloft.

"Power on," yelled the tower. "Power . . . level out . . . left rudder."

"I can't see a bloody thing," Kris said, his teeth grating from the shock through our bodies.

"Power . . . POWER . . ."

Kris pushed the throttle open and held the nose steady, and again we hit the ground with a frightful crash, though this time we bounced off grass, not off the hard runway, and were heading heaven knew where, still with a lethal but necessary airspeed giving us lift enough for a livable landing and still with the setting sun golden red in our eyes.

Kris said loudly, "To hell with this," and pulled the throttle right back, chopping off the fuel and stopping the engine, which would have been fine if we'd had any wheels on the ground, instead of ten feet or more of air beneath us.

Normally Kris's landings consisted of a smooth nose-up float followed by a feather-soft transference of wheels to earth. This time with the speed dropping off alarmingly fast, leaving Kris progressively without any effective control, we hit the ground again and bounced again into the air and bounced again, slowing, slowing, each bounce shallower but at the wrong angle for the wheels to stay down.

Kris from instinct finally pulled the control column yoke right back, raising the nose until the wings stalled and, with no lift left, the airplane's propeller dipped down and dug a deep groove in the earth. There was a screeching and a banging of metal and there were human bodies being flung about. There was a terrifying sudden and final standstill with the fuselage and tail pointing halfway to the sky.

The oil on the windshield still shone radiantly, the glass unbroken, the last red-gold gleams of sunset slanting across towards a motionless dusk.

Silence. Stillness. My head rang.

It had been a miraculous deliverance and a splendid piece of flying, and within a minute we were surrounded by foam trucks and ambulances and police cars and half of the county of Bedfordshire that had been listening on the so-called "private" frequency dedicated to our troubles.

9

KRIS HAD BEEN knocked out by the last going-nowhere impact and was half hanging in his seat belt and half lying on the control column. I'd felt in myself a sort of resilient cracking bounce in my chest, disorienting but not disabling, nothing to stop me from trying to unlatch the door, which when it came to the point I couldn't do, as it seemed to be bent.

I'd reached a woozy level of thinking "fire" and "dammit we have fuel in both wing tanks this time," and various comforting little items along those lines, but the rescue mob outside jimmied the door open and scooped us carefully and quite fast out of our nose-down cabin and covered the fuel leaks around them and us with foam and expedition.

Kris woke up moaning, a noise that shocked him into silence and a weak grin. By the time the first news camera with microphone was seen advancing among the uniforms, his concern had been wholly transferred from the living to his mangled treasure, which no one would let him inspect.

I could have told him that the obvious damage was a nose wheel with broken struts, three burst tires and propeller blades bent into right angles.

I stood on the grass, shivering, while someone with kindness wrapped a blanket round my shoulders; and I watched Kris lose the battle against stretcher-bearers and other good-natured forms of restraint.

It was inevitable, I supposed, that the question of *why* had the oil leaked out of the engine should be one of the first needing an answer and almost the last to get it.

For some reason my mind was inclined to clear sharply sometimes in a crisis, and it was then with a jolt that I remembered Kris's friend setting out the landing lights at White Waltham. Our savior from the Luton tower, coming down from his heights, promised amiably to alert him, with a consequent widening of the bad and good tidings, and no chance of a modest disavowal. Everyone at White Waltham chatted onwards and agreed that the weathermen had nine, or better, twenty-nine lives.

Being carried off by paramedics—against his will—Kris urgently told me as he passed to stay with the Cherokee to the death (or to the scrap heap), as oil should *not* have got past his eagle-eyed checks; and indeed I was well aware, as he was carted protestingly to onward transport, that we had in fact flown safely to Doncaster a few hours earlier with the engine oil intact.

I folded the blanket from around my shoulders, returned it noncommittally to an ambulance and, covering most of my too easily recognized face with a hand, became a gawping bystander among others. Never mind that Kris wanted to know, I too was fairly anxiously curious. Except for the direction-finder and its operator in Luton's control tower, and but for Kris's "give-it-all-you've-got" semi-crash landing, the BBC would have lost two forecasters permanently, and on a cloudless fine evening, no less.

INEVITABLY IN THE end Kris and I became news fodder with names, but I did stay with the Cherokee to the crane-lifting stage, for which

Kris next day (out of hospital custody), said, "Thanks, kiddo," absentmindedly and demanded to know what I'd learned.

I said, "When we . . . er . . . landed, there was no dipstick in the engine."

He stared at me fiercely. We were up in my attic surrounded by the Sunday papers he'd brought with him. All the later editions had given us front page slots with a frame or two of the nose-down wreck and our best BBC faces, with unstinted and not unduly complimentary comments on our recently reported escape from our flight through a hurricane. *Two* crashes within two weeks was excessive.

"It was *not* pilot error," Kris asserted, deliberately ignoring any possible embarrassing reference to fuel tanks. "You saw me use the dipstick yesterday morning when we took off. I wiped the stick clean and put it into the engine sump to make sure there was enough oil, and there *was*. And I put the dipstick back and screwed it up tight, and no oil came out on the way to Doncaster."

"No," I agreed.

"And I didn't look at the oil level again at Doncaster. Go on, say it, I didn't do that check again

as we hadn't come far from White Waltham—
like I didn't check the oil that day for coming
home from Newmarket. No one checks the oil
after such a short flight."

I said, "You certainly did not remove the dipstick at Doncaster and not put it back."

"You'd swear to it?"

I'd been semi-asleep at Doncaster but I would
have bet my life on his carefulness . . . as indeed I
had done in Odin . . . and nearly drowned for it . . .

At Doncaster there had been no pressure on
him. The panic scale had registered zero. He
wouldn't have made an elementary mistake.

The alternative had to be faced. Someone else,
not Kris, had taken out the dipstick at Doncaster
and not put it back.

Kris shook his head to any question about
Robin Darcy, but in good spirits collected his
newspapers and went down my stairs, slowly for
him because of the medics' warning of dizziness
and concussion; and I finally admitted to myself,
chiefly as a result of a stabbing indrawn breath,
that I'd possibly cracked a rib or two at Luton.

I'd been treated well there, courtesy no doubt of
my employment by the Weather Centre, and I'd
learned how very lucky we had in fact been, as

the single wide runway and the airport itself lay on a hill above the town. The control tower people, aghast, had seen our first heavy bounce throw the Cherokee off its straight course, and we'd been heading across grass towards a steep downwards slope when Kris had opted for his dramatic full stop.

Kris's Cherokee would be stowed safely in their hangar, they said, and there it would stay until the accident inspectors came to write their report. I would please meanwhile not talk about no dipstick. Silent as mushrooms, I said.

I called my grandmother and dispelled a flourishing outbreak of heebie-jeebies. The Stuart feet, I assured her, may have been in the recent wars but were this time safely on the ground. She could however hear the lighthearted relief in my voice and unerringly understood it.

"You might not always escape," she said worriedly. "Wear a bulletproof vest."

BY MONDAY MORNING we had yielded the front page to an eloping heiress and there was no denying the fact of my cracked ribs. Maybe two, I thought: not more. And no lung-piercers, the really extremely bad news.

I'd done much the same damage once before by falling down a Welsh mountainside. A visit to a doctor resulted at that time in "grin, bear it and take aspirins" advice: after Luton there seemed nothing to improve on that, except the distraction attained by looking up snowfalls in Europe.

Glenda surprisingly was apparently right. If her dominating George had reported icy temperatures as an excuse for infidelity, he hadn't been truthful, regardless of faithful.

I made a list of the actual air temperatures and inches of snowfall for all the places and cities I'd been given, and none of them matched. Either Glenda or George, or both, was playing winter games.

I telephoned Belladonna, reckoning to catch her at breakfast after she'd come in from riding morning exercise, and I located her with Loricroft and Glenda, eating cornflakes in the Loricroft kitchen. Racehorse trainers, it seemed to me, led half their days in the kitchen. It was warm there in winter, Bell explained.

Kris had refused sick leave, she said, and would be forecasting on Radio Four, as scheduled, and he had already told her that for the five weekdays ahead, starting on that day, Monday, I would be doing television forecasts in the evening after the six o'clock and nine o'clock news.

"Mm," I agreed. "Could you and Glenda spare me any time tomorrow morning, if I come over?"

"Is it good news for Glenda? Do you want to talk to her? Will you be bringing Kris?"

I said, "Maybe. Perhaps. And no."

"Hang on," Bell said and put her hand over the microphone, I guessed, while she asked her boss and his wife for their reaction, because in a minute or two she was saying, "Perry? How about Wednesday? George says if you're here early enough you can see his jumpers going over the schooling fences."

I gathered I was being offered a medium honor which it would be impolite to refuse: I agreed on eight-thirty Wednesday, though I would rather have gone a day sooner.

Until then . . . Until then there was first of all Jett van Els, whose third week with my grandmother had concluded that Monday morning. At ten she had changed places with another of my grandmother's "dear girls," and at one o'clock she met me in a sandwich bar for lunch.

She came dressed not in the nurse's uniform familiar to me, but in black pants, a thick white sweater and a boxy scarlet coat with black and gold buttons. I greeted her with frank admiration and the first thing she said was, "You're not well."

I kissed her anyway.

"I'm a nurse, remember," she said, "and I've seen pallor in too many faces."

She made no more fuss about it, however, but hung her coat on a nearby peg and read the possible menu with half her attention.

"What job do you start next?" I asked, settling on cheese and chutney in brown bread for myself, but not caring much what I ate.

"I'm taking a week off, and next Monday I'll be back with Mrs. Mevagissey." She spoke calmly as if this program were usual. Normally, if a nurse returned, it would be after at least a month.

"Did she agree?" I queried, my eyebrows rising.

Jett smiled at my surprise. "Your grandmother warned me severely not to grow fond of you, as you were inconstancy personified, or words to that effect."

"She doesn't want you to be hurt."

"And will I be?"

It wasn't the sort of exchange I'd ever before embarked on.

I said weakly, "It's too soon to tell."

"I'll negotiate terms of disengagement."

We ordered food. She chose tuna, which I'd never liked, and I found I hoped her future plans wouldn't take her far away. Jett van Els, with or without Belgian father, was more likely to leave Perry Stuart in tatters than the other way round.

"Seriously," she said, having healthily dispatched the tuna, "what's hurting you?"

"Onset of broken heart?"

She shook her head, smiling. "I saw the papers yesterday, with your grandmother. It's amazing you and your friend Kris survived at all."

I said I'd probably cracked a rib or two, which could be a bit frustrating in the active love department, for a couple of days.

"Think in terms of a week or two," Miss van Els instructed. "Or a month or two." She smiled with composure. "The first rule of disengagement is to take your time at the beginning."

"How about lunch tomorrow, then?"

"All right," she said.

ALTHOUGH I WOULDN'T do my act before the cameras until well after six o'clock, I was always at work in plenty of time before two, when the twice-daily conference on world atmospheric conditions took place.

One had to consider as a whole the jacket of air swirling round the spinning planet and to foresee if possible how far the low pressure systems in hot areas might deepen further still, to give rise to gales.

I had always found it extraordinary that people turned their backs on physics as a subject at school and university, even if public opinion was at last gradually changing. Physics was the study of the hugely powerful invisible forces that ruled the way we lived. Physics was gravity, magnetism, electricity, heat, sound, air pressure, radioactivity and especially radio, the mysterious forces that clearly existed, whose effects were commonplace, whose powers were unlimited, and which could not be seen. Every day I dealt with them as friends.

No one at work made much comment on Kris's or my Saturday escapade, as our colleagues seemed to have exhausted their "welcome backs" after Odin. Their matter-of-fact approach suited me fine, though perhaps I would have preferred a more concerned response to inquiries into the fate of a missing dipstick further north. When I telephoned for news, I got nowhere, as it wasn't my dipstick, I was told. When Kris telephoned, at my prompting, he still got nowhere, as nothing could be discussed unless he made the journey to talk to them in person.

"Get Luton to ask," I suggested, but Luton received only a suggestion that Kris himself should be more closely questioned.

"What does *that* mean?" Kris demanded.

I said, "It means they haven't found a dipstick at their end. It means they think you didn't screw your dipstick in tight and they are trying to say it was your fault the oil came out."

Kris scowled, but when I went to Kensington on Tuesday morning to pretend to be engaged on a textbook, John Rupert took the leaking oil to be a bona-fide attempt to put Kris and myself underground.

"I fly my own plane," John Rupert said. "I've been a weekend pilot for twenty years, and I wouldn't like to try to land blind. A year ago, oil on the windshield killed four people who crashed into English cliffs on their way back from France. Their dipstick was found on the ground where they'd topped up their oil before setting off for home. It was in all the papers."

"Poor sods," I said. "I remember it."

"No one," John Rupert observed with conviction, "could have expected you both to be back at work unharmed."

The door opened quietly for the advent of Ghost. He shook hands with stretched sinews and finished off the single ginger cracker overlooked by John Rupert himself.

"News?" Ghost suggested laconically, quietly crunching. "Thoughts?"

"Apart from attempted murder by oil," John Rupert said.

"Because you both lived," Ghost said dryly, "no one will consider it an attempt . . ." He broke off and asked me straightly, "Could it have been by any means an accident?"

"Only if it was random mischief by a stranger, which is, I believe, what the local investigators think."

"But you don't?"

"No."

"And is that why you've come back to us?"

I blinked. "I expect so," I said.

Ghost smiled: a fearsome facial expression threatening the wicked with decades in limbo.

I said, "I don't know exactly who whisked out

the dipstick, but I've brought you a list of possibles."

They read them. "All from Newmarket," Ghost commented. "All except this last one, Robin Darcy."

"I don't think it was him," I said.

"Why not?"

"He shook hands with both of us. Separately, that is."

"You're old-fashioned," Ghost said. "Shakespeare was bang up to date. One can smile and smile and be a villain."

"I don't want it to be Darcy," I said.

"Ah," Ghost sounded satisfied. "Gut feelings . . . those I believe in."

John Rupert studied the list. "Tell us about these people," he said. "What about Caspar Harvey? And Belladonna, his daughter?"

I was surprised at how much I'd learned about each of them and it took me a good hour to roam round the perimeter of quivery Oliver Quigley (old and new perceptions) and George Loricroft, a bully who believed himself entitled to dominate his semi-bimbo wife, who was much brighter than her husband realized or allowed for and who half-understood too much but not quite enough, and was therefore a danger to herself, though she didn't know it.

"I don't think the dipstick was Glenda's doing," I explained, drawing breath. "I don't think she wanted Kris and me dead. She wanted us to be alive, to be weathermen, and to check on her suspicions."

I explained about the snow and ice discrepancies in Loricroft's actual and professed journeys.

Ghost listened intently. John Rupert said merely, "Expand."

"Well . . ." I collected a few thoughts. "When I came to you . . . sought you out . . . I knew the names of three of the Traders, and I didn't tell you them because . . ."

"Because," Ghost said disapprovingly, as I hesitated, "you sentimentally wanted to save them from prosecution, as they hadn't killed you when they had the opportunity. Correct?"

"I guess so."

"And?"

"And that was fact, but what I can tell you now is inference and supposition."

"Glad to have them," John Rupert said with mock formality. "Fire away."

"You may ridicule . . ."

"Leave that to us."

"The Unified Traders . . ." I said slowly. "Well, these Unified Traders, it seems to me, are more amateur than professional. That's to say, they're dishonorable enough in intent, but not slick or hard enough in performance. For instance, leaving their folder of *essential* information lying about for so long was plain stupid, so was engaging Kris to collect it. On the surface it seemed a reasonable quid pro quo, as Kris would have done more or less anything in exchange for a chance to fly through a hurricane."

John Rupert nodded.

I said, "Caspar Harvey and Robin Darcy are very longtime colleagues, and apart from Harvey's barley and Darcy's turf farm, they are both used to handling things in small packets. Harvey sells birdseed and Darcy sells vacuum-packed exotic mushrooms. Darcy set up a small mushroom operation on Trox Island, but I was told, secondhand, by full-scale mushroom growers, that the Trox operation was too small to succeed. In the end it was used, as I told you before, to frighten away the whole population of the island. But it was their ability to think small that started them off, I reckon, on arranging the introduction of buyers to sellers of tiny amounts of radioactive materials."

John Rupert said, "I suppose if you put enough small packets together you get a haystack."

"Or a bomb," said Ghost.

"Or enough of a bomb," I said mildly, "to raise the bargaining power of that amount. But I don't think the Traders actually handle the uranium or plutonium themselves. It's very dangerous stuff. But they do have small-scale know-how."

I stopped, but both men wanted more.

"I think," I said, "and frankly I'm guessing, that Darcy recruited Caspar Harvey as a Trader, and Harvey drew in Oliver Quigley and George Loricroft . . . and for a while the middlemen operation ran smoothly and immensely profitably with the three Traders across the Atlantic, each of the group of six acting on the old musketeers' principle of 'All for one and one for all.'"

Ghost, his eyes shrewdly narrowed, asked, "Why did the original Traders need more recruits? Why didn't Darcy and Harvey keep the proceeds to themselves?"

"I think . . ." I found all my thoughts coming out as speculations. ". . . I think Harvey found Loricroft had a gift for sniffing out the truffles.

George Loricroft has traveled all over Europe—
and especially throughout Germany—telling his
wife lies about the local weather to explain why
he hadn't been where he was supposed to have
been, and always treating her as an idiot, and
in fact it's possible that all those places he lied
about were trading posts. They were nearly all in
Germany, and as Loricroft is internationally
known as a racehorse trainer, there is nowhere in
the world more suitable or less conspicuous for
him to trade and exchange information than on
racetracks."

I looked down at my shoes, dodging their un-
doubted incredulity, but I'd gone too far to with-
draw.

"I told you I could remember only Hippostat as
a word in the heading of one of the letters, but I
know another—it came to me when I wasn't concentrating . . . it just drifted back from my sub-
conscious memory."

Ghost said impatiently, "What is it?"

"Well . . ." I looked up, "it's Rennbahn. It's
Baden-Baden Rennbahn."

John Rupert smiled vividly. "And do you know
what Rennbahn means?"

"Racetrack," I said. "I've looked it up. Baden-

Baden Racetrack. It was written in German script in a letter in another language that I didn't know."

"We have German dictionaries downstairs, and every other sort of dictionary you care to mention," John Rupert said. "Would you remember any more if you . . . er . . . browsed?"

I said doubtfully, "I don't know."

"We can try."

"Meanwhile," Ghost said, "tell us about the other two Traders in Florida; Robin Darcy's colleagues."

"They're in the Cayman Islands, not Florida," I explained, and described Michael and Amy Ford. "And they may be in the game because of idealism or political motives . . . I simply can't tell, but they also may be the original Traders. In any case, they are, I'd say, the richest of the whole group."

"Why do you think so?" Ghost wanted to know.

"I stayed in their house . . . and Amy's airplane, that we ditched in the hurricane, that plane was a perfect beauty. They said Amy had sold it to Darcy."

"But you doubt it?" John Rupert asked.

"Well . . . I do, yes. But that's only an impression. None of them seemed to be terribly upset by losing it. I don't know about insurance. None of them mentioned it."

There was a pause. John Rupert then said, "Is that the lot?" and prepared to rise, and I said with diffidence, "One more thing . . ."

"Yes?" He relaxed in his chair, attention unending.

I picked at my fingers. "Well . . . it's only that the Unified Trading Company doesn't have a boss. They don't have a hierarchy."

"Are you sure?" John Rupert inquired doubtfully. "Every organization I've ever dealt with has had a hierarchy."

"I'm sure." I nodded. "In an ordinary company, the lower members report upwards, and then receive their instructions from above. But in the Unified Trading Company they each act on their own ideas and report afterwards what they've done. They act first and tell the others after. As a result they duplicate some things and omit others entirely, and they get in a muddle."

Both John Rupert and Ghost were showing more and more doubt.

"If both of you had been for a long time accustomed to rule," I said, "which of you would make the decisions?"

They answered quickly and in unison, "I would."

"Who would?" I asked. "Which of you would give commands?"

"I would." They answered as one again, but more slowly, and then both of them looked thoughtful.

"The Traders so far identifiable," I remarked, "have each run their own business, and are accustomed to command. Michael Ford owned and ran a chain of profitable gymnasiums. His wife, Amy, made a fortune from video rental stores. Robin Darcy farms turf, which in Florida is like growing gold. Caspar Harvey too is a farmer, but also makes trillions out of birdseed. Both George Loricroft and Oliver Quigley are racehorse trainers and both succeed only by controlling their workforce. All of those six people are accustomed to making the decisions. They're not used to being told what to do. Also they don't *like* being told what to do, so they do what they think is best, independently. And because of that, things, overall, go wrong."

"It's an interesting theory," Ghost said.

"For instance," I said, "Robin Darcy expected Kris to be able to pick up the folder without difficulty because he'd left it in a desk, but someone else, unknown to him, had removed the desk and installed a safe, using Darcy's own password. Like I said, they get things wrong, and Kris didn't find the folder at all."

I was fast running out of energy and felt sore along the protesting ribs. More than ready to leave, I asked, "Is there anything else I can do? If not . . ."

They indecisively shook their heads. "Only the dictionaries . . ." So I went downstairs with them into a busy world of books. There were indeed dictionaries by the hundred, but after a survey of incomprehensible scripts, with no reliable recognitions, I finally scraped together enough impetus to leave and meet Jett in her scarlet coat for lunch.

"You're ill," she said over curried egg salads, and I hadn't the vigor to deny it.

"Tell the BBC you need sick leave."

"It's only ribs. They'll be better tomorrow."

"Let me drive you to Newmarket, then, in the morning."

I'd told her I was going to Newmarket to see

George Loricroft's horses school over fences. She'd wanted to come anyway, and although I thought it incautious, I gratefully accepted her offer.

I got through the working day somehow, but when Jett arrived at my front door at six-thirty the next morning she said I wasn't fit to travel anywhere and should see a doctor.

We had agreed we would go in her own Honda as she felt happier driving it than sitting behind the wheel of my compact runabout. She said she knew a good doctor and I said we were going to Newmarket, and maybe for the last time with Miss van Els, I got my way.

At George Loricroft's house Bell greeted me with a kiss, switching her gaze past me to see how Jett reacted to that embrace. Waste of time. Jett was cool.

Glenda wrapped her arms lavishly around me so that her mouth ended up by my ear.

"Don't tell George . . ." It was scarcely more than a whisper. Then more loudly she said, "How *divine* of you to come, luv." And George himself, unenthusiastic about me at all times, cheered up considerably when introduced to Jett. A thoroughly sex-conscious bunch of hellos, I thought, and couldn't eat any breakfast from nausea.

Glenda and Bell rejoiced again about the landing Kris had achieved on Saturday, and George, looking at his watch impatiently, crossly said that in his opinion Kris had been in too much of a hurry to set off from Doncaster before dark and that he'd left the dipstick on the ground and clipped the engine cowling shut without it in place.

"Easy done," he said. "Get ready, girls. It's time to go." And he strode out to his horses without looking back.

George, with well-developed brusqueness, had seemed considerably out of tune with his wife, and she from time to time had shot him searing glances of anxiety mixed with ill will. Neither was any longer bothering to pretend devotion to the other, an awkwardness for everyone else.

At a moment well out of her husband's sight, I gave Glenda her list of the icy venues George had sworn to that were contradictory to the freezing truth, and I watched her cheeks flush with justification and—I thought—with a sort of disappointment and disillusion that she'd been right.

Bell put an arm round Glenda's drooping shoulders and walked with her into the depths of the house, returning alone to mount a horse out in the stableyard and to lead Jett and me (driving George's Jeep) to the schooling grounds for the promised jumping practice. I was glad Jett seemed genuinely interested and that Bell, though herself due to ride one hustling breath-stopper over three rattling flights of hurdles, spent time explaining schooling routine in advance to me and to the next-best-thing to Florence Nightingale, the Miss van Els, who was that day wearing olive-drab trousers and jacket over the thick white sweater. She and I walked from the Jeep to a vantage point nearer the hurdles, to hear and be a part of the noise and commitment.

After the jumping and out of breath from the speed, Bell trotted her mount over to where we stood and dropped down from his back, surprisingly saying to us both with a smile, "I've not known you long, brother Perry, but I know a good brain when it flashes under my nose, and you and your Jett van Els, you're both loaded."

Bell started walking her horse round in a small circle nearby, to cool him, while I tried to keep up with her and talk as well.

"Like Robin Darcy?" I suggested.

She took ten seconds of silence to surf her memory, and came up with a straightforward account of bits of her father's lunch party. "I told you not to be fooled by his cuddly shell."

"Yes, you did."

"And I tried to warn Kris that Darcy was way outside his league, but that day Kris wouldn't have listened to me if I'd been the angel Gabriel."

Kris had listened to Robin that day and ever since.

"Kris and Robin talked for ages at Doncaster," I said.

Bell nodded. "They talked when I went to the loo. Darcy asked Kris to spend another holiday with Evelyn and him, and to take me with him!"

"A marriage trip?"

"Sometimes I think we'll never get to the wedding." She looked undecided herself, and then unexpectedly said, "Stay here with Jett and hold my horse by his bridle and I'll go and fetch George's Jeep. Honestly, you look pretty gray."

I couldn't understand it, because the cracked ribs in Wales hadn't caused sickness but only discomfort, but I did accept her offer and stood beside her steaming mount, pleased to be near the great primeval creature under the wide, cold, cloudless skies of Newmarket Heath.

Bell brought the Jeep and we exchanged conveyances; she rode the horse and I drove myself and Jett back to George's yard and felt awful.

In the warm kitchen George and Glenda were standing rigidly opposite each other, glaring as if ready to kill, and the reappearance of others hardly began to melt the cutting edges of hate.

George, in his mid-forties, always emanated heavy forcefulness, but at that moment the handsome set of his shoulders, thick smoothly brushed dark hair, the thin fingers clenching and stretching with tensile grace, all the stylishness served only to intensify the positive malevolence of his intention.

George's anger would, I thought, have erupted already into a physical attack on his wife if it weren't that she herself seemed to wear an impermeable and invisible armor.

Jett and I silently retreated, with Bell on our heels looking worried and trying to say, "I'm sorry . . . I'm so sorry . . ."

"Don't be," I said, but I couldn't reassure her, not with only two brief words.

We walked across George's parking area and stopped by Jett's Honda. I looked back at the big Loricroft house and saw only prosperity and peace. Tissue paper over an abyss, I thought.

"Bell . . ." I begged her uneasily, "leave New-market and move in with Kris in London."

She was shaking her head before I'd finished speaking.

"I can't leave. And what for? Kris doesn't need me, he said so."

Neither Bell nor Jett felt any of the urgency making my intestines cramp and my scalp itch. My grandmother, I realized, would have recognized this deep unease as heebie-jeebies, but I didn't know whether the feelings I was having derived from reason or instinct or simply queasiness.

I said only, but with as much persuasion as I could manage, "Bell, I mean it. Leave Newmarket. I have an intuition . . . you could call it premonition . . . call it anything, but leave here . . ."

Jett said, "You're ill."

"Maybe . . . But ill or not . . . Bell, leave Newmarket *now.*"

Both she and Jett, puzzled by my vehemence, nevertheless began to waver. I found it impossible to tell her that her father and her employer and Quigley and Robin Darcy were all involved in a conspiracy to supply to many lawless parts of the world and to many a clique and brotherhood the information needed to acquire tiny quantities of the highest-grade fissile material for weapons. Tiny quantities, if enough of them were gathered together, made a threat, an aggregation . . . a bomb.

All four men, and surely they knew it, were dealing in death.

One or two of them were themselves personally lethal.

Loricroft, the seeker and collector of the stuff of profitable deals, he certainly, with his conviction of his own superiority, with his wife ever nearer on the trail of his transactions, he most of all was closest to detonation.

I thought him dangerous, as likely to cause heartless damage as any of his cold-blooded customers.

I said to Bell, "If Glenda wants out, take her with you."

Bell shook her head.

"I'll come back in an hour," I said, and asked Jett to drive me in her car through the town.

"To the hospital?" she asked hopefully.

"Sort of," I said.

10

THE HOSPITAL I sought cared for horses.

I'd made a telephone call to prepare the way, and was greeted inside the main door of the Equine Research Establishment by a woman whose given name was Zinnia. Although a research veterinarian in general, she introduced herself as a specialist in poisonous plants and on their effect on any horse that ate them.

It had been she who'd been given the task not just of saving if possible the life of Caspar Harvey's filly but of finding what was wrong with her to begin with.

Zinnia had already attained fifty, I guessed, and wore a professional white coat over a gray flannel skirt. In spite of her colorful name she had short

gray hair, no hint of lipstick, flat-heeled shoes
and an air of tiredness, which I discovered to be
a permanent mannerism, not a pointer to lack of
sleep.

"Dr. Stuart?" She greeted me with a toe-to-head
inspection but no enthusiasm, and raised her eyebrows over Jett, who'd declined to be left outside
in her car. A recital by me of Jett's nursing
certificates brought the eyebrows down again,
and we were invited to follow the flower into a
laboratory equipped with a herd of microscopes,
centrifuges, measuring devices and a gas chro-
matograph. We all sat on high laboratory stools,
and I went on feeling lousy.

"Mr. Harvey's filly," Zinnia said without emotion, "presented with severe symptoms of intes-
tinal distress. By the time I was called in to see
her here, late on a Sunday afternoon, she was in
a state of collapse . . ." She detailed her actions
and her thoughts at the time which, as in nature
horses had no provision for anti-peristalsis, or in
plainer words, couldn't throw up, had consisted
to a great extent of purging and of offering copious amounts of water, which the filly fortunately
drank.

"I thought it certain that she'd eaten some form

of plant poison that had been ground up into chaff and mixed into her hay, as there were no whole specimen leaves or stems in the haynet that came with her. I expected her to die, when of course I would have analyzed the stomach contents, but as she clung to life I had to make do with the copious droppings . . . I thought that she might have ingested ragwort, which is extremely poisonous and often fatal for horses. It attacks the liver and is usually chronic, but it can have acute effects, as with Harvey's filly."

She paused, looking from my face to Jett's and seeing considerable ignorance in both.

"Are you cognizant of *Senecio jacobaea?*" she asked.

"Er . . ." I said. "No."

"Better known as ragwort." She smiled thinly. "It mostly lives in wasteland and was designated an injurious weed under the 1959 Weeds Act, so it's your duty to pull it up if you see any."

If she'd said that neither Jett nor I had any idea what it looked like on the hoof, so to speak, she would have been absolutely right. We asked, and she described.

"It has yellow flowers and jagged leaves . . ." She broke off. "Ragwort has to do with cyclic diesters, the most toxic of pyrrelizidine alkaloids, and it causes the symptoms shown by the filly, the digestive tract upset, the abdominal pain and ataxia, the lack of control of the legs."

We listened respectfully. I wondered if I'd been eating ragwort myself.

"The leaves can be dried and will keep their poisoning capacity for ages, unfortunately making it all the more suitable for chopping and mixing with other dried fodder, like hay."

Jett said to Zinnia, "So you found ragwort in the filly's droppings?"

Zinnia glanced from her to me. "No," she said without dramatics. "There was no identifiable ragwort in the filly's droppings. We treated her with a series of antibiotics in case an infection was present, and she gradually recovered. We sent her to George Loricroft, having been given instructions to do that by the owner, Caspar Harvey. The filly had been trained by Oliver Quigley before that, of course, and we made inquiries in that yard from the head groom downwards, but the whole workforce there strongly denied that anyone could possibly have tampered with the filly's haynet. None of the other horses showed any symptoms like the filly, do you see?"

"What was wrong with her, then?" Jett asked. "Did you ever find out?"

"There are other theories, I believe," she said, sounding as if any theory advanced by anyone except herself would automatically be wrong. "But the filly isn't here, of course. If you want to do blood tests for antibodies, Dr. Stuart, we have already suggested that course to Caspar Harvey, but so far he has declined the procedure."

Zinnia was saying, in her meticulous way, that if a horse—or a human—had had a disorder successfully treated, then that creature's blood would likely forever contain the antibodies summoned up to defeat the infection. The presence of the antibodies to any disease proved that the individual had been exposed to that disease.

"No, I don't want to test for antibodies," I said, "but . . . did you keep any of the droppings? Do you still have any of them here in the research lab?"

Zinnia said with starch, "I assure you, Dr. Stuart, we tested the droppings for every infection and every poison in the book and we found nothing."

My forehead was damp with sweat. I felt more or less on a par with the filly. No cracked bones that I'd heard of gave one such unquiet guts.

Zinnia with surprise agreed grudgingly that the Research Establishment had indeed retained some of the material in question, as the riddle of the filly's illness hadn't been solved.

"Caspar Harvey might change his mind," Zinnia said.

I thought Caspar Harvey most unlikely to want light poured onto the filly's ailment, but regardless of his feelings, I said to Zinnia, "Does the Equine Research Establishment by any chance have a Geiger counter among its equipment?"

"A Geiger . . ." Words dried in Zinnia's throat.

"I believe," I said without emphasis, "that someone here reckons the filly was suffering from radiation sickness."

"Oh no." Zinnia shook her head decisively. "She would have deteriorated and died from that, but she recovered within days when treated with antibiotics. We have a research scientist here who advanced the radiation theory, chiefly I think on the grounds of some of the filly's hair dropping out; but yes, to answer your inquiry, we do have a Geiger counter somewhere, but the filly showed no abnormal count when she left here."

There was a pause. I had no intention of annoying or contradicting her, and after a short while she raised an at least semi-friendly smile and said she would go and find the researcher in question. Within five minutes she returned with another white-coated lady, whose knowledge of radioactivity could have done with a dusting off.

Her name, she said, was Vera; she was earnest, thorough and a cutting genius in bad cases of colic.

"I'm a veterinary surgeon, not a physicist," she explained, "but since Zinnia found no trace of poison—and believe me, if she couldn't, then no one could—I began to think of other possibilities, and I just floated the idea of radiation sickness . . . and of course it generated an instant atmosphere of fear, but we called in an expert on radiation and he did tests and told us not to worry, neither radiation sickness nor the filly could have been infectious. I wish I could remember everything he said."

"Dr. Stuart is a physicist," Zinnia smoothly remarked.

"He reads the weather on the BBC," the second veterinarian contradicted flatly, unimpressed.

"He's both," Jett assured her, "and a lecturer also."

I looked at her in surprise.

"Your grandmother told me," she smiled. "She said you lecture on physics in general and radiation in particular. Mostly to young people, like teenagers."

Vera, the second white coat, showed none of Zinnia's constant tiredness, but quite the opposite. She woke to see me as a different creature.

She said, "Give me a sample of your lecturing wares and I'll lend you my records of the filly's droppings."

"That's totally reprehensible," Zinnia reproved. "Unacceptable."

Her friend nodded, unabashed.

"Promise?" I said.

"Of course."

I thought it might take my mind off greenish gills, so I started on a portion of the lecture I'd given so often that I knew it by heart. "This is about uranium," I said. "It's from a lecture I give to sixteen- and seventeen-year-olds usually."

The second white coat approved. "Right. Carry on."

In a conversational voice I did her bidding.

I said from memory, "Just one gram of uranium ore contains more than two thousand million million million million atoms; that's a two with twenty-one zeros after it; too big to imagine. Even though natural uranium is not very radioactive compared to some other really dangerous stuff, a couple of grams of it, less than half a teaspoonful, will emit about thirty thousand alpha particles every second and will go on doing so at almost that rate for millions of years. Thirty thousand alpha particles attacking your guts every second for a couple of days might certainly make you feel sick, but I think you would recover eventually."

I stopped. I certainly did feel sick, but I hadn't touched uranium that I knew of. Jett looked alarmed, however, and Vera, evidently considering the bargain kept, made a short exit and returned carrying a buff folder that to my eyes looked the exact double of the one that had agitated the Unified Traders.

The contents, alas, were not twenty letters offering for sale or offering to buy any of the enriched version of the ore I'd just been chronicling, but a scholarly account and graph of the amount of radioactive waste expelled by a two-year-old filly over the short number of days she'd spent in recovery.

By the time Vera had thought of radiation sickness the Geiger count was already on the decline.

The source of it, I reckoned, had been passed by the filly very early, maybe even in diarrhea during that first Sunday afternoon, while she lay and groaned in her stall in Quigley's stable.

As a charming gesture Vera also gave me a parcel of shoe-box size which she said not to open in polite company. Zinnia, still disapproving, pointed out that the contents of the box were the property of the Research Establishment, or perhaps of Caspar Harvey, or even, arguably, of the filly, but not, definitely not, mine.

I stood up abruptly and asked for directions to the bathroom, and through the closing door behind me heard Jett thanking the two white coats and saying goodbye, and shortly, still unwell, I was sitting beside her on the way back to Loricroft's yard.

"Is that what's wrong with you?" Jett asked anxiously.

"Radiation sickness?"

"You have the symptoms."

"I simply don't know."

She braked to a halt on Loricroft's gravel. There was no one about.

"Don't argue," she said. "I'm coming with you into the house."

I felt too rough anyway to demur. I slid out of the Honda and with Jett firmly alongside crossed the gravel and, after the briefest of taps on the door knocker, walked into the kitchen.

George Loricroft himself, to my enormous relief, wasn't there. I'd had visions of having to deal with him physically, and, apart from my persistent and weakening nausea, George was taller and stronger, and had already tried once to see me off.

The only person there was Glenda, who sat beside the big central table shaking with apprehension and looking a light shade of gray. She was clearly relieved that it was we, Jett and I, who had come.

She said, "George isn't here. He said he was going out with the second string to jump them on the Heath." Her voice sounded flat, without life.

"And Bell?" I asked.

Glenda sat motionless, her stiff eyelashes unblinking. She still wore the semi-bimbo trappings of a too-tight sweater, high-heeled clattering boots, and the puffed-up glittery blonde hair arrangement, but the Glenda of before Doncaster had vanished. The woman who had enraged and stripped away the shaky facade of Oliver Quigley was now wholly in charge, except that she hadn't yet settled entirely into the role.

"Bell went to her house to pack a suitcase," she said at length. "She's coming back here to take me with her."

After a pause I asked Glenda if she had discussed with George the list of frosty discrepancies I'd brought for her.

"Discussed!" She almost laughed. "It wasn't anything to do with girls, you know." In bitterness it sounded as if she wished it was. "There hasn't been any racing at Baden-Baden since September."

I nodded. I'd looked it up.

"George is a traitor to his country," she declaimed, and I murmured, "That's a bit dramatic, don't you think?"

"He knows I think so. I'm going to London with Bell because I don't want to be here when he comes back. If you think I'm afraid of him, you're right, and I'm going to tell you things I never meant to tell anybody."

She swallowed, paused, screwed up her nerve.

"All those places, where I thought he was with girls, he was buying and selling nuclear secrets." To do her justice, she sounded scandalized.

"And once"—her disgust intensified—"once he brought home a heavy little package and because I thought it was gold . . . a gold present for a girl . . . I was so furious . . ."

She visibly drew in an outraged gulp of air. "How *could* he . . . we've always had good sex . . . I took the packet out of his briefcase and opened it, and inside there was only this heavy gray box . . . So I opened that too, and right in the middle of some foam packing there was only this tiny twist of a coarse gray powder, but it was wrapped up tight in a tissue and I couldn't wrap it back again the way it had been before, and then George came in."

"And he noticed you'd opened his parcel?" I suggested, as she paused to draw breath.

"No, he didn't, but I was afraid he would, because he stuck around . . . and I had this stuff out of its box, so I popped it into my handbag in the tissue paper and it was still there when we went round to Oliver Quigley's yard on our way to Nottingham races on the day before Caspar Harvey's lunch. When I was looking for my lipstick . . . the tissue fell out of my bag and the powder went into a feed bowl full of oats lying on the ground ready for one of Oliver's horses. I didn't do it on purpose and I didn't know the horse would be sick. But I didn't tell George as I was frightened of him. I just left it."

"And," I asked, completely stunned but also believing her, "did you see which horse got that particular bowl?"

Her eyes were wide, and she said, "No."

"Glenda!" I protested.

"All right then, you've guessed. I saw which stall it went to, but I didn't know it was Caspar's filly that was in that one. I didn't even think of it until Bell said the filly could have had radiation sickness, and then I really knew what George was probably doing in all those places and lying about it. He was buying stuff to make bombs with, so I asked you to sort out what he'd said about where he'd been. And I do wish Bell would hurry up."

So did I.

I asked Glenda, "Did George know at Doncaster that I'd said I would look up those weather discrepancies?"

"He sure did. I told him. He wasn't going to do me any harm as long as he knew someone else could give him away."

Glenda, the new lesser-varnished edition, was

still far too naive. I was less and less inclined to be in George's house when he returned, but Bell at last arrived, saying she'd packed a suitcase, argued with her father and talked to Kris on the telephone to persuade him to give her bed room.

Without urgency she loaded Glenda into her car while protesting that none of this haste was necessary.

"It will avoid a scene," I pointed out, and with the equivalent of "wagons roll" we at last set off in two cars towards London.

Jett glanced over at me and said, "How are you feeling?"

"Don't ask."

"I didn't understand everything that Glenda said."

"You came in halfway through the movie."

"Was that powder uranium?"

"Judging from its wrapping in tissue paper and lead—that heavy container sounds like lead—I'd guess it might be perhaps ordinary basic uranium ore, but also it might have been some other radioactive stuff giving off alpha particles."

Jett said, "And is George buying and selling uranium? Is Glenda right?"

"She's half right. He's putting in touch with

each other people who know where to buy enriched uranium and enriched plutonium with
people who want to buy it. The gray powder
wasn't bomb-making stuff, though, since the filly
recovered."

I told Jett about the Unified Traders frightening
away the residents of Trox Island, and she said it
explained why my grandmother spent her days
biting her manicured nails.

"Then don't make it worse for her . . . but
about that dipstick . . ." I stopped, in hesitation.

"Do you know who took it?" Jett asked.

"Do you remember what George Loricroft said
at breakfast?"

She wrinkled her forehead. "Something about
Kris must have left the dipstick on the ground at
Doncaster when he clipped shut the folded-back
engine cowling."

"Absolutely right, but Kris didn't unclip or fold
back the engine cowling at all at Doncaster, so
George couldn't have seen that. Add to that a few
more facts, such as George's car was in the park
near Kris's private airplane. Glenda had just told
him that I would have him investigated. He knew
I'd been to Trox Island, but didn't know what I'd
learned there. And he could have known oil on

the windshield could kill, as he could have read about a case of it that was in the news last year."

"That's damning," Jett said.

"And all circumstantial. He *could* have folded back half of the engine cowling and taken out the dipstick. Also he might not."

It was a bit later that I asked why we weren't on the right road in London. Wait and see, Miss van Els uttered calmly, and soon after that she found a parking place in a side street near wide busy Marylebone Road.

"Follow me . . . in sickness and in health," Jett said with humor, and I found myself in a medical specialist's waiting room in an annex to a small private hospital that I certainly couldn't afford. The specialist's name, a placard informed me, was Dr. Ravi Chand, citizen of Uttar Pradesh.

"I can't stay long," I warned. "At two-thirty I'm due in Wood Lane."

Jett didn't answer but was some sort of miracle worker, as in a very short time I was prodded, inspected and generally turned inside out by a briskly competent Indian practitioner with a wide grin of splendid teeth. To Jett, summoned as my nursing companion, the odd news was delivered in the neat accent of New Delhi.

"My dear Jett, your impatient Dr. Stuart isn't suffering from radiation sickness of any sort, nor are his troubles to do with fractured ribs. He is developing a rash which is still under his skin but may erupt into sores in a day or two, or perhaps later today. He has been infected with a disease I can't readily identify. I need to grow cultures and take blood tests. Meanwhile, he shouldn't go to work, but I can give him prescriptions to allay the severe nausea . . . This may be unwelcome news to you, my dear Jett—and how nice it is to see you again—but I would advise you not to sleep with this young man until we know how infectious he may be."

Demurely she said, "He hasn't asked me yet."

"That's unfair," I protested. "Who said don't hurry? Consider yourself asked."

Ravi Chand smiled, ruminated, inspected his nails, which were lighter against the brown of his fingers, and told me to rest in bed (alone) in the hospital next door for at least a day or until he knew what was wrong with me.

"I can't afford it," I said, and got overruled by Dr. Chand's quick reply that money came tailed off compared with health. He himself called the BBC and alarmed them far too much. So I spent a worse pincushion and pill-popping afternoon with X rays, C.T. scan and embarrassing interior searches, and wrote as requested a long list of where I'd been in the past two months. Halfway through the list I realized what might be wrong with me, relaying the revelation to the gleeful satisfaction of my Indian inquisitor.

"Cows!" he exclaimed. "I thought so. Unpasteurized milk! Paratuberculosis!" He frowned. "You do not, though, have any ordinary form of tuberculosis. I had you tested for that routinely, to begin with."

He bustled away, thin, good-humored, dedicated to mystery solving.

In a bedroom that would have honored a hotel for comfort I watched someone else on television foretell cold showery periods for the following day with a chance of sunshine in Wales, later, and I recognized with gratitude that the feeling of abject illness had abated to a much more bearable level. Jett, returning to visit briefly in the evening, wore an anti-infection surgical mask, and having incautiously asked what she could do for me, made a face at the length of my list.

"In sickness and in health," I reminded her teasingly.

"For richer, for poorer," she replied, nodding. "I promised Ravi I would pay your bill here, so you can cross off number one on your list, 'bring credit cards over.' You don't need them."

"Bugger that," I said. "Please do get the cards."

"I'll pay your bill out of the money I earned looking after your grandmother. That," Jett explained, "came from your BBC salary, didn't it? I know it did."

I said, shaking my head, "After all those dreadful tests today, you must leave me at least a little pride."

"Oh." She blinked. "I'm not used to your sort of man. I'm not used to self-sufficient survivors. I'm used to adult little boys being brave but needing succor. Needing comfort. Needing their hands held. Why don't you?"

I would give it a try, I thought, one day.

"Please bring my cards," I meanwhile said.

THE LOOKING GLASS in the morning (Thursday) confirmed the Indian doctor's prognosis. There were three sores round my mouth and several small outposts of the same bad news from forehead to chin, from chin to waist, and other places besides. The knowledgeable product of

New Delhi seemed quite pleased however, and sent in well-protected and gloved nurses with relays of pills, needles and swabs.

He hustled in again himself at what would have been lunchtime if I'd felt like it, and with obvious pleasure rattled off his diagnosis.

"The already good news is of course that you don't have straightforward tuberculosis, as we'd established already," he said. "The rest of the news, my dear Dr. Stuart, is that you have a variation of an already rare complication of *Mycobacterium paratuberculosis.*"

He waited quizzically for some sort of reaction from me, but all I was numbly thinking was that it seemed to be my week for long incomprehensible medical terminology and other words to that effect.

"The point is," the precise voice confided, "that an absolutely positive culture may take weeks, as this is a bacterium that's uncommonly difficult to grow in a Petri dish."

I said, horrified, "I can't afford weeks away from work."

"No, no, of course not. We have already started you on antibiotics, and as far as can be seen up to now, you are not developing Crohn's disease—

good news—or Johne's disease, which is more or less endemic in cattle—more good news. The best of all news is that on present showing, you should make a full recovery." He paused, considering, then said, "This infection you have, this unusual variant of *Mycobacterium paratuberculosis* . . . it's from a strain that was developed originally for measuring how much or how little heat was needed to achieve viable infection after pasteurization. I would say that you might have drunk raw milk from a cow with yet another new variant . . ." He broke off, then continued, "I see you understand what I'm saying."

An experimental herd, I thought. A mixed herd, with specimens of several breeds: Charolais, Hereford, Angus, Brahman . . . *Friesian* . . .

A herd isolated on an island, breeding only among itself . . . The presence and the purpose of the cattle on Trox abruptly made sense.

"Very little is known about the human incidence of paratuberculosis," the Indian said cheerfully. "I'll bring you some information booklets, if you like. In return, you might tell me where I can find this cow."

"Thank you . . . yes, O.K. . . . When can I leave?"

He looked at his watch, but dashed my hopes.

"Sunday," he said. "Perhaps. The tests I'm running will not be conclusive until Sunday morning, and even then I'm accelerating them." He smiled primly. "I will eventually publish my results. Until then I will keep my findings thoroughly locked away, and I'm afraid even you won't know every detail before I publish . . ."

"Do you mean," I asked slowly, "that you will meanwhile lock your findings . . . in a safe?"

"Certainly. There is fierce competition among researchers. I do not want any competitor to scoop me, now do I?"

The word *scoop* sat amusingly on his tongue, but did explain the purpose of the safe on Trox Island. The results from the experimental herd were worth a lifetime's fortune in prestige. I'd been grateful to those cows. Too late to wish I'd starved.

"Am I still likely to infect anyone else?" I asked.

He took longer to answer, then he said, "Just bear in mind that no one knows. Among cattle the basic disease—Johne's—is only spread through ingesting either feces or infected milk." He grinned broadly. "You should be all right here. Visitors may come without a mask."

Jett came often, usually with my grandmother's

gifts of a book not too heavy for holding when sitting in a wheelchair or bed, or anywhere with gin and tonic or busted ribs. Even though upright and walking round and round a civilized room, I learned from Wednesday to Sunday an approximation of my grandmother's restricted life.

I talked to her on Thursday on the telephone, and I sent her a bowl of Christmas roses and a spray bottle of cologne.

On Friday morning early, colleagues at work called to urge my a.s.a.p. return, as it seemed I had won the annual Bracknell Meteorological Office sweepstake by guessing which day in the year would register the hottest shade temperature on the roof (September first) and they wanted to help me with unpopping the cork of the prize bottle of fizz.

They had barely left me smiling when I had Bell exploding in trouble in my ear, almost unintelligibly full of a five-star disaster.

"Slow down, dearest Bell," I begged, hoping that what she'd just told me pretty hysterically was at least only half true. "What did you say about Glenda?"

"I *told* you," she shouted. "Why don't you bloody *listen?* Kris is *frantic.* She stole his trains . . ."

"*Bell.* Slow down."

"She jumped in front of a train." The words still tumbled out.

"*Glenda?*"

"Of course, Glenda . . . Stop being so stupid. An underground train. Late last night. The police came here this morning. She's . . . terribly . . . dead. They've not long gone."

Bell swallowed between words to get them out, but she was audibly crying. "I've talked to Dad . . ."

"Bell . . ." I had at last, and with growing dismay, taken it in. "Where are you? Is somebody with you? Kris? Jett could be with you . . . I could come myself."

"No, you can't, you're in hospital. Glenda yattered all the way to London on Wednesday and honestly I got fed up with her—oh hell . . ." She gulped, but the tears wouldn't stop. "I wish I had been nicer to her, but I've never truly liked her . . . I've done my best while I've been working for George, but I was going to change jobs—but that's only half of it and the rest is *worse.*"

It couldn't be much worse, I thought, and of course I was wrong.

Bell said, "Glenda went on and on about

George being a traitor. She said she couldn't bear to be married to a traitor. She said she'd told you all about it, and you knew it was true—and she couldn't bear the shame of having a trial . . . she couldn't live with the disgrace . . . and I thought . . . I thought she was exaggerating, you know how she always rattles on and swings her arms about . . . Oh dear. Oh dear . . ."

I'd tried Kris's flat several times without reply, so into the pause for sobs I asked again, "Bell, where are you right now?"

"In your attic." Bell said it matter-of-factly as if I should have expected it. "We moved in here yesterday evening. Kris had a key," she added. "He said you wouldn't mind. We'd got so utterly *bored* with Glenda going on and on all day yesterday, so when she finally went out at last we just came here to get away from her and of course we never *dreamt* . . ."

The unstoppable sobs, I thought, might almost have a compound of guilt.

"When Glenda was with you," I asked, "couldn't you in any way have calmed her about George?"

"*Perry.*" Bell's voice on the telephone was a wail. "You don't understand. The Newmarket police went to George's house to tell him Glenda was dead. They didn't go to arrest him. They just went because of Glenda . . ." Bell fell into a silence that seemed past even sobs.

"Go on," I said, "What did George say?"

"He was dead," Bell said.

"Dead?"

Bell said jerkily, "He was upstairs in his bedroom. He had been hit on the back of his head. His skull was crushed. The police went round to see Dad because of me working for George, and they told him George was dead . . . and Glenda had left a letter in the bedroom saying she couldn't bear the disgrace . . ." She wept. "Dad told the police to look for us here because I wasn't at Kris's place."

"Are you saying," I asked her plainly, "that while Glenda sat in Newmarket, in her kitchen, telling Jett and me how she'd given radiation sickness to the filly, George was lying dead upstairs?"

"Yes." Bell's distress carried its own measure of horror. "He must have been. When you and Jett drove off to the Equine Research place and I went home to pack a case . . . we left them in that state of really murderous fury . . . she must have killed him during that time when we weren't there . . .

and then she packed a few things and went down to wait for us." Bell still couldn't quite control her voice. "Kris thinks she told George she was going upstairs to pack as she was leaving him, and telling the world about his trade in uranium, and he went upstairs after her to stop her."

One could imagine George, in a rage, leaning over Glenda's suitcase to take things out of it . . . and one could also imagine Glenda, snatching up a heavy object . . .

"What did she hit him with?" I asked.

"I don't know. Hell, Perry, what does it matter? I've hardly ever been in their bedroom . . . they have a heavy brass clock . . . modern . . ." Her voice was cracking, and Jett would have reckoned she needed a tranquilizer, or better, a hug.

"Is Kris with you now?" I asked.

"He went to get some food."

"Then eat it."

"Glenda!" she said miserably. "And George!"

Disbelief racked her, and she felt more pain for them dead than she'd felt affection for them while they lived.

It would be no use telling her not to think about them. She had known them for most of her life.

I thought of them myself as I had seen them first at Caspar Harvey's lunch, no odder than many a bickering married couple, and I thought how their central cores had slowly begun a meltdown after that, until the bedrock character had clarified in each.

George's innate villainy had taken over from the still respected racehorse trainer until he was ready to try killing with blinding oil. Glenda with her foolish unfounded sexual suspicions had uncovered not the lover but the traitor in her house, and in shame and disillusion had both killed and died.

I thought of the manifest instinct to destroy that had throbbed between the pair of them in that kitchen. There had been, that Wednesday morning, the basic bloody urge of nature . . . all red teeth and claws.

Did a murderer, I wondered, live deep within us all?

11

AT AROUND NOON I ran dear disheveled
Melanie to the other end of the wire and asked if
I could speak to my ghostwriter about my book
on storms. "Sure," she blithely replied and in a
moment Ghost himself was saying, "I thought
you'd come out in spots."

"Spots don't gag you."

"So I gather you want to talk."

"There are storms present and future," I said.
"There are things you should know."

"On our way."

They both came, long John Rupert and insub-
stantial Ghost.

I invited them to sit down, and apologized for

the imitation measles I could well have done without. Ravi Chand expected the rash would fade by Sunday, but Sunday seemed a long way off. I looked a mess.

"What's wrong with you?" John Rupert asked.

"*Mycobacterium paratuberculosis* variant X."

"Ah," one said and "Yes, of course," said the other. Neither had ever seen it before, but then, nor had anyone else.

"Last night," I said, trying not to make it sound too theatrical, "Glenda Loricroft, wife of George, jumped in front of an underground train." Their mouths opened speechlessly. "On Wednesday morning in Newmarket it seems she had bashed in her husband's skull. He lay undiscovered in his bedroom until the police found him this morning, when they went to tell him his wife had killed herself."

John Rupert and Ghost started breathing again, and I said, "Before you ask, he had not been unduly missed by the staff of his racing stable, because he constantly traveled overseas without saying where he was going. He supervised a schooling session early on Wednesday morning—I was there myself. So was Belladonna Harvey, his assistant, but when neither she nor

George nor George's wife appeared yesterday morning, or today, the head groom simply carried on with the stable routine as he'd done several times before."

They listened intently while I told them about Glenda, the filly, the alpha-particle powder and the lead container. I asked them, after that, if they had any authority to search Loricroft's world? The answer seemed to be somewhere between "No" and "It depends" and "It's up to the Newmarket police." There was no simple "Yes."

"Of all the possible Traders," I remarked, "George Loricroft might have been the one most likely to handle and keep orders from foreign sources . . . but he's been dead two days."

John Rupert nodded, "His Trader colleagues will have picked the body clean. But what would you have hoped to find? He would have been too careful. They always are. The real question now is, who will take his place?"

A thoughtful silence ensued. Glenda's spurious snowfalls, Ghost said, had put more than a husband out of action. There would be a pause for regrouping. A vulnerable period, he thought, for the Traders.

John Rupert asked me again, "What would you have hoped to find at Loricroft's place?"

"I suppose names and addresses would have been too much to hope for," I said. "Glenda herself might have got rid of anything obviously damaging. She had time. But how about a dipstick in the trunk of his car, say, with smears of oil matching that in the crunched airplane? How about bank statements, phone bills . . . a paper trail?"

They shook their heads, thoughtful and depressed. John Rupert said, "Even though the Traders aren't a hundred percent professional, Loricroft will have known better than to leave damning paperwork lying around."

Ghost agreed. "Do you know what I think?" he said. "I really do think we may have them undecided at this moment and not knowing what to do next, but it won't last long. So what we need now are some good sound ideas. Fruitful ideas. It's time for genius."

John Rupert smiled lopsidedly. "We need someone they would never expect to be actively working against them."

I found both visitors turning their heads until their eyes focused on my face, and I thought that if they expected fruitful ideas from me, they had come to a dry well.

"I," I pointed out, "originally sought *you* out for help. My province is as a forecaster of wind and rain and sunshine, not as an ideas man in antiterrorist country. You must know better than I do how to profit from a Trader's death."

I waited for a good while during which they unhelpfully offered no suggestions even in the fruitful category, never mind genius, and with disquiet I realized that they had begun to rely on *me* for direction, not the other way round.

"I need a few answers," I said reluctantly. I had to be crazy, I thought, even to begin on such a journey, but unless I knew where I was going, I would no longer agree to go anywhere at all. Only an idiot would set out without a map.

I said, "The chief question I want answered is what exactly do you expect from me? Then . . . are you two part of a large organization? Do you pass on to others what I tell you? Who is 'Us'? Am I useful, or shall I just nurse my myco-dots and forget about the Unified Traders?"

I watched their changing expressions and realized I was in effect facing them with their most difficult of decisions, the question of what did and what did not fall into the category of "need to know."

John Rupert glanced at Ghost and uncoiled slowly to his feet. Ghost followed him silently to the door.

"We'll consult," they said. "We'll be back."

Life would be simpler, I thought, if they stayed away. Much simpler if I disentangled myself altogether. Much simpler if I'd never gone to Kensington in the first place. What did I now want to do? Extricate or dive in?

I walked over to the window and looked down into the street that ran along the side of the building. Taxis often decanted and picked up fares there, but I was unprepared for John Rupert and Ghost to run across the sidewalk, flag down the first taxi to come along and set off to realms unknown. Ghost's white hair, three floors down, had been unmistakable, and John Rupert's long legs exaggerated from above his storklike stride.

Their taxi had barely cleared the first corner before Jett arrived in my room, saying, "Have you heard?" and with eyes stretched wide, in disbelief, "George Loricroft was actually dead upstairs . . ."

She brought a fax from the BBC to the hospital saying that as Dr. Chand had requested a further week of tests for my tubercular illness, I would not be expected back at work until I'd fully recovered.

"Don't worry, please," said Ravi Chand, looking in and reassuring his protesting patient. "You can still probably leave on Sunday, but you obviously need rest. You have a strong constitution but also you don't know when you are in danger of overtaxing yourself. Illnesses like this deplete muscle power, believe me."

He swept out again at his usual speed, white coat floating, waving a hand to Jett.

"You know him well," I commented, and added in his own chirping accent, "my dear Jett."

"I've nursed several of his patients after they've left here," Jett said, smiling from past familiar moments. "Ravi's terrifically well thought of. I brought you here because he's a top man for radiation sickness, which I thought you had, but he's mega thrilled to find you've got something he's never met before. He's going to write you up for publication, did you know?"

She stayed, good company, until John Rupert and Ghost returned, and then left, saying she would be back in the evening.

The two men brought cold November air in with them, but little in the way of fruitful aid.

Ghost studied his toe caps, smoothed a hand over his hair and did his best. "We have consulted our—er—superior officer, and the answers he told us to give you are . . ." He still hesitated, as it seemed telling nothing at all was a near-unbreakable habit. "The answers are . . ." He pulled a small neat sheet of paper out of his breast pocket and read in a strangled voice, "Yes, you are useful, yes, your information is passed on, and as for our ultimate aim . . ." He hesitated yet again, and I waited in persuasive silence until he managed to resume. Then, looking down at the page, he read, "We do want to put the Unified Trading Company out of business, but we also want more, we want the people behind them, the unknown mostly foreign groups who are constantly planning and putting together the threat of a bomb. It's like infiltrating a drugs ring, to get beyond the pushers to the main suppliers."

"Except," I said dryly, "that your suppliers are trading in enriched uranium and plutonium, not in fairly harmless stuff, like cocaine."

Ghost wriggled in his chair and read again directly from his paper.

"As Dr. Stuart is primarily a meteorologist he is not expected to proceed any further in this matter." He folded the paper and tucked it away. "That's all I have," he said, sighing. "John Rupert has a shorter message."

I turned to John Rupert, who, also with hesitation, issued a much briefer instruction. He read, "Win quietly. Look sideways, at what you learn. I have faith in you. If you can swim through a hurricane, you can find a way through a maze."

I said, "Are those the exact words?"

John Rupert nodded. "When I asked him what he meant, he said you would understand."

He looked uncomfortable, and I saw that even for "authorities" there were baffling acres of "need to know." One thing that these two apparently didn't know was the identity of their superior officer. I asked who he was. They numbly shook their heads and confessed ignorance, but owing to the overall secret nature of their business, I wasn't sure whether or not to believe them.

They both expected (and said) that in the absence of fully satisfactory replies to my questions, I would retire from the field at once; but in a minor fashion I was addicted to crossword puzzles, and as I'd been invited to find a way through a maze that might not exist, I thought it wouldn't hurt to discover more about how the undercover mind worked. Rather to the surprise of publisher and ghostwriter, I asked them about books.

Ghost knew hardly enough about storms to blow the head off a dandelion, but said if I talked onto a tape the way I could talk in their office, with all my best stormy dramatics topping high C, we might even hit best-sellerdom, and John Rupert good-humoredly worked out how many tons of paper it would need. The book that had started out as camouflage unexpectedly struck flint and caught fire.

I learned from my visitors' increasingly relaxed lightheartedness during the next hour that the lady "authority" at the Health and Safety Executive who had originally sent me to Kensington hadn't steered me very high up the antiterrorist ladder. John Rupert, all the same, had proved a reliable middle rung, leading upwards to a loftier level, and had given me a path now if I wanted to take it.

"What have you decided?" he asked.

"Have to think," I said.

When he and Ghost had left I sat in an armchair in the dusk and let the meaning of the answers I'd been given filter through into a clearer understanding.

First of all, I thought, I'd been told incidentally that I might already know by sight the person who stood on the next rung up. Next-rung-up most likely had, like myself, a recognizable face . . . Maybe next-rung-up was a politician.

Next-rung-up, far from choking me off, had more or less urged me to go on. It seemed to me that the main message that had been delivered could be interpreted as "Destroy the Trading operation, but don't let the Traders know how you did it."

I drifted from the possible future back to the unexpected past and tried without stress to see if a pattern would emerge that I could trust, like laying down random-seeming threads on a loom that all of a sudden revealed themselves as a piece of whole cloth in three dimensions. There had been a whole lot of "magic illusion" pictures like that once, which gave three-D effects if one looked beyond the close and obvious and focused on the distant. A lot of weather forecasting fell into atmospheric pressure pictures of close and distant fronts, three-dimensional and always on the move.

The close and obvious in Unified Trading terms—as I saw now, when it was too late—had been George Loricroft with his multiple contacts on European racetracks.

If I'd been a Trader I would be searching now for either a dishonest physicist or a linguist or preferably both in the same man. Yet George

Loricroft had been neither . . . perhaps a race-horse trainer then . . . perhaps the Traders were indeed solely middlemen, and George had broken the company's own rules of never taking the merchandise home, especially if you have a jealous wife.

Jett arrived when I reached that unfruitful point, slapping on hospital-bright lights and asking why I was sitting in the dark.

I blunder about in the shadows, I thought, but made do with "Hi" and "You know those crossword puzzles with no black squares and not even black lines?"

"They're impossible," Jett said. "I can't do them."

"They sometimes take me a week and a reference library," I said.

"What exactly is the point?"

"The point is, where in the world is one across."

"Do you mean you don't know where to start?"

I said, "Dearest Jett, you're right. Where in the world would you look for a folder full of orders and invoices? Where would you keep it if it was yours?"

Jett said she didn't know, but asked if I meant Vera's Equine Research Establishment folder full of records of Harvey's filly. That folder and the box of fragrant droppings were still in her car.

"No," I said, though struck by the similarity. "The last time I saw the one I mean, it was being stowed aboard an airplane on Trox Island. Where is it now?"

"On the airplane?" She was puzzled.

I shook my head. "That plane was rented, and everything on it would have been cleared out between flights. I'd expect that one of the Traders still has that folder. Nothing else makes sense, unless . . ." I broke off in half sentence and only after a short-breath recovery said, "Let's call Kris."

"You've lost me," Jett said, but I at least found Kris. He and Bell were both in Kris's apartment eating Thai rice and sounding glum.

Their reaction to the suggestion of a little hospital visiting brought them rapidly round with a six-pack of Heineken, though inevitably vivid memories of George and Glenda hovered over the room, forbidding much in the way of laughter.

Bell had brought Glenda's suitcase with her, as I'd asked, and it was Bell who opened it, but inside there were only rudimentary overnight clothes and no folder. A good idea, but no good fruit.

"Funny you should ask about a folder," Bell said. "You know I talked to Dad this morning about Glenda and George—and I'm so sorry that I couldn't stop crying—well, Dad called again and asked me if there was a folder in Glenda's case and he positively begged me to go and look at once—"

"And was the folder there?" I interrupted.

"You're as bad as Dad. He was in a frightful tizzy. And, if you want to know, everything that's in the case is more or less all she brought with her, which isn't much, but then she'd just killed George . . . Oh dear . . ." Tears welled in her eyes, unstoppable.

"You didn't even *like* him," Kris said crossly, handing her tissues.

Kris liked Robin Darcy.

"Robin Darcy was in Newmarket . . . wasn't he?" I asked Bell.

"Yes, he was," she said. "But he went back to Florida."

"Which day?"

"Ask Kris."

Kris said, "Tuesday," sounding bored. "Long before Glenda pinched the folder."

"Why do you all fuss so much over a folder?"

Bell asked, irritated. "You'd think it held the crown jewels. All it had in it was a bunch of shopping lists, but they were mostly in German, or some language like that." She seemed unaware of my own state of pole-ax and blithely continued. "Dad practically zoomed off to outer space, but he came down to earth again when I told him the folder had gone back to Newmarket and was quite safe."

I took a steadying breath and asked more or less calmly who had taken it back to Newmarket.

"One of those motorbike delivery boys," she said. "A courier."

"And . . . er," I asked, "where was he going with it?"

"It was a bit odd, really," Bell thought, "considering Glenda was practically scratching his eyes out at Doncaster races."

"Oliver Quigley?" I said it jerkily, enlightened but horrified.

Bell nodded. "That's right. The courier came with a big envelope for it this morning, with everything paid for in advance, so of course Kris put the folder into the envelope and stuck it up, and we gave it to him. Actually I haven't thought about it since. The courier came before we knew about

George. Before we knew he was dead. When we heard, it put everything else out of our heads."

"Um . . ." I cautiously asked, "did Glenda herself say anything about sending a folder to Oliver Quigley?"

"It was about all she didn't gabble on about, but yes, she did talk to Oliver, but not for long. Talk . . . it was more like a shouting match . . . but she told us to give the folder to the courier if he came for it, and then she went out for some air . . . and oh dear, poor Glenda . . . She didn't come back . . ."

Kris raised his eyes heavenwards and passed tissues. He said, "The courier was waiting here on my doorstep when we got back from your place. He'd been waiting for ages, he said. He wasn't best pleased, but we gave him coffee and toast and stuff, and I gave him a big tip when he left because he'd recognized me, and he went off quite happy."

"Ridiculous really," Bell said, "but we were pleased to have done something for Glenda, even though she was dead." Bell meant it seriously but Kris hid a giggle.

"Drink the beer," I told him, but he gave his second can to Bell.

He was perched on the windowsill, long-bodied, pale-skinned and incredibly sane. His own near-death at Luton and Glenda's actual acting out of the chief threat of his suicidal nature had, in an extraordinary way, flattened out his wilder self, and it was he who gave me a thoughtful stare and said, "Let's start at the beginning, kiddo, and we'll find your bits of paper for you, and you'll explain why you want them, and then I'll give them to Bell's father, to make him like me a bit as a son-in-law."

"So the wedding's on?" I asked.

"At the moment," Bell agreed.

"Folder," Kris said flatly, coming back to basics. "Glenda brought one with her in her suitcase, and I'd guess from the ruckus that she'd pinched it. How am I doing?"

"Terrific," I said.

"How about this, then? There were things in the folder that she knew Oliver Quigley wanted back . . ." Kris stopped and scratched his head and then doubtfully went on. "They had a slanging match which Glenda lost, and she agreed to courier the folder back to Oliver if he sent a prepaid envelope for it, which he did, but it was just one thing too much for poor old Glenda."

Both Bell and Jett were nodding and I wondered if Kris really believed his edition of things, or was deliberately trying to mislead us all . . . and I regretted how suspicious I had become after barely four hours as an unofficial snoop.

By nine o'clock all three of my visitors had voted for more lively entertainments than rash-watching, and by midnight I'd discovered the loneliness woven into problem-solving, when success meant that no one knew there was a problem to begin with.

On Saturday morning a spot check persuaded me that perhaps there was an improvement there, though the rash now itched under a three-day beard. A week after Luton, I still had black rib bruises with accompanying painful reminders if I forgot to move slowly. Only in the vomit department had things unmistakably improved. All in all, apart from Jett's cheerful visits, it hadn't been the grandest seven days ever. More like a long lesson in my grandmother's lifetime philosophy: if you can't fix it, think about something else.

I spent most of Saturday morning running up a frightening hospital telephone bill in a search for a motorcyclist who had, on Thursday, ferried a large envelope to Oliver Quigley in Newmarket, but learned, when I at last found a courier company who'd even heard of Oliver Quigley, that they were now being accused of nondelivery, even though the package had been duly delivered and signed for.

They were upset, and at times incoherent with anger. Would they please, I asked them, slow down and start again?

Yes, agreed the Zipalong Couriers. Yes, they had been engaged to collect and deliver the package I described, and yes, their man had unfortunately had to charge a good deal extra for waiting time. But Mr. Ironside had made it worth his while. Yes, their man motorcycled to Newmarket and identified Mr. Quigley's house, and yes, a Mr. Quigley had received the envelope, and signed for it, and it wasn't their fault that Mr. Quigley was now complaining that the Zipalong courier hadn't arrived, and that at the time of delivery he, Quigley, had been at Cheltenham races.

"What had been the delivery time?" I asked.

"Noon."

By the time they thought of asking what my interest was in the affair, I'd learned enough courier etiquette to fill a "how to" book for Ghost.

I disconnected from Zipalong with fulsome

thanks, and called the cell phone number of Oliver Quigley, anxious racehorse trainer, all now, it seemed, restored to his normal self of trembles and shakes.

When my phone caught up with his phone, he was again at Cheltenham races, outside the Golden Miller bar. He offered a stuttery greeting that ignored the stripped-down personality I'd seen at Doncaster.

"As a matter of fact," I said, "I wondered what happened with Zipalong Couriers."

The stuttering reply included stableyard language at its roughest, but meant in essence that when Oliver Quigley was reported to be receiving and signing for couriered envelopes in Newmarket at noon yesterday, Friday, he had been at Cheltenham races saddling his runner in the three-year-old hurdle. A pointless exercise, as the horse in question had one speed only—slow—and wouldn't have won even if Perry Stuart had been where he ought to have been—in front of the cameras with details of the weather—instead of fussing over a couple of bruises in hospital.

At my third try of "Mr. Quigley?" he slowed down and said "What—what?" If he had been at

Cheltenham, I asked, who had signed for Glenda's package?

Oliver was inclined in bad temper to think it was none of my business. I would be happy to help him with last-minute underfoot forecasts, I murmured. In that case . . . Oliver Quigley believed that when the courier found no one at home yet again, he was so pissed off (Oliver said), he just signed as if he were Quigley, and took the package away with him and chucked it in a ditch.

"Do you really think so?" I asked.

"Mark my words," Oliver said, the receiver clattering with shakes against his teeth, "they never delivered that parcel and I'll sue the pants off them until I get it back."

"Good luck," I said.

"I could kill that bitch Glenda," he said. "If she weren't already dead I'd kill her. If Zipalong don't find my package soon it won't be worth suing them . . . but I'd do it anyway. I'll get that thief of a motorcyclist run off the road."

I was glad, while listening to him moaning on and on, that Cheltenham racetrack was a hundred or more miles west of where I sat.

After Oliver I spent a silent hour or two by myself while smooth cogwheels like quiet fruit machines clicked gently into place, and I made at the end of that time two telephone calls, one to the Bedford Arms Hotel in Newmarket and the other to the Meteorological Office at Bracknell.

John Rupert and Ghost had got things right. The murder of one of the Traders was splitting the others apart.

As John Rupert had given me his own cell phone number ("in case," he explained), I called him in the middle of a golf game, which he put on hold with good grace.

"You're not worse, I hope," he said.

"No, the opposite. Can I ask you a question?"

"Always ask."

"Then how serious are you about the book on storms?"

"Oh!" I'd really surprised him. He said guardedly, "Why?"

I said frankly, "Because I need a contract . . . actually I don't need a contract, I need an advance."

"An advance . . . for anything special? I mean, is this urgent? It's Saturday afternoon."

"I think I can get you another Trader, but I need a ticket to Miami."

He took barely ten seconds to make up his mind.

"Tomorrow do?" he said.

By lunchtime on Sunday ("tomorrow") Ravi Chand was peering at my fading rash with a magnifying glass, a bright light and a disappointed expression.

"What's wrong?" I asked anxiously.

"From your point of view, nothing. From mine, my laboratory animal is walking out with only half of my investigations complete." He sighed. "Jett promises she will week by week bring you back for continuing treatment. I will publish as soon as I can."

I asked diffidently, "What about the owners of the herd that gave me this disease? Doesn't my rash belong to *them?*"

"The owners, whoever they are, are using that herd as a living laboratory totally isolated from outside factors. Ideal. They might stand to make millions from new pasteurization methods."

"How so?" I said.

"The present law states that raw milk has to be raised to 71.7 degrees centigrade, that's 161 degrees Fahrenheit, for a minimum of fifteen seconds to be pasteurized. If anyone could patent a new procedure which reduced the temperature or the time, then they would make a fortune due to the fuel saving. That's what they're after. They are not interested in, or experimenting on, a new disease infecting humans. If they were, there would be immense interest in any affliction resembling your illness. Instead, there has been no reaction at all to your progress. The incubation time was short, the onset sudden, and now the speed of your recovery is conclusive. This illness is new. It's different. You are unique. I have incidentally named your illness in our joint honor, *Mycobacterium paratuberculosis Chand-Stuart X.*"

He shook my hand warmly. "I cannot lock you in a safe with my notes, but please, please, dear Dr. Stuart, dear Perry, keep yourself alive until I publish."

When Jett drove her car to collect me, Ravi Chand in his white coat stood on his doorstep waving us a sorrowful if temporary goodbye. I'd been in his care so far only from Wednesday to Sunday, but the swift Chand-Stuart disease (curable, thank the fates) struggled in many a Petri dish in his laboratory towards universal recognition.

Jett drove to my grandmother's apartment, where she was due to start work again the next day. She seemed pleased at the prospect, but to me it meant an end to the nearness I'd valued all week. Jett had definitely burrowed far under my unattractive skin.

My grandmother exclaimed in alarm at my thinness but was enjoying the company of John Rupert, who had postponed another game of golf on my behalf and was covering every surface in sight with contracts for a gathering of *Storm*.

With everything signed he shook hands with my grandmother and left me with a vast check made out to a credit card company to cover every expense.

"Instant money and more to come," he promised, "when Ghost starts Page One."

When he'd gone my grandmother asked the resident "dear girl" to give me the little parcel the postman had delivered for me the morning before. According to its postmark it had been sent from Miami, and only to one person there had I given my grandmother's address.

Unwin of the yellow-toothed grin had amazingly sent me the best gift he could, because when I'd threaded a way through yards of bubble packing I found a note wrapped round a plastic sandwich bag, and, inside that, my small old familiar mud-filled camera. With surprise and jubilation I opened and read the note.

Perry,

I flew a load of people to Trox. There was a woman in charge. She says the island is hers. She was the pits. I found your camera where you said. All the pax were bloody rude all day, so I didn't tell them I'd found it. Best of luck.

Unwin.

Explaining to the others where it came from, I put the camera contentedly in my pocket and on a different tack set about making calls to find Kris and Bell. Result, Bell had gone home to Newmarket, where she and her father were now presently in unofficial charge of the Loricroft stable.

"It's all *dreadful*," Bell said, tears in the offing. "Oliver Quigley and Dad are *singleminded* about this wretched folder, which still hasn't turned up anywhere. They've both gone to Cheltenham again today and left me looking after things. Dad's berserk with worry and he won't tell me why."

"Where's Kris?" I asked with sympathy, and she said he would be at the Weather Center doing radio forecasts until midnight; and he would be sleeping in his own apartment, as far as she knew.

"Are you better?" she remembered to ask, and I thanked her and said I'd been let out of the cage.

"What does pax mean?" Jett asked, reading Unwin's notes.

"Passenger," said my grandmother, who'd been one most of her life. "And Perry, after supper from the take-away, and when you've said good night later to our dear Jett van Els, you can lie down here on the sofa and have a good restful sleep. Don't think of going home. You look far too frail for climbing all those very steep stairs."

I never entirely disobeyed her but I wasn't bad at finding ways to modify the format, so that when I asked to borrow her warm deep-pocketed Edwardian Sherlock Holmes look-alike cloak, all she said was "Take some gloves" and "Come back safe." Nothing, I was encouraged to hear, about heebies or jeebies.

I kissed her on her forehead, our tiredness mutual, and traveled with Jett in her car to Paddington Station, terminus of trains to the west, playground of suicidal manic-depressives (but not of Glenda) and home of a simple coin-in-the-slot photocopying machine.

After a Romeo and Juliet length and intensity of good nights, Jett confessed to receiving a Ravi Chand medical opinion, Sunday morning edition.

"What was it?"

"Wait a week."

I had already waited too long.

"With such a slow start," I said, "our disengagement should take fifty years."

Smiling with shiny eyes she helped me make a set of copies of Vera's equine research work, and when she finally left me two short streets later I had a set of Vera-copies in a buff folder in one deep front pocket, and Vera's originals in a paper clip in the other.

By midnight or soon after I was sitting on Kris's doorstep waiting like the Zipalong rider for the weatherman to come home.

He stopped, key in hand, surprised to see me there so late.

"I locked myself out," I said, shrugging. "Do you mind if I sleep here?"

He looked at his watch. He said "O.K.," without huge enthusiasm, but he'd landed on my own doorstep often enough at midnight.

"Come on in," he said. "Take your coat off. You look awfully ill. Coffee or tea?"

I said I was too cold to take my coat off. He boiled water and clattered some mugs.

I said, faintly smiling, "Whatever you sent to Newmarket with Zipalong's motorbike, it wasn't what Glenda took from George."

He stared. "How the hell do you know?"

"Well . . . who else but you could make sure that Zipalong's motorcyclist reached Quigley's house at the right time? You kept the poor man eating toast and generally waiting about until you were sure that he would arrive after Quigley had gone to Cheltenham races."

Kris said, laughing, "It was only a joke on fussy old Oliver."

I nodded. "He's easy to make fun of."

"Glenda," Kris said, "drove us half crazy all day Thursday saying she'd got a whole lot of George's papers that were proof of his out-and-out treason in Germany. We got fed up with it. Then Oliver called and he and Glenda had a frightful row. He told her what she'd taken was a list of horses that would be running in Germany, and it was his, Oliver's, and he wanted it back."

"But you didn't send it back," I said.

"Well, no." He grinned. "It stirred silly old Oliver up a treat."

"What *did* you send with the courier to Newmarket?"

"A list of horses. I clipped them out of newspapers. What else?"

"Did you read the list you were supposed to have sent?"

Kris said, "Of course not. It's all in German."

"Show me," I asked persuasively.

He nodded, and, willingly moving into his spartan bedroom, pulled open a drawer and picked out a completely ordinary buff folder from underneath his socks.

Without any sort of dismay he handed it to me, and one brief glance verified its contents. Different from those on Trox but for the same purpose.

"There you are," Kris said. "Love letters, Glenda had once thought. But they're really only lists of horses. See that word?" He pointed. "That word means racehorses."

The word he pointed to was *Pferderennbahn.*

"That word," I contradicted mildly, "is Horse-racetrack."

"Well? So what?"

"So . . . er," I asked, "who met the motorcyclist at Oliver's house to sign for the package?"

"Guess."

"I'd guess . . . how about Robin Darcy?"

"You're too bloody smart."

"You and Robin are friends and he was staying at the Bedford Arms Hotel, which is barely a hundred yards down the road from Quigley's stable, I'm told. So who else was more likely? It was obvious, not smart."

"Yeah . . . well, it was only a joke. How did you get it right?"

"You told us Robin left for Miami on Tuesday . . . what does it matter? I happened to be phoning that hotel and they said he left yesterday. Never mind. How about if we made a copy of these German letters. We can do it easily along at Paddington, and then you can see Oliver's face when you show him you've got his precious list safe after all. It's always prudent to make copies. It would be a disaster if Oliver could sue you because you'd lost the originals."

Kris yawned, sighed and agreed.

"I'll do it for you," I said, "if you like."

"I suppose I'd better come. Let's go now and get it over."

"Right."

I picked up the folder and, summoning energy

I didn't think I had, headed out of Kris's bedroom, down the hall and out of the front door without looking back, happily humming a marching tune as if the whole thing were a prearranged jaunt.

I could hear Kris behind me saying, "Well . . ." doubtfully, but it wasn't far to the station, and my enthusiasm kept us both going the whole way.

I sent Kris off to get more coins for the machine and made copies quickly with a German list on top for all the world—and Kris—to see. We set off back to his apartment with me grasping a folder inside my grandmother's cloak and Kris clutching Glenda's folder to his chest.

The impetus was draining away in us both and the night suddenly felt very cold indeed when Kris uneasily said, "I hope Robin will think these copies a good idea. Anyway, he'll be coming for the folder at any minute now. Any time after one o'clock, he said, when I'd finished my shift for the day."

"I thought he was in Miami," I said, uneasy in my turn.

"No, he's going tomorrow. He changed his plans, I think." He looked at his watch again. "Any time from now on, he'll be here."

"Really?"

I didn't like that. I needed a peaceful retreat, and a gentle walk away.

Kris was in front of me, suddenly deeper in doubt, equally suddenly taking quick steps ahead and saying, "I don't know . . . There he is!" he joyfully shouted, pointing. "Let's tell him now . . ."

I stopped walking, stopped listening, turned fast on my heel and started back towards the station at a paratuberculosis effort of a shambling run.

It was my day for spending another of those twenty-nine lives.

Kris could always run faster than I could, but not faster than a roving taxi whose driver was convinced he was saving his passenger from a mugging. As I scrambled untidily into the cab it circled on two wheels into a side road, and I glimpsed the two figures stop running after me and stand with arms akimbo just short of Kris's apartment, looking along the road in my wake, deprived of their quarry.

Under the lights the heavy dark spectacle frames flashed on the round head of the short, unmistakable Robin. Behind him stood the tall, blond, frustrated, godlike Norseman.

Kris still firmly clutched Glenda's buff folder,

though it now contained, not dangerous requisites in German, but the plain English copies made, with Jett's help, of Vera's records of the filly's radiation history at the Equine Research Establishment.

In one deep pocket, I carried Vera's originals, as before, and in the other a true Trading gift to mankind, the Loricroft legacy of the where, the how much, the how soon and the strength of available U-235 and Pu-239.

THE CAB DRIVER asked where I wanted to go, which if answered literally would have meant to bed with Jett, warm, loved and healthy. Instead I opted for round the block and back to the station, where warmth in some places kept total misery at bay.

I sat on a bench in a waiting room, sharing limbo with bona-fide travelers and the hungry dispossessed.

My immediate impulsive reaction, to run away from Kris and Robin, was on reflection stupid, and could quite likely never be explained or given an adequate apology. Temporary madness, that flight had been. True, I had in my pocket lists of illegal materials, a damning piece of evidence, but evidence against whom? To whom should I give the folder? To someone one rung up from John Rupert? So where would I find him? And who would he be?

I thought for a long time about the enigmas that had been handed down.

Win quietly.

Look sideways at what you learn.

I had done neither.

If there was a path through a maze—if there were a maze—would the riddle be solved by going outward, or by searching deeper in?

The folder with the Vera copies in it could have been explained as a further teasing of Oliver Quigley. I had meant to laugh it off and could have done. *Why* had I run from Robin?

I chased the reason in the end to a dream of delirium, when Robin and Kris stood hand in hand beckoning me towards a gun to end my life. Subconsciously from then on I'd thought of them as allies, yet not believing Kris capable of real atrocious crime. Believing two opposite things at once was highly common though, like people who couldn't abide the rich but bought lottery tickets every week, hoping to become what they said they despised.

Look at things sideways . . . What did he mean?

I tried looking sideways at the island of Trox. At mushrooms and cattle and worldwide anarchy.

Looked sideways at Odin . . .

Went to sleep.

When I woke at six I found that my sleeping brain had sorted out the sideways factor. Sideways, I yawned, was fast asleep.

No one had disturbed me during the four or five hours I'd spent in my huddled corner, but a quick glance in a looking glass disguised as a beer advertisement on the wall there revealed that although the rash had faded to a mottled pinkish brown, my eyes had now swollen to puffballs and my unshaven chin was a stubblefield in black. As no one, I imagined, would recognize this wreck as the well-brushed me, I left things as they were and sorted out the contents of my grandmother's Sherlock Holmes cape-coat pockets, which I'd filled the evening before.

Apart from the folder of Loricroft's German papers and copies, they chiefly contained Vera's originals, my camera and my wallet. Camera contained Trox Island mud, but the wallet, more helpfully, disgorged passport, credit card, check, phone card, international driver's licence and a fistful of cash borrowed from Jett.

As soon as lights came on in a nearby photo shop which boasted of its eight o'clock "instant passport photos," I was knocking on its door, aiming to test the abilities of the sloppy-looking teenage boy in charge, who astonished me by actually waking up to interest when I asked if he knew anywhere that I could get specialty work done at this early time of day. He looked at the camera and peered more closely at me.

"I say, aren't you Perry Stuart?" he said. "Something wrong with your face, isn't there?"

"It's getting better," I said.

"I can lend you a razor," he offered, absentmindedly prodding the camera with a pencil. "Do you want to see if there are still O.K. exposures under this muck?"

"Do you know anyone who could do it?"

"Do me a favor!" He took my question as an affront. "I spent four years in night school learning this job. Come back in an hour. And it's an honor to do your work, Mr. Stuart. I'll give it my best shot."

My expectations sank. A sloppy voice; a sloppy mouth. I wished I'd gone somewhere else.

There were more advantages, though, than drawbacks in a face. When I went back an hour later I found a tray, laid with a cloth, bearing a pot of coffee, a basket of hot rolls, and many other comforts. Even a cleaned electric razor in a folded and frilled paper napkin. I thanked the shop's incumbent for his thoughtfulness and then had to listen to multiple detail while he told me how to resurrect negatives from a cow-pat tomb.

I ate, I shaved, I admired his skill sincerely. I watched him make expert color prints, and I signed autographs for him by the dozen when he refused to be paid any other way. His name, he said, was Jason Wells. I shook his hand, speechless, and asked for a card with an address.

"It's my uncle's shop," he said. "I'll get my own, someday. Do you mind if I take a photo of you, so I can hang it on the wall?"

He snapped and snapped away, and seemed to think himself well rewarded for the thirty-six clear clean negatives and the amazing enlargements I presently bore away.

12

IN SOME STRANGE way the adulation and respect shining out of Jason Wells's sloppy face, together with his professionalism and dedication, reawoke in me the feelings of self-worth that had slept through a wretchedly debilitating illness and had for far too long let a brain used to ten thousand revs a minute waste time looking for one across.

Jason Wells might find that a sloppy exterior was right for him, but it didn't match my normal onscreen self. It was time, I decided, for the onscreen self to go to work.

My grandmother's grand tweed cape-coat wasn't just Edwardian, it was splendid; it had presence. My clean-shaved chin was after all much better smooth. My hair, recombed, fell naturally again into its usual shapely BBC cut. I bought enough in a pharmacy for cleanliness, and a shirt, tie and pants in an outfitters, in order to look pressed. I acquired an overnight bag to contain everything, and some films, a new camera and batteries from Jason Wells.

All I needed after that was to stand up straight, give out my name, explain my needs and *ask*. Never mind that I still felt uncomfortably queasy. I'd forgotten, during the past battering weeks, the extent of my clout.

I wish to take a train to Heathrow airport, I said.

"Certainly, Dr. Stuart, this way. We have the Heathrow Express which takes fifteen minutes nonstop to the airport."

I want to fly to Miami.

"Certainly, Dr. Stuart. First class, of course?"

I need to deposit this check with the credit card company in order to be in funds for the whole of my trip.

"Certainly, Dr. Stuart, the credit card company will send a representative to the first-class lounge at once to arrange it. And you'll need some dollars, of course."

I have time for a shower before boarding.

"Certainly, Dr. Stuart. Our Special Services Department will see to your every need."

I have to make a phone call to my publishers in Kensington, and I would like to use a private room for a business meeting.

"No trouble at all, Dr. Stuart. Our business center is in the Executive Club lounge."

Cosseted in every way I found myself inevitably watching a television set. Equally inevitably, someone had switched on a channel showing the weather in store across the Atlantic.

"Bad weather ahead in Miami, Dr. Stuart," I was told, with happy nods. They thought bad weather was naturally the motive for my journey, though only my last call, to the Met Office, had given me even a five-day notice of coming trouble.

Standing in front of Heathrow's best accurate weather update I heard that a weak cyclonic system might be developing in the Caribbean very late in the season. If it developed, which on past probability was unlikely, it would be designated tropical storm Sheila.

At present the millibar pressure of 1002 looked bound for a fizzle-out, but then so had Odin not so very long ago.

An announcer was explaining how modern methods of storm prediction saved money and lives. Preparedness, he said, couldn't deflect a storm but it could lessen some of its effects. Knowing in advance was invaluable.

A world-weary businessman standing beside me, glass with ice in hand, looked with cynicism at real advances in atmospheric technology, and in boredom said, "So what else is new?"

Doppler radar was new, I thought, and research had led to new satellites and computer-generated three-D models . . . and there were idiots like hurricane hunters who flew into hurricane eyes and all but drowned. All those tremendous efforts had been made so that bored cynical businessmen could keep their gin and tonics dry.

Special Services collected me from there, offering armchairs, things to eat, newspapers with crosswords . . . London area telephone calls. I punched in my grandmother's number and, as I'd rather hoped, found my call answered by Jett, who'd started her week there and sounded relieved to hear my voice.

"Where did you get to last night?" she asked

anxiously. "Kris says he has been looking for you everywhere. I was talking to him just ten minutes ago. He thought you might be here."

"And I don't suppose," I said regretfully, "that he was at all pleased with me."

"I wouldn't have told you, but no, he was very very angry. So where are you, anyway?"

I thought: if I can swim through a hurricane I can find my way through a labyrinth. I'd begun to understand where I was going, and I felt a shade reckless and light-headed.

"Wait for me," I said, smiling. "Forsaking all others . . ."

"You'll be lucky!"

"Keep thee only unto me." Why in hell, I thought, did I ever say that?

"For as long as we live? Do you know what you're quoting from?"

I answered her this time with conviction, "For better or worse."

"Are you sure?" she said uncertainly. "Or is this just a joke?"

"No one jokes about marriage on a Monday morning. No or yes?"

"Then . . . yes."

"Good! Tell my gran that this time it's for keeps ... and ... er ... if I solve that crossword I'll be back later this week."

"Perry! Is that all? It's not enough."

"Take care of yourselves, both of you," I said, and put down the receiver as she said protestingly, "Perry!" not wanting me to go.

Did I mean it, I thought wildly? Did one really coolly suggest marriage on a Monday morning? Was it a stupid impulse or a forever sort of thing? Impulses like that, I answered myself, that seemed to come from nowhere, they weren't really impulses at all, they were decisions already made but waiting for an opportunity to be spoken aloud.

WHILE I DAYDREAMED about Jett both John Rupert and Ghost traveled to Heathrow, finding their way to the business center, and both, from their expressions, were unprepared for the grandeur of my grandmother's cape-coat and the tidiness, strength of purpose and revived power of Stuart P.

I smiled. How did they think I had ever climbed the meteorology ladder? And, thinking about ladders, were my publisher and my ghost-writer on rungs going up or going down?

On the telephone I had promised them an interesting package if they would drive to Terminal 4, and when they arrived I gave them the German orders and invoices, and also fresh copies I'd just made on the machines all around us.

I said, "These copies are enough to madden Oliver Quigley and Caspar Harvey, the Traders who are searching for them day and night. The originals were the collected works of George Loricroft, Trader deceased. He collected these orders from customers who met him for the purpose on racecourses, mainly in Germany. If he hadn't died he would have distributed these orders, one by one, to those who could either fill the order themselves, or pass it to someone who could. I suppose the contents of these folders are always fluid—I should think the number of buy or sell items is sometimes small, but this time, by good luck, there are fourteen." I briefly paused. "Belladonna Harvey," I said, "doesn't know what's going on. Nor does my fellow meteorologist, Kris Ironside. If you have any influence at all with whoever you call in to unzip the Traders, see if you can keep those two out of trouble."

My "authorities" said they would try: but even if they succeeded, I thought, I'd lost two friends for ever.

I looked at John Rupert and at Ghost with respect and growing affection. Few enough people gave their time as they did, living double lives without recognition. Ghost, as if feeling for me something of the same emotion at the same time, said he hoped we really would, one day, get to writing *Storm.*

"You'd better, after that huge advance," John Rupert said with irony.

Ghost, with a sudden urge, broke all secret-operative rules. "Perry," he said, his face full of private liking and professional indiscretion. "Feel better, your friends aren't likely to be prosecuted. Nor are Harvey or Quigley, unless they do something foolish. Our superior officer has decided to leave those two in place to start again. What we actually stalk the Traders for is what you've just given us, the written lists of the materials they are currently expecting their clients to buy and sell. If we manage to acquire a list—like this one, pure gold—we send each order, each component of the package, to our counterparts in Germany or wherever the activity is taking place, and they prosecute or close down or use whatever force they like. We, John Rupert and I and some others, we see our job as identifying Traders (or whatever they happen to be calling themselves this year, this month, whatever) and then from that identification we set out to obtain or copy their requisitions, preferably without them knowing. Very often, like we'll do this time, we leave the Traders in place and active, so we can steal from them again. Those German letters you've found for us will put all those people who wrote them, who aimed to buy or sell—it will put all those people in court or out of business, some in a violent way, and it will collect and put into safe storage the materials they were offering for sale. Acquiring papers like those you have just given us, that is our job. That's how we choke off acts of terrorism, even before the terrorists get as far as their own detailed planning stage. You can't make a nuclear bomb if you can't get the hot stuff."

He stopped, but not from regret at what he'd said: more in satisfaction.

John Rupert, the one who might more likely have disapproved of this frank disclosure and have tried to stop Ghost's abandonment of "need to know"—even John Rupert was nodding in approval.

"You'll see now that we know more about uranium and so on than we admit to," he confessed. "We hide behind ignorance to be safe. We wanted to enlighten you on Friday in the hospital. Our superior officer won't be pleased that we have."

"Don't tell him," I said.

I shook their hands, one by one, with commitment and warmth.

John Rupert said, "What we're always looking for are red-hot letters like those in the folder you first came to tell us about. All those foreign scripts!"

"As far as we know they've never resurfaced," Ghost said. "They are so sensitive they must be in someone's safekeeping. Funny if they're back where they started."

John Rupert thought the idea frivolous. Ignoring it, he said, "There are antiterrorist governments in Russia and in Germany and of course in many other countries. They welcome what we can send them. We never know exactly when we prevent sabotage or blackmail, but we receive intense expressions of thanks."

"But," Ghost warned, "do you remember we told you about the man in the Everglades?"

"The one who was shot for seeing too much?"

"That's right," Ghost said. "We knew him. So

take care, Perry. The Traders are sometimes not lethal, as you know, but the basic bomb merchants, the ones who physically write their orders for enriched uranium, they almost always *are.*"

Before I could make any promise the Special Services man bustled up kindly to fetch me, and he set off at a fast walk, carrying my holdall and telling me the airplane had boarded all except for me.

I waved briefly to John Rupert and my ghost. They'd told me for certain what I'd mostly surmised. The Traders were middlemen, and John Rupert, Ghost and others like them, were middlemen catchers.

I walked into the humming engine noise of the almost full airplane to be greeted by a chorus of knowledgeable eyes staring and elbows going nudge-nudge, and I wondered how many million years made up the half-life of a Trader-hunter.

THE SPECIAL SERVICES Department had outdone itself by arranging a rental car to be ready for me to collect at Miami, and the one I picked up had the added unexpected blessing of a talking map display. "Turn left at the next intersection for the Federal Highway to Sand Dollar Beach . . ."

I twiddled knobs and found a radio weather channel busy with things to come.

An extremely rapid voice rattled off, "There has been a weakening trend and a change in the direction of the upper winds over the western end of the Caribbean, with a consequent strengthening of the cyclonic system further east, which we have just heard has now officially been designated tropical storm Sheila, with sustained winds of over fifty miles an hour. Coordinates of Sheila, as of four o'clock Eastern Standard Time this afternoon, were sixteen degrees north, seventy-eight west, moving northwest at approximately ten miles an hour. Now we'll bring you your local forecast, after these messages . . ."

The voice sounded as if he were uninterested, except for trying to complete the weather bulletin as quickly as possible, so as to get back to the commercials, always (as the source of the channel's income) more important than the formation of gale-force winds.

The coordinates given put Sheila about four hundred miles southeast of Grand Cayman Island; not enough of a threat yet for Michael and Amy Ford to nail onto their huge house panels of sea-repelling plywood.

I switched channels.

"Continue down Federal Highway, straight ahead over the next intersection, take the left fork ahead . . ."

The car took me to the street and a memory for numbers took me to Robin Darcy's spreading house.

It was dark by then. I rang the bell with a feeling of stepping off a cliff.

It wasn't Robin himself who opened the heavy medieval-type front door. Evelyn, slender in floor-length black and iridescent with long ropes of bugle beads and pearls, had been expecting someone else. Her welcoming smile faded to a shrewd inspection of me from toes to eyebrows while she acknowledged unwillingly to herself that she knew my name, that I'd been a guest in her house three weeks earlier and that she now regretted it. "Perry Stuart," she said accusingly, "why are you here? Surely Robin can't be expecting you."

Robin himself appeared, framed in a double doorway across the marble-floored hall. There was an essential stillness in him, none of the flutter of host toward valued guest.

"Yes," he said calmly. "Perry Stuart. Yes, I was expecting you. Maybe not tonight; maybe to-morrow; but yes, expecting you. How did you get here?"

"British Airways and Hertz," I said. "And you?"

He smiled faintly. "Come in," he said. "American Airlines and wife."

I walked forward into the center of the entrance hall and stopped under the lit chandelier. Ahead, as I remembered, lay the sitting room, with, beyond that, the terrace where we'd sat in the evening, and below that, the pool. Standing where I was, I had the bedroom I'd slept in on my right. Robin and Evelyn inhabited unmapped regions to my left, along with kitchens by the square mile and, in its furthest reaches, the big room allotted to Kris.

"Well?" Darcy asked.

Behind me, unmistakably, Evelyn cocked a handgun.

"Don't shoot him." Darcy said it without heat. "It would be unwise."

Evelyn protested, "But isn't he the one . . . ?"

"He's the one," Robin Darcy agreed, "but he's not much use to us dead."

I was wearing the new white shirt and dark gray pants, but not the Edwardian greatcoat, and in general looked as I had at Caspar Harvey's lunch.

Robin too, conventional, unimpressive, chubbily round, Robin with tepid eyes behind the black owl frames—he too looked as if his day-to-day business occupation, his propagation of sods, made up the total pattern of his life.

I stood quietly under the chandelier thinking I would have miscalculated disastrously if his curiosity wasn't strong enough to keep me alive. After a tense little pause he walked round to his wife, and although I couldn't stifle an involuntary swallow altogether, I managed not to move or speak.

"Hmph," he said. "Cold under fire." He walked round in front of me, holding the gun loosely and removing the bullets.

"What do you think of," he asked with evident interest, "when you're not sure the next instant won't be your last? I've seen you twice stand motionless like that."

"Petrifaction," I said. "Fear."

He twitched his mouth and shook his head. "Not in my book. Want a drink?"

Evelyn made a no-no gesture, but Robin turned and walked back into the sitting room where a champagne bottle stood open alongside four crystal glasses.

"As you ran away from me last night in London," he said to me as I followed him, "or to put it more accurately, early this morning, I am to

conclude, am I not, that you have come to apol-
ogize and return what Kris wanted to give me?"

I tasted the champagne; dry but with too many
bubbles. I set the narrow flute down. "I don't
think you should conclude anything like that," I
said peacefully.

"Get rid of him," Evelyn urged, looking at her
watch.

Robin also looked at his watch and then, nodding to Evelyn, said, "Of course you're right, my
dear," and to me, "Can you come back tomorrow? Same sort of time?"

It sounded a most normal invitation. Which of
us, I wondered, looked the more trusting and
meant candor least?

Evelyn ushered me fast to the front door.
Robin, when I glanced back, was watching my
departure with expressionless eyes. Whatever he
wanted to say to me could not be said in front of
his wife.

Outside in the warm night, with the door
closed firmly behind my back, I retrieved the
rental car, drove it to the nearest busy shops,
parked it outside a four-screen cinema and
walked the short distance back to the Darcys'.

Bright lights now shone on the driveway and

on the heavy door. I waited concealed in rampant greenery across the road as near as possible to the house, knowing the expected guests could be strangers but from Evelyn's urgency, hoping not.

Evelyn the Pearls had done a splendid semaphore act with her watch, and also Robin with his four waiting champagne glasses, but they had flagged only half of the story. When the guests arrived both Evelyn and Robin appeared in the brightly lit doorway to greet them.

The guests, unmistakable anywhere, were Michael Ford and Amy. Evelyn and Robin welcomed them effusively, and the car's driver, in a black baseball cap, slipped quietly out of the long vehicle and into hiding not far from where I crouched, stepping out later from deep cover to move in and out of the striped shadows of palm fronds, slowly making a bodyguard's circuit to keep his employers safe.

The only real difference between him and me was that he carried a gun and I didn't.

The bodyguard-chauffeur finished one of his mostly invisible circuits and stopped in the roadway by Darcy's gates, directly opposite my own patch of concealment. In the deep starlight he leaned against a tree and lit a cigarette, and there he stayed on watch, without alarm of any sort, the sweet smell of burning tobacco drifting across as the evening's sole entertainment.

He and I both waited two and a half hours for Michael and Amy to reappear. The chauffeur came to life with ease to open rear car doors and drive away, and I, still pinned with stiff muscles, was about to cross the road to where Robin stood in his doorway looking at his guests' departing car when Evelyn, appearing behind him, put her hand persuasively on his shoulder and drew him into the house.

The inside lights went off progressively until they shone only in their owners' bedroom, and I saw no likelihood that night of getting Robin on his own. Evelyn was a complication and a nuisance.

Thanks to her I'd wasted a long time learning the leaf-shapes of enveloping Florida bushes, and thought them a poor exchange for the rear end registration number of the visitors' car, which showed its home state unsurprisingly to be Florida. To Michael and Amy, I learned later, the Cayman Island house was a weekend cottage. An equally grand house north of Miami was home.

My rental car, collected from outside the cinema, had been too far away for me to be able to follow Michael and Amy if I'd tried, but it was Robin alone I wanted. I hadn't known Michael and Amy wouldn't be in their house on Grand Cayman, and they weren't anywhere in sight when I returned to the middling motel one road back from the beach that had seemed to me a faceless place to stay.

In the frugal but reasonably comfortable motel room I wrote a long letter to Jett, telling her on paper all the loving things I found it difficult to say to her face. My dear grandmother might warn her that I'd loved and left three times in the past, but Jett was different . . . and how did one define "different"? Except that anyone who could love *Mycobacterium paratuberculosis Chand-Stuart X* was as different as Pu-239.

The television in my room predicted a short life for tropical storm Sheila, now located over open water at sixteen degrees north, seventy-nine degrees west, and still traveling northwest at ten miles an hour. A map was screened briefly, with a storm warning issued for a place called Rosalind Bank.

By morning it was raining on poor old Rosalind Bank, but tropical storm Sheila, although now circling with sixty-mile-an-hour winds, showed few serious signs of organization and was traveling north.

Tropical storm Sheila, I mentally calculated, was about six hundred miles due south of Sand Dollar Beach. If she went on traveling due north (very unlikely), she would hit the Darcy house in roughly sixty hours, or nine o'clock in the evening on Thursday, two and a half days ahead.

Tropical storm Sheila perversely then wriggled round to northwest again and, speeding up, earned hurricane status, Category 1.

Apart from swimming in the still blue and tranquil Atlantic I spent a good part of the day filling hours as profitably as possible by buying and making revealing lists from a detailed Florida racing form newspaper. I sent a copy of my labors to West Kensington by courier and then spent time repacking both clothes and mind, and used some of the hours left talking to Will on the phone at the Miami Hurricane Center (Sheila strengthening nicely) and to Unwin to thank him for the camera.

Unwin had an answering service that said he was out, but at my third try he lifted his receiver and after surprised hellos said he was real pleased to hear I'd got pictures out of that little mud-bucket.

I asked him about Amy's day on Trox and learned some new four-letter profanities. Never again, Unwin said, would he fly that woman anywhere. And yes, he agreed, she had had the safe open and shut again, and wouldn't let anyone else near it.

He listened carefully to what I suggested, and after he'd thoroughly sucked his long yellow teeth and considered things he said there would be no difficulty, and he would call me back.

It was much later than I'd intended to be still at the motel when he at length came on the line, but the delay had been worth it. Tomorrow was all fixed. He'd completed the paperwork.

"Sleep well, Perry," he said.

I DROVE AND walked to the same place as the evening before, and at Robin Darcy's house pressed the bell.

This time, as if he'd been waiting there, Robin Darcy opened the heavy door himself immediately, and stood there unmoving, the light from inside shining on his back making his whole body immobile in silhouette.

He looked not exactly deadly, but most definitely a threat.

From his point of view he saw, lit from in front against darkness beyond, a man taller than he, and younger and thinner and certainly with better eyesight, but one with only a fraction of the knowledge and experience he needed.

Darcy didn't ask me in. He said, "Where are George Loricroft's letters?"

I replied flatly, "Germany."

"For whose benefit?"

"If you don't know," I said, "I'll go home."

A triumphant voice of West Berkshire origin grated suddenly and loudly behind me, "You're going nowhere, mate. And this bit of hardware jamming into your kidneys, this is no toy, it makes holes in silly boys."

I said lightly to Robin Darcy, "Do you have an endless supply of these things?" and I saw the flash behind the glasses that perhaps meant a warning. In any case he turned on his heel, jerked his head at me to follow and walked silently in felt slippers across the marble and into the distant sitting room.

I didn't need to be told that it was Michael Ford's shoes squeaking behind me, nor that it was Amy's sandals tip-tapping away beside him in an echo of Glenda Loricroft's high-heeled boots.

"Stop there and turn round," Michael ordered, and the brief view I had of anxiety on Darcy's face, as I did what I was told, reminded me unsettlingly of alligators.

Michael wore khaki-colored knee-length shorts with a white short-sleeved top that purposefully revealed his weight-trained biceps. The slight bow to his legs gave, as before, the impression that his muscular shoulders were too heavy for his knees, and his thick neck left no doubt that, in general, opposing his strength was futile.

Amy, her small-boned pared-down little face smiling with satisfaction, clearly thought me a total fool to have walked into such a simple ambush. She, in fawn pants and look-alike white shirt like Michael's, carried also a look-alike gun.

Ignoring the gun as if it were invisible I said to her with gushing pleasure, "Hello, Amy, how lovely to see you! It seems so long since I stayed with you the night I was rescued from Trox Island."

I meant what I said as simply a way towards sheathing the swords, so to speak, but Amy frowned and snapped back very sharply, "You were *never,*" she said, "on Trox Island." Into my obvious amazement, she said, "Trox Island is mine, and no one has any claim to anything on it since Hurricane Odin. I repeat, you were NEVER there. You must have been saved from some other island. You have got them mixed up."

Michael nodded in agreement with watchful eyes, and said, "Everything on Trox Island is Amy's. If you have never been there, which of course you have not, you cannot claim it or anything on it."

"Kris . . ." I began.

"Your friend Kris agrees he never went there either."

My friend Unwin might tell it differently, I thought, and put Trox for the while on hold. The immediate present needed more like an intensive care unit, emergency-room treatment. I still wanted to get Darcy alone.

Michael, Amy and Robin Darcy, I thought in clarification: these three were active Traders, active middlemen. Then there were three more, at least, in their group. There was Evelyn, and the one who had done bodyguard duty the evening before, patient and loyal and carrying a gun. A sixth was perhaps the pilot who had flown the Downsouth rental aircraft that I had ridden in blindfold.

All of them at times had borne arms, but I

judged Evelyn in her jewels and grooming and forceful opinions to be most trigger-happy. She, of them all, I feared most at my back.

I said to Michael, turning in the sitting room to face him, "Why the artillery? What's the point?"

"Letters in German."

I said, "What letters?"

Even Robin Darcy didn't know exactly, I saw. If Kris hadn't told him about his joke on Oliver Quigley, the others probably wouldn't have known the German letters existed.

Probably . . . but nothing was certain in their mixed-up world.

Michael said, "Who did you sell those letters to?"

Shit, I thought. I said again, "What letters?"

Darcy said to me, "Tell him for your own good."

I thought only that the conversation, if one could call it that, was on many levels unsatisfactory. They wanted one thing, and I another. My turn. Plunge in.

I said to Amy, "How did your horse run at Calder races on Saturday?"

I might as well have thrown a bomb myself. Shock waves visibly ran down Amy's shooting arm until the round black hole at the end of the barrel pointed to the floor instead of my navel. Her intense reaction proved satisfactorily to me that she too used racecourses as trading posts. The long list that I had sent to Kensington had been of dates and places where, as an owner, Amy had cover. The lists had been, in my mind, one of the possibilities awaiting proof. After this, I thought, John Rupert and Ghost might know where to look.

Robin Darcy stiffened.

Michael Ford flexed his awesome muscles.

Evelyn walked in with the uniformed chauffeur-bodyguard–general purpose help. No one introduced him, though the others called him Arnold. He no longer wore the baseball cap or showed any sign of being a servant, and I wouldn't have recognized him if I hadn't watched him smoking a whole packet of cigarettes for nearing two hours.

Arnold, in his black shirt, wore his pistol holstered under his left arm with straps like braces to hold its weight.

Brought up from childhood in a no-handguns culture, I'd never fired a shot, and had never before regretted it, but in the Darcy house I felt naked. To go barehanded into a gunfight promised a shortcut to the hearse.

Evelyn carried—of course—her weapon of yesterday, presumably now refilled with bullets. It would be pointless to ask her to lower the rising temperature of threat in the room when she was more likely with her loud menacing voice to stoke things up.

Only Robin Darcy, at the moment unarmed, made anxious attempts at common sense.

Michael Ford's opening attitude of belligerence had increased as if self-generating. He bunched his muscles repeatedly until it seemed it was solely for destruction's sake that he had developed them. Those descriptive words "spoiling for a fight" flickered across my own pacific mind and I sought automatically for body language that would defuse him.

The Perry Stuart of his grandmother's greatcoat, however, thought cringing to be not much of an option. Whatever Michael read of involuntary defiance in my face, it only enraged him more.

Amy, who seemed to read her husband as clearly as the *Racing Form,* quite obviously put her money on the champ, not just to win but to deter any thought I might have had of taking him on again afterwards. She was smiling. She likes to see him fight, I thought. She's aroused by it. She would have howled for blood in the Colosseum.

"Go on, Michael," she urged him. "Make him tell you what he really did with those German orders. You can't let him get away with it. Chop him up, Michael."

None of them bar Robin Darcy showed any wish or indeed any ability to discuss anything, including the German letters, except at the point of a waving firearm. They violently invented gruesome threats (but not about alligators) until, encouraged and wound up by noise and shouting from the others, Michael's core of basic lawlessness let go like an avalanche, at first beginning in a slow slide and then pouring itself out at an increasing speed until its momentum couldn't be stopped.

In Michael Ford terms an avalanche meant a full heavy attack with bunched fists and with lifting his victim clean off the floor and throwing him against sharp-edged furniture to the accompaniment of cheering from his wife.

Evelyn and Arnold applauded.

Only my host was silent.

My efforts at lessening Michael's onslaught by punching where I could, at dodging and at kicking or crashing his head on the wall, weren't enough. I couldn't ever at the best of times have beaten him at his own professional skill.

He took his time. He was deliberate. He made every contact count.

At one point when I'd escaped from him across the room, and he was pausing to take breath, I rolled on Evelyn's best rug and kicked Darcy's feet from under him, pulling his head down by the hair, his ear to my mouth, and I said clearly but intensely, and with no little desperation, "Open the terrace door and go to bed."

I saw his eye-widening astonishment before Michael came roaring back from his breather, and with increasing mindless urging from his cohorts set about proving again the pulping potential of his muscles, and it seemed that he himself was unleashing his maximum power simply because he had so few opportunities for it in real life.

Exhausted defeat was already a close certainty, and I was on my knees, both in fact and meta-phorically, when Darcy reached the heavy sliding glass doors to the terrace. I couldn't by then have pulled even one of those open myself at any speed, but when I saw Robin Darcy yank a huge glass panel aside against friction and heard the grate of the door's gliders, when I heard the waves down below on the shore and smelled the salt air, when a way out of being kicked to extinction lay there for the taking, then from somewhere I scraped up every vestige of resilience uneaten by myco-bugs, and I rolled under Michael's hammering foot and crawled a yard like an infant and thrust every enfeebled sinew into panic action . . . and I was out through the glass door and halfway across the terrace before they began with shouts to follow.

I stumbled as if inebriated down the stone staircase from terrace to pool deck, and untidily fell rather than dived into the water, horrified by the weakness that made a futility of my efforts to swim at even half of my normal speed in my own natural element.

If I'd hoped the one-sided fight would end at that point, I was wrong. Michael Ford's appetite merely changed direction. He decided against following me fully clothed into the water but instead snatched his gun back from Amy and shot at me, the bullets splashing with appalling heat a great deal too close.

The prospect of a dead well-known meteorologist in a private pool in Florida, a body moreover plugged with bullets from a registered gun, still seemed not to deter Michael, nor get it through the thick skulls of Michael's pack that his success would be their time in jail.

I no longer tried swimming in fast circles to avoid straight lines from his barrel. I could no longer work out lines of refraction. I simply clung in wretched feebleness to the bar round the inside of the top of the pool and I shrank into the too-small shadow of the tiled overhang while Michael whooped with undiminished bloodlust, and, having no success from where he stood, galloped round the pool deck to get at me from the other side.

The water slowed the bullets' speed, but not enough. Refraction as a really useful shield in water worked better the deeper the target, as the bent rays of light made the target appear where it was not. If one shot at the apparent victim, one would miss the real one. Deep water . . . I gulped air and swam downwards, and the bullets missed, but Odin hadn't taxed my lungs more.

It seemed ages, this time, before the floodlights poured onto the terrace and pool, until the swarm of navy blue uniforms erupted from the bushes with sirens and bullhorns and shouts and meaningful guns . . . It seemed familiar that I should be ordered at rough gunpoint to get out of the water and to kneel and be pressed down with a heavy hand at my neck, and be screamed at in gibberish in my ear and have handcuffs clicked onto my wrists behind my back.

The police weren't the same ones as those that had come before. These were if anything more afraid and in consequence more bullying. As I'd virtually summoned them to save my life, I couldn't complain.

Across the pool, Michael, in the same igno-minious kneeling position, was talking his way out, "A bit of fun, officer, merely a game," and claiming friendship with the police captain and with the commissioner further up the scale.

Arnold, along with Evelyn and Amy, could none of them understand why they should be treated this way. It was outrageous. The police would be demoted, every one.

"What's your take-home pay?" Michael was asking. "I could double it."

Into this overdramatic scene ambled Robin Darcy, yawning, clad in a silk dressing robe, seek-ing out the highest blue rank and apologizing that his guests should have set off all the intruder alarms. "Very sorry, lieutenant. The alarm sets it-self on a timer to summon you automatically." Darcy promised the false alarm wouldn't happen again. He was afraid his guests had been playing boisterous party games. It was his fault entirely for having forgotten to switch off the system. He would of course be pleased to contribute as usual to the Police Ball Fund.

Robin Darcy, with small anxious-looking steps, then accompanied the lieutenant around, followed by a disappointed blue uniform wielding an undo-handcuffs key. They came with liberation via a spitting-mad Amy, a loudly furious Evelyn ("in my own house!") and a growling deep bass from Arnold.

Michael, though violently threatening unspecified revenge on everyone, was unlocked also, to my extreme dismay.

"We might have booked all your guests for aggressive behavior," the top rank said, slotting away his notebook and pen, "if it weren't for Sheila."

Darcy reminded him that I still knelt there patiently, though in fact at the time the patience was at least half too much tiredness to do anything else.

"Who is Sheila?" Darcy asked.

The blue uniform raised his eyebrows. "Hurricane," he said succinctly. "We don't want our cells filled with playboys."

His assistant unlocked my wrists, but Michael had more or less pulverized my ability to stand. The lieutenant, seeing it, warned that hurricane or no hurricane Mr. Ford would find himself behind bars if there was any more trouble.

The policemen, job done, put up their guns and departed, and Evelyn, in bossy hostess mode, shepherded her guests, even including Michael, back into the house. She gave me merely a furious glance and left me outside.

I SAT IN one of the pool chairs and gazed at the peaceful sky.

I supposed I could put up with the discomfort that washed in waves through my protesting body; I could put up with it better if anything had been achieved, but it was too soon to say.

Somewhere distant in the house a telephone rang and was answered. The security firm, I remembered, checked that all was well in the household, after a police raid ending without arrest.

It was thanks to Sheila that there had been no arrest.

Robin Darcy, alone, came down from the terrace and took the chair beside me.

"Thank you," I said, and he nodded.

He sat for a while without speaking, watching

me as if I were some kind of beetle. All he could see, I imagined, was the stiff soreness that made movement a trial, the legacy of Michael's ferocious fists and feet.

I asked if Michael was still around, and Darcy said no, because of the police warning Michael had gone tail-down to the house he and Amy owned north of Miami.

Like a fed lion, I thought. Sated.

"He can be brutal when he gets going," Darcy said.

"Yes."

Minutes passed.

I said, "Will you fly with me tomorrow to Trox Island?"

He stood up abruptly, as if I'd drawn a knife on him, and jerkily walked a circuit round the pool. Returning, he sat as before and asked, to my surprise, "How do you see me?"

I smiled involuntarily. "When I went to Caspar Harvey's lunch that Sunday," I said, "Bell Harvey told me you'd been born clever, and I wasn't to be fooled by your cozy appearance."

"Bella! I didn't think of her as so perceptive." He sounded put out by it.

"I listened to her," I said, "but on that day I

didn't imagine I needed to pay much attention to what she said."

"And on the whole, I thought you were hardly bright enough for your job."

He sounded suddenly depressed, saddened beyond expectation, as if he'd lost a major game. He had believed in himself too much, I thought.

"I listened to Bell," I said, "and during our stay with you and with Michael and Amy, and after our disaster in Odin, where I learned about the Unified Trading Company, I saw that you were the one who knew how to achieve things, and because I liked you, I regretted very much that you dealt in deadly metals."

He said, "And do you now think I don't deal in those metals?"

"Oh, no," I said. "I'm certain you do."

"I don't understand you."

I said, "Your purpose is inside out."

"Perry . . ." He was restless. "You talk in riddles."

"Yes, so do you. You sent me a message to find my way through a labyrinth, and . . . well . . . I have."

Robin Darcy looked stunned.

I said, "You are John Rupert's superior officer."

I waited for him to deny it, but he didn't. He looked pale. Breathless. Horrified.

"John Rupert and Ghost consult you," I said, "and you tell them what to do. They are part of a hierarchy of which you are the top."

Robin Darcy stared, blinked, took off his owl frames, polished them needlessly, replaced them, cleared his throat and asked how I came to such a conclusion.

I merely said that that morning I'd understood the workings of instinct and impulse. "And it simply crept into my mind," I said, "that if I trusted my instinct in liking you, then you weren't evil, and if you weren't evil you weren't selling death, you were more likely defeating those that did. If you see things that way round it means that when you gather together a whole lot of destructive transfers, you prevent the worst ones from going through, and sometimes you manage to lose others, but you yourself remain unsuspected by your fellow Traders. You lead a very dangerous double life. Michael would probably kill you if he found out. So you needed me . . . or someone like me . . . to be your eyes, without me knowing it. Everything I told John Rupert and Ghost went straight to you." I smiled ruefully. "We'd have done better if we'd talked face to face."

Robin was shocked. "I couldn't have done that."

I guessed, "It was outside 'need to know'?"

He heard my irony, but he'd long trodden a double path where "need to know" divided life from death.

"So . . . will you come to Trox?" I asked again.

"What about Sheila?"

"I'm afraid she may be along for the ride."

"Who's going with you?" he asked.

"You, me and the pilot."

"What pilot? Not Kris?"

"Not Kris," I agreed.

He sat in another long silence, then he said, "You're not fit to go anywhere. Why are we going?"

"Hope," was all I said, but he turned up the next morning at the General Aviation aircraft park at Miami Airport, early, as arranged.

I INTRODUCED HIM to Unwin and reunited him with the airplane, which was the same one, chartered from Downsouth, that he had flown in to Trox before.

Unwin gave me a broad grin and patted Robin Darcy on the back. Amused at the mixed Darcy expression at this piece of presumption, I checked again with our pilot how our trip looked for weather as I stowed my holdall in the cabin.

"The lady Sheila," he said, "has overnight picked up her skirts and hiked northeast. She's Category 2 and building, and if I lived on Grand Cayman Island, I'd be hiring me this morning to go and fly me out."

Long years a professional, Unwin moved economically around the airplane and forgot nothing. I'd thought Kris a good pilot, but Unwin flew like silk. In his hands Trox Island appeared punctually in its coordinates and the solidified grass strip accepted the rented turbo-prop twin without lurch or slither. When he had braked to a standstill near the ruined church, Unwin climbed down alone and walked off by himself towards the remains of the village.

It seemed strange for me to be back on that land and stranger still to have Robin Darcy beside me.

As we sat in the seats behind the pilot's, I said to Robin, "You heard Amy say the island's hers?"

He nodded. "She maintains it's hers as no one else had set foot on it for months. Some sort of ancient law, I believe."

"She said I'd never been here."

"Yes," Robin said, explaining, "she wants her claim unopposed."

"I suppose you know," I said to Darcy, "she

stands to make a million or so from pasteurization techniques if she can keep that herd of cattle isolated. You must actually know that, as you helped her chase off the whole population with your radioactive mushrooms. You came back and tested that herd again in radiation protection suits the day you took me blindfolded to Cayman. The herd isn't radioactive and will be worth several fortunes . . . maybe."

"How do you mean . . . maybe?"

I said, resigned, "I drank the milk of those cows, and it gave me a unique illness now called *Mycobacterium paratuberculosis Chand-Stuart X.*"

He said with understanding, "So that's why you were in that hospital! But you've obviously thrown it off. That won't prove that you were on the island."

"The antibodies will."

He said, "Oh," and then, "Oh," again. "And culture dishes by the hundred, I suppose."

"Those too."

"So you can prove you were on the island."

I said, "Not only that. Amy won't like the illness you can get if there is a glitch in pasteurization. It's a fierce disease, acute at first and lingering after. It seems I still have weeks of treatment ahead before I'm cured."

I didn't care much to think about it, and to change the subject I said to Robin, "What became of the original folder full of letters in strange foreign scripts?"

"The one you saw here, that you managed to get out of the safe?"

"That one," I agreed.

"I was astounded when John Rupert reported you'd seen it."

"But you came back here for it," I said. "And you took it away the day you shipped me blindfolded to Cayman, and thank you for that."

He smiled. "It didn't fool you, though."

"Just saved me from a watery grave."

"Michael was all for dumping you"—Robin nodded, and went on with gloom—"and he was also keen to get on with making profits from the orders in the folder, as there had already been too many delays, so he took it when I wasn't looking."

Robin had had trouble with the Traders insisting on doing their own thing. He said, "Only last night Michael told me he wasn't very good with all those different scripts so he had given the folder to Amy to put it back in the safe here on Trox Island with all her cow stuff while he worked out what to do, and as far as I know it's still there. That must be one of the reasons why Michael will fight anyone anywhere, because he's made a fool of himself."

"Do you want that folder?" I asked.

"Of course. But the safe won't open."

"Who says?" I asked.

"Amy says it won't open so no one can take her cattle records."

"It might not matter," I said. I brought Jason Wells's careful envelope of photos out of my hold-all. "I took all of these on the island," I said. "The first ones are of the raked clean mushroom sheds before the hurricane, and of the village and cattle before the hurricane, and the last one of cows and the three of the foreign scripts are from after."

Robin looked with fascination at the pictures of the scripts.

"I'll use these," he said. "Better than nothing."

I opened the aircraft's rear unfolding door and stairs and, blown sideways by the wind, I walked down them, not blindfolded and with clothes and shoes on, and Robin hesitantly stopped, holding onto the handrails.

"Come on," I encouraged him. "There's no danger of radiation. The residents here were scared away by something like George Loricroft's little packet of alpha particle powder, which gave off a lot of noise but made no one sick."

Robin shrugged and followed me down the steps, and we walked in the blustery wind together towards the second of the thick-walled huts.

There were bulls about in the ruined village, and Friesian cows that mooed and rubbed against me, as I patted them with fondness despite the rotten time they'd given me. They were, after all, the world's only source of *Mycobacterium paratuberculosis Chand-Stuart X.*

Robin and I went into the hut away from the gathering gale, and looked at the safe.

Robin tried 4373 3673 (HERE FORD) and nothing happened.

"Amy's right," he said, frustrated. "It doesn't open."

"Try 3673 4373," I said, "FORD HERE."

Robin gave me a gruesome look of skepticism but punched in the numbers. Still nothing, still immovable door.

"Hopeless," Robin said. "Amy was right."

"Amy was right," I agreed. "Amy knows her way about video rentals, and she may know about pasteurization, and she also knows about safes."

"How do you mean?"

"There's no electricity on this island," I said.

"I know that . . ."

"So what powers the safe door?"

Robin, clever in all ways except in elementary science, frowned and didn't answer.

"Batteries," I said.

I slid downwards the small metal plate located under the display of numbers and letters, and there, side by side, stood a row of three very ordinary double-A batteries.

"But," Robin objected, "it's got batteries in it, and it still doesn't open."

I said, "It's got three batteries, but it's got space for four." I fished in my holdall, brought out the unopened pack of four double A's that I had bought with my camera, and, removing the three old ones, I pushed the four new ones into place and closed the flap.

I pressed 4373 3673, listened to the sharp click, lifted the flat lever upwards and opened the door.

Inside there was Amy's row of cattle files and one familiar buff folder. I lifted it out, checked its contents and with a slightly ceremonial gesture handed it to Robin.

Astonished, he said, "How did you know how to open it?"

I answered him, "I spent four days alone on this island. I know this safe well. I discovered its password. I checked its batteries. I just couldn't decipher the scripts."

"I'll get that done," Robin said. "I'll use them. Nothing you have done will be wasted."

EPILOGUE

Unwin flew through Hurricane Sheila.

He flew three straight passes through the eye at ten thousand feet and leveled the fuel in the tanks as a matter of course. Downsouth's turbo-prop twin, in his hands, took Category 3 pressures and wind speeds as merely numbers that he dictated for me to write down.

I didn't weep in the eye. The science was accurate, but the heart-wrench was missing.

Robin looked thoughtful and was airsick.

I carried the rescued folder in the holdall and Robin showed me, a few weeks later, several short handwritten notes in Hebrew, Greek, Russian and Arabic.

"They say thank you," he said.

By then I'd returned to the BBC and put on for the winter the Edwardian cape-coat version of me, and over in Kensington John Rupert in pleased surprise said his superior officer wanted Perry Stuart raised to "need to know" status.

I and Ghost, thin white-haired grandfather, bounced vigorous young tempests into unput-downable textbooks that I signed by the hundreds in schools, and after that in five hundreds in bookstores.

I seldom saw Kris. One sordid anecdote too many scuppered his job finally with the BBC, despite his Norse god look-alike presence. No longer talking of trains, he spent the insurance from the Luton crunch on a drama course and let out his extravagant nature playing superheroes.

Bell, who phoned me often for advice as a brother, swung as ever between love and exasperation, nuptials on, nuptials off, indecision rules, O.K.

Behind my back my faithful Jett van Els conspired with my grandmother to make my Monday morning impulse irreversible, but with contentment we came in time to "I do," "I do," and I gave her a ring and a promise.

Under the successful exterior, the damage inflicted on me by Michael Ford still stung as a painful memory, try as I might to ignore it. To have been smashed to a standstill by a thug, I told myself, wasn't an abject disgrace, it was one of life's little hiccups. Try telling that to the winds!

In Robin's dangerous double life, the Unified Trading Company faded away, to be replaced by new recruits who understood from day one that action first, report later was the wrong way round.

The Traders atrophied, the Select Group bloomed.

Evelyn left Robin with a goodbye note.

Jett stayed at home when Robin Darcy and I drove from his home in Miami to Florida's capital, Tallahassee, to hear Amy's claim to be the owner of Trox Island.

I gave evidence with photographs of having been there. Ravi Chand clinched things with New Delhi grins, and Amy lost her claim but kept her cows.

Michael came to the hearing, too close on my horizon.

Michael's hunger, like a lion's, was awake and prowling.

He hadn't properly understood Ravi Chand's explanation of antibodies and in fury began taunting the Indian birth and skin color of the world expert witness. Who was he, Michael shouted, to interfere and to say his wife's cattle carried a sickness?

I left Ravi trying in vain to explain pasteurization techniques and went back into the room where the hearing had been held. I picked up the small churn of raw unpasteurized Trox milk that Amy had lied on oath was safe, and I took it outside and put it on the table near to Michael, and using a dipper, filled a glass and set it down.

Michael looked at the glass with disgust and at me with a sneer as an adversary well beaten and now afraid of a replay.

It was worth a try, I thought.

"Don't drink that," I warned Michael. "It's unpasteurized. It will make you ill."

I spoke the truth but, as I hoped, he didn't believe me. Michael wouldn't have believed me if I'd said the sun was hot, and in arrogance and bravado, he drank the milk.

THAT EVENING, MICHAEL, about to become the second-ever case of *Mycobacterium paratu-*

berculosis Chand-Stuart X, lost his cool, shot an intruder and was having to answer the difficult question—why did the bullet in the intruder match the one removed from a man discovered facedown in the Everglades with his legs half eaten by alligators?

It wasn't Michael's day.